Craig Harris

White Cliffs Media Company
Crown Point, IN

White Cliffs Media Company
P.O. Box 561, Crown Point, IN 46307

Distributed to the book trade by
The Talman Company
150 Fifth Avenue, New York, NY 10011
(212) 620-3182

Printed on acid-free paper in The United States of America.
10 9 8 7 6 5 4 3 2 1

**LIBRARY OF CONGRESS
CATALOGING-IN-PUBLICATION DATA**

Harris, Craig 1953–
    The new folk music / Craig Harris
        p.   cm.
    1. Musicians—Portraits. 2. Folk music—History and criticism.
3. Popular music—History and criticism. I. Title.
ML87.h243 1991
781.62'00904—dc20
ISBN 0-941677-27-3
ISBN 0-941677-25-7 (pbk).   90-44717
                                                              CIP
                                                              MN

Dedicated to Ina Lavin.

Contents

The New Folk Music
An overview of trends in contemporary folk music featuring
photographs and interviews with pacesetting musicians.

Many familiar performers continue to influence contemporary
folk and acoustic music.

*Ronnie Gilbert / John Stewart / Peter, Paul and Mary
Odetta / Dave Van Ronk / Tom Paxton / Guy Carawan
Tom Rush / Arlo Guthrie / Joan Baez / David Bromberg
Bill Staines / John Hartford / Waylon Jennings / Jerry Jeff Walker
Buffy Sainte-Marie / Jesse Colin Young / Leon Redbone*

Singer-songwriters comprise the most durable branch of tradition-
rooted music. Many rising stars carry on the songwriting tradition.

*John Gorka / Shawn Colvin / Patty Larkin / Greg Brown
Fast Folk Musical Magazine / Christine Lavin / Rod MacDonald
Bob Franke / Fred Small / Bill Morrissey / Cormac McCarthy
David Buskin and Robin Batteau / The Indigo Girls
Kate and Anna McGarrigle / Loudon Wainwright III
Michelle Shocked / Cheryl Wheeler / Nanci Griffith / Aztec Two-Step
Livingston Taylor / Ferron / Holly Near / The Washington Squares*

Bluegrass continues to evolve from the string-band oriented
sounds of America's hill country.

*The Seldom Scene / Ron Thomason / Doc Watson / Northern Lights
Peter Rowan / Hot Rize / The Nashville Bluegrass Band
Matt Glaser / Alison Krauss / Cathy Fink and Marcy Marxer
Bryan Bowers / Robin and Linda Williams*

African-American music's folk legacy continues to thrive, affecting
every form of popular and traditional music in the United States.

*John Lee Hooker / James Cotton / Clarence "Gatemouth" Brown
Moses Rascoe / John Hammond / Bonnie Raitt / Rory Block
Geoff Bartley / The Dixie Hummingbirds*

Acknowledgments

Much credit is due to the many concert and festival promoters who have allowed me to document the New Folk Music. These include Harry Lipson of Folktree Concertmakers, Richard Lizotte and Steve Colborne of Nightstage in Cambridge, Massachusetts, Flo Murdock and Carla DeLellis of Johnny D's in Somerville, Massachusetts, Bob and Rae Anne Donlin of Passim's Listening Room in Cambridge, Massachusetts, Tim Mason and Robert Haigue of The Old Vienna Coffeehouse in Westborough, Massachusetts, Chuck Wentworth and Franklin Zawecki of The Cajun-Bluegrass Festival in Escoheag, Rhode Island, Mary Tyler Doud of The Winterhawk Bluegrass Festival in Hillsdale, New York, Howard "Bub" Randall and Anne Saunders of The Falcon Ridge Folk Festival in Hillsdale, New York and Liz Bralow of The Philadelphia Folk Festival. Special thanks to Mike McGovern for his technical assistance.

Thanks to all the newspaper and magazine editors that have offered me their encouragement and wisdom. Much appreciation is due the musicians included in this book, who consented to interviews and photographs. Thanks are also due my parents, Stanley and Ida Watsky, my brother, Lance Watsky and my sister, Robin Malley, for helping me to reach this point.

Introduction

During a recent telephone interview, Garrison Keillor tried to explain what constitutes a folk song. "(Folk music) really needs no promotion," he explained from his home in New York. "It's immediately recognizable. I recently did a show in Memphis. I was, of course, aware of Memphis as a music city. But I was also thinking of the fact that Martin Luther King Jr. was shot in Memphis. I wanted the audience to sing a song but I didn't want to fool around with telling them the words. I didn't want to have to teach them anything. So, I thought of 'We Shall Overcome,' that Black spiritual and civil rights tune. Of course, they all knew it. They all knew it without being aware that they knew it. They knew all the verses. They knew how to sing it in harmony. This was nothing that anybody did. It was something that was simply inside of them. It was the most emotional moment in the show. Tears came down people's cheeks, mine too. Well, that's a folk song."

THE NEW FOLK MUSIC

Folk songs were once defined as songs that were passed by word of mouth from generation to generation without any remembrance of the original composer. Since the late 1940's the definition of folk music has changed. Most of what we now call "Folk Songs" can be traced to composers such as Leadbelly, Woody Guthrie, Bob Dylan, Phil Ochs, and many others. Beatles songs, for instance, are ingrained in the collective memories of even the most conservative audiences, providing a kind of folk memory that was once provided by indigenous musics.

The New Folk Music reflects modern changes of circumstance and is played by people who incorporate a diversity of musical influences. Although many folk purists and academics debate folk music's proper definition, we take a direct and pragmatic view for the purposes of this book. Folk music is what folk music does; The New Folk Music is tradition-rooted music as it is performed in the 1990's.

I first became aware of the endless variety of music when I hosted college radio shows that continued the old "Free-Form" FM Radio style of playing the best music regardless of whether it was rock, folk, jazz, country or some kind of fusion.

The music market changed radically in the mid-1970's. Tradition-rooted music, which had played such an important role in the late 1960's, had led to the saccharine sounds of soft rock. When this had sufficiently bored listeners, radio responded with a move towards disco and, then, to punk and new wave. Folk music suffered until the mid-1980's when a new breed of tradition-influenced musicians began to emerge. At first, post-war babies were the prime audience for this New Folk Music. Performers like The Indigo Girls and Michelle Shocked are now attracting a younger following.

My own involvement with the music has grown. Since 1983, I've written for many of the daily newspapers in the Boston area including The Boston Globe, The Tab, The Patriot Ledger, The North Shore Magazine and The Attleboro Sun Chronicle. This has given me access to many pacesetting musicians. In addition, I've been the staff photographer for several of the major Folk Festivals in the Northeast, including The Cajun- Bluegrass Festival, The Falcon Ridge Folk Festival and The Winterhawk Bluegrass Festival.

I've approached this book in the same way that a folk festival represents the music's diversity. By touching on as many directions as possible, I hope to offer a taste of the wealth of what I call "The New Folk Music." If, after reading this book, you are inspired to seek out other musicians and other recordings, then, my goals will have been met.

Craig Harris, Brighton, MA 1991

The name of this book, The New Folk Music, is an oxymoron. How can a music be both New and Folk Music at the same time?

The New Folk Music incorporates a diversity of musical influences.

Pete Seeger

The Old School

The revival of folk songs began in the nineteenth century. In 1898, Francis Child traveled throughout the British Isles and collected three hundred and five tunes that were published as *The English and Scottish Popular Ballads.* In the United States, musicologists John Lomax, his son Alan, and Charles Seeger (Pete's father) researched and collected folk songs in America. When Cecil Sharp (founder of the English Folk Dance Society) traveled through the Appalachian mountains in the eastern United States, he noticed that traditional songs were much better preserved there than in his native country.

In the early twentieth century, folk music became the background for union and labor songs. Most notably, the simplicity of the music proved adaptable to the topical lyrics of Joe Hill and other members of the I.W.W. (Industrial Workers of The World). In the 1930's, Pete Seeger joined with Woody Guthrie and Lee Hays to form that decade's most politically outspoken group, The Almanac Singers. It was not until the late 1940's, when Seeger and Hays formed The Weavers, that the tradition of socially-conscious folk music which they represented began to hint at commercial success.

The current folk and acoustic music reflects a continuing link to the traditions that flourished from the late 1940's through the 1960's. Many familiar performers—from Ronnie Gilbert of The Weavers and John Stewart of The Kingston Trio to Dave Van Ronk and Joan Baez—continue to influence the contemporary scene.

RONNIE GILBERT AND THE WEAVERS

Born in New York, Ronnie Gilbert's earliest musical leanings were toward classical and pop music. "I was a city girl," she recalls from her home in California. Although she had sung folk songs with the Washington, D.C.-based band, The Priority Ramblers, Gilbert didn't reach her stride until joining with Pete Seeger, Lee Hays and Fred Hellerman to form The Weavers. The Weavers' singing style was infectious, making it almost impossible to resist singing along. "We had the uncanny ability to make it sound like a big chorus," Gilbert explains. "We could really harmonize."

"I felt like I was falling into heaven," Gilbert recalls. "We heard each other from the beginning. Pete and Lee made a natural duo. They had previously sung together with The Almanac Singers. They were kind of the core. I learned so much from them. I learned, from Pete, about music and, from Lee, I learned all about the shape of the world. He was incredible. What America lost from the blacklist was this amazing man with so many connections. He knew all about The South and tenant farmers. I met Fred at a summer camp. He was just learning to play the guitar. By the time that we were getting together, he knew what he was doing. His voice and mine blended well."

The turning point for The Weavers came when they were booked to play The Village Vanguard in New York. "We came in to play for ten days," Gilbert remembers, "and ended up staying for six months." Gordon Jenkins, who was House Arranger for Decca Records, saw the group and signed them to a record contract. Jenkins added string sections to The Weavers' early records. "I had misgivings about the strings," Gilbert says, "but Gordon had respect for folk music. I'm not ashamed about anything that we did with Gordon. A lot of people heard us that wouldn't have had the chance."

The Weavers' recording of Leadbelly's "Goodnight Irene" remained the number one song in America for an unprecedented fourteen weeks in 1949. The group was not prepared for their popularity. "Had we not been blacklisted, I don't think we would've been prepared for stardom. I don't know if we would've stayed together," Gilbert recalls. "It wasn't our major thrust to find our place in the mainstream but I enjoyed it a lot."

Ronnie Gilbert

The Blacklist

The rise of the Weavers' popularity paralleled the era of anti-Communist government blacklisting. It came as no surprise to Gilbert when The Weavers were blacklisted. "We were outspoken peaceniks," Gilbert reflects. "We came from a background of labor unions. We were involved in the campaign to elect Henry Wallace for president. We were dissidents against the growing push for the cold war. We thought it was better to sit around a negotiating table and talk instead of building up armies and stockpiling weapons. It was a very unpopular stance with the powers-that-be. The Korean War was going on. It was an undeclared war but American men were being sent over to fight. Our message of peace was not welcome."

The blacklist had a devastating effect on The Weavers. "It was an almost immediate loss of work," Gilbert recalls. "The record company didn't drop us, but, they just didn't record us anymore. Disc jockeys were forbidden to play our records. Nightclub owners were threatened with picket lines. The House Committee on Unamerican Activities hounded us."

Seeger Defends First Amendment

Pete Seeger suffered the worst at the hands of the blacklist. "Pete took a stand," Gilbert says. "Most people that were called to testify took the Fifth Amendment and refused to answer any questions. If you answered any question at all, they forced you to answer every question. Pete decided to take a position on the First Amendment. It didn't fare well and he was cited for contempt of Congress. He was convicted." The decision was later overturned."

"Had we not been blacklisted, I don't think we would've been prepared for stardom."

Seeger's problems put a temporary end to The Weavers. Gilbert, who had recently married, moved to California and tried putting music behind her. In 1955, Harold Leventhal, The Weaver's manager, convinced the band to reform. "Harold called me and asked me to do a concert at Carnegie Hall," Gilbert recalls. "I took my two year old child with me."

The Weavers stayed together, performing occasional shows at colleges and concert halls. Seeger left to concentrate on his solo career in 1958 and was replaced in succession by Erik Darling, Frank Hamilton and, in 1963, Bernie Krause. "Pete has always been a loner," Gilbert says. "He likes to bring people onto the stage with him but he's very much an individual. It's hard for him to function in a group."

DISSOLUTION AND REUNION: Wasn't That A Time

By the mid-1960's, it seemed that The Weavers had run their course. "We tried to keep the group together," Gilbert remembers, "but there wasn't so much energy anymore. Fred Hellerman was doing a lot of writing and had opened a publishing company with Harold Leventhal." Although Gilbert recorded a solo album, she felt herself being pulled away from music. "I was always 'the girl singer,'" she reflects. "On my own, I was totally unprepared."

The Weavers held their final reunion in 1980. "Lee Hays had been ill for years," Gilbert remembers. "He was in a wheelchair minus both legs. He had a severe heart condition and had to wear a pacemaker. He was never one to get much exercise anyway. People around him took such loving care. He was very much loved by his neighbors. The kids would always be hanging out with him. One, Jim Brown, turned into an ace film maker. He really loved Lee. He and his wife even moved into a house near Lee so that he could be close by. When he saw that Lee was on his last legs, he decided that he wanted to film him at a party. He got all of Lee's friends together, including The Weavers. Pete (Seeger) did an annual Thanksgiving concert at Carnegie Hall," Gilbert continues, "and he asked us to play with him. That was filmed also."

The resulting film, *Wasn't That A Time*, was an award-winning musical documentary. The film also led to Gilbert's collaborations with vocalist and political activist Holly Near. "I thought she was fantastic," Gilbert recalls. "We sang together while we were filming *Wasn't That A Time*. The little bit that was shown in the film was so exciting." Gilbert and Near are featured on two albums, *Lifeline* and *Singing With You*. "Both came out of the tours that we did together in the early 1980's," Gilbert says. "*Lifeline* is still a favorite of mine. It was originally going to be a double album but the record company didn't have enough money."

Gilbert and Near also worked together, along with Pete Seeger and Arlo Guthrie, in the short-lived folk music "supergroup," H.A.R.P. The group was named after the initials of the performers' first names. "H.A.R.P. didn't last long enough," Gilbert reflects. "We only did six concerts."

Gilbert remains active in the musical world. *Love Will Find A Way*, her latest album, is her first self-produced outing. "My partner, Donna Korones, did most of the work," she says. "It was a very exciting album to record. It's all about love. I think I'm old enough now to see love in a much wider way. There are some funny songs, some very tender songs. It's the record I've always wanted to make."

JOHN STEWART

Although their career was cut short by the Blacklist, The Weavers inspired many young musicians to rediscover traditional music. In the late 1950's groups such as The Kingston Trio, The Chad Mitchell Trio and Peter, Paul and Mary began to perform a commercial-sounding form of tradition-rooted music. "We would find songs by writers who were unknown," recalls John Stewart, who joined the Kingston Trio in the early 1960's. Stewart initially attracted the trio's attention as a songwriter. Managing to get backstage at a Kingston Trio concert in 1959, he was able to convince the group to adapt some of his material for their repertoire.

After the Trio's manager told Stewart that Roulette Records was interested in signing a folk group, Stewart formed The Cumberland Three. During the two years The Cumberland Three was together the group recorded three albums. In 1961, however, original Kingston Trio member Dave Guard left the Trio. Stewart was brought in as his replacement.

Nick Reynolds and John Stewart

Although he stayed with the trio until they disbanded in 1967, he occasionally toyed with the idea of leaving and forming a group of his own. One such group was scheduled to bring Stewart together with John Phillips and Scott MacKenzie. "I was thinking of leaving the trio," he says. "I was tired of not making any money. John (Phillips) and I were best friends—we had written "Chilly Winds"—and it made sense for us to play together. But there were some emotional problems and I went back to the trio. It really came down to the wire."

Daydream Believer

Stewart's most memorable composition—"Daydream Believer"—was written right before the trio broke up. "Songs just come out sometimes," he recalls. "I wrote it in twenty minutes. I was going to play in a duo with John Denver after the final tour so he came out on the road with us. We had two songs that we were rehearsing—'Leaving On A Jet Plane' and 'Daydream Believer.' No one knew that they were going to be hits. A friend of mine was producing The Monkees and he asked me if I had any songs that they could record so I gave him 'Daydream Believer.'" A month later, it was number one. It happened that fast."

Stewart released several solo albums after leaving the trio. He didn't reach his commercial potential, however, until recording *Bombs Away Dream Babies* in 1979. Fleetwood Mac guitarist Lindsay Buckingham produced the album. "Lindsay learned to play by listening to Kingston Trio albums. There's a feeling of indebtedness for old heroes. When we first met, it was painful. I was totally in awe of Lindsay. He turned me around musically. He taught me the magic of recording studios."

Stewart recently reunited with original Kingston Trio member Nick Reynolds. "It's the first time in twenty years that Nick has been on the road," Stewart explains. "When you're as young as he was when the trio broke up and you try to do something else, you get bored and start to miss singing. I'm amazed it took him as long as it did."

PETER, PAUL AND MARY

Peter, Paul and Mary were the most successful of the early 1960's folk groups. "We always included some traditional songs," Noel Paul Stookey says from his home in Maine. "By virtue of the acoustic instruments and a lack of desire to explore different mediums, we stayed in that genre. Political commitment was also calling us. Folk music says that if you sing it, you've got to believe it. We were in Washington, D.C. in 1963 and in Selma, Alabama. We protested the war in Vietnam because of what the music said. We believed in the music."

Noel Paul Stookey

"Folk music says that if you sing it, you've got to believe it."

The trio came together during the heyday of the Greenwich Village scene. "(The Village) was like a bunch of classrooms," Stookey recalls. "I really miss it, not only for the nostalgic reasons, but, for the kids today. There was no booze at the coffeehouses. That meant there were ten places of entertainment that had listening crowds. They weren't drinking crowds. They weren't singles crowds. A performer could leave one place and go right down the hall to another coffeehouse to hear one of his friends. There was a great fraternity between all the performers and a great exchange of ideas. There was a sense that we were holding hands, in a metaphorical sense, for a better world. We felt that we had seen the Emperor's new clothes and that it was up to us to point it out. Much of our songs and much of our beatnik behavior was flying in the face of the Eisenhower era. The Baroque idea of American culture was caving in."

Odetta

Peter, Paul and Mary formed as a group at the suggestion of Albert Grossman (who managed Peter Yarrow and, later, Bob Dylan) and record producer Milt Okun. "Mary (Travers) lived two floors up from where I was working (as a stand-up comedian)," Stookey remembers. "Eventually, I worked out a couple of guitar parts for her. When Peter's manager introduced him to Mary, with the idea of putting together a group, she said 'Let's call Noel. He'd be terrific.' I remember Albert asked me if I'd like to be in a group."

The group helped to introduce and promote Bob Dylan's songs. "(Dylan) wandered into the Gaslight Cafe," Stookey says, "on his way to a folk music club in New Jersey. Albert saw him after I did. I introduced him a few times. He used to do 'Talkin' Bear Mountain Massacre Blues.' I couldn't stress to Albert the importance of Dylan's music. We did a lot of Dylan's material," he continues, "before a lot of people even heard him do it. We had the same management so we were privy to acetates of upcoming albums or demo tapes." Although they disbanded in 1970, the trio reunited in the late 1970's. "Mary called me and asked if I'd like to perform at a benefit to protest the nuclear power plant in Diablo Canyon," Stookey explains. The group recently released their thirteenth album, *Flower And Stones.* "The three of us are more equally balanced powers," Stookey reflects.

Bodyworks

"(My own band) Bodyworks was conceived by me and is more like a family situation with me, sometimes just as a token, leader. I've been asked if there's a conflict between the message of Bodyworks and Peter, Paul and Mary. There's not really a conflict but there's a frustration on my part, not feeling as free to be specific about my faith. Just about anything that I can sing with Peter, Paul and Mary, I can sing at a Bodyworks concert, but not vice-versa."

Stookey and Bodyworks recently released an album, *In Love Beyond Our Lives.* "It was a labor of three years' work," Stookey says. "I've traded in my personal vision for better ears. I've been so pleased and I've enjoyed my life so much, by virtue of what circumstance has presented to me, that I'm less desirous of enforcing my own vision and my own faith. We are, after all, humans with fancies and desires and preferences. In the personal decisions of my life, I find that if I wait and just do what seems to call for my participation, the net result is always more pleasant, not only to me, but, to the people around me. I get a sense of a cosmic connection."

ODETTA

When folk music started breaking into the coffeehouses in the early 1960's, Odetta was already a star. In the forty years since she made her professional debut in *Finian's Rainbow*, she's never slowed down. As a singer, actress, guitarist, songwriter, recording artist, voice teacher and performer, the Birmingham-born, California-raised and New York-based songstress has embodied a continuing link to the traditional melodies and spirit of the Afro-American experience.

Combining gospel hymns and spirituals, work, prison songs and folk ballads, Odetta shades each tune with her strong, distinctive personality. Accompanying herself with the fingerstyle strums of the acoustic guitar that she affectionately calls "Baby," she reaches into her deepest gut and consistently produces emotional intensity.

Odetta's Background

Despite her natural affinity for folk music, Odetta was initially attracted to piano and classical music. "From the time that I was four years old," she recalls from her home in New York, "I would pretend on my grandmother's piano. I can still remember that I was deadly serious about it. I was always pretending. When I was six, I found a music book and a pencil and pretended I was writing music. Maybe that's why I'm such a good actress today."

Odetta has always been gifted with an amazing voice. "I was a coloratura soprano. In the Black communities, the very high voice was especially admired. A teacher at school told my mother that the body wasn't ready to study voice until the age of thirteen—that, in fact, it was harmful. But when I became thirteen, I got very serious. I've gone from the highest voice to a bass baritone—the range is very wide."

"Folk music is about human concern, struggle and attempting to improve it."

Although she maintains her love for classical music, she's become one of folk music's most influential practitioners. "We sang some folk songs in school," she explains. "Then, later, in San Francisco, I heard people standing on street corners with guitars singing. I had no clue that there was such a wealth of material."

Folk Music Becomes the Focal Point

Folk music would become the focal point of Odetta's performances. Leaving *Finian's Rainbow*, she returned to San Francisco and began her career as a folksinger. Performances in Bay area clubs brought her almost immediate critical acclaim. Following a year-long engagement at The Tin Angel, she was booked for two weeks at the prestigious New York nightclub The Blue Angel.

From the moment that she hit New York City, she made a lasting impression. Befriended by Pete Seeger and Harry Belafonte, Odetta became one of the driving forces behind American folk music. She recorded at a voluminous rate—nineteen albums by 1975—but she became discouraged by the formula-conscious record industry. "I did an album of songs by contemporary songwriters," she says. "It came out at a time when the music business was trying to find a niche for itself. But it was whatever a producer with gold records on his wall said that the niche should be. I'm not one to put on a gold lamé suit or be a punk rocker, although I could sing songs by anyone. The music is the thing."

Odetta released her first album in twelve years in 1986. Recorded during a concert performance in Madison, Wisconsin, *Movin' It On* reflects back to her 1956 debut album *Ballads And Blues* and is a sensitive tribute to the strength of a very powerful performer. "It began with an incredible woman—Elizabeth Karlin. The people that she wanted to hear weren't appearing in Madison, so she began producing her own concerts. I played one of her first shows. It worked out well. While she was driving me back to the airport, she suggested that we do a live recording."

Odetta has subsequently released an updated version of her early 1960's album, *Christmas Spirituals*. "The songs are the same, but I'm a different person now," she says. "I know so much more about how to approach a recording studio. I used to think that you sang in the studio like you sang on the stage. But that doesn't really work. It's a completely different medium."

Odetta's Current Work

Odetta is currently preparing album-length tributes to the songs of Pete Seeger and Jimmy Driftwood. "We've heard a song from Pete here, a song there. Doing a record as a retrospective would put them into a grouping," says Odetta. "Many, many, years ago I met Jimmy Driftwood and his wife at the Newport Folk Festival," she also explains. "They said, 'Oh, you must visit us.' Thirty years went by, and I heard on (radio station) WBAI he was having his eightieth birthday. I said, 'My goodness, if I'm going to visit them, I'd better do it now.'" Odetta's visit to the Driftwoods resulted in a wealth of material. "I wanted to use his tall tale songs to make a children's album," she says. "He was a school teacher who started writing songs to keep kids interested."

Odetta also dedicated an album to the works of Bob Dylan. "To me, (Dylan, Seeger and Driftwood) are a continuation of the focus of folk music," she states. "Folk music is about human concern, struggle and attempting to improve it. Though their songs can't be called 'folk music,' it's a true continuation."

DAVE VAN RONK

The folk revival inspired many solo performers. In New York's Greenwich Village, Dave Van Ronk was at the center of the movement. Van Ronk's earliest professional playing was as a member of New Orleans-style jazz bands. "It was my first commitment as a musician," he explains from his home in Brooklyn.

Van Ronk attracted attention when he performed with Odetta in 1957. "There was a coffeehouse on Third Street," he remembers. "The owner was the landlord of a place in Soho that was sort of a folksinger's commune. He brought in a lot of better-known acts and Odetta was one. He tapped me as opening act."

Dave Van Ronk

Early Success

Van Ronk proved so successful that he was asked to record an album with Odetta. "I was awestruck," he recalls. "I'd listened to Odetta on record and admired her. I still do. The idea of even making a record was so remote. I suppose if somebody had told me that I'd be recording myself in a couple of years, I would've been somewhat surprised. Odetta liked my music and gave me a lot of encouragement. It probably turned me around."

Josh White's folk-blues was a major influence on Van Ronk's music. "I met Josh at the same place that I met Odetta," he remembers. "He was with his son, Josh Jr., who was only twelve years old. He was a pretty strong inspiration. I thought I'd outgrown Josh until a few years ago. I started to listen to myself. It's still there. I liked the way he phrased as a singer. I still do a lot of the same songs that he did, although I didn't learn them all from him. I knew 'St. James Infirmary' from working with jazz bands."

Van Ronk worked in several jug bands with Sam Charters. "He was a friend of a friend," he says. "One time, when Sam was in New York, we were introduced. It began a long association that's still going on. Sam has his own record company (Gazelle Records). I just finished an album of jazz standards (*Hummin' To Myself*) for him. Sam's a very good musician. He knows all kinds of musical forms. When we did the jug band, he was the resident scholar. He knew the classic recordings inside and out. In some cases, he knew the people that had made the records."

Van Ronk Turns Down Invitation to Join Peter, (Paul) and Mary

Van Ronk turned down the chance to perform as a member of what became, Peter, Paul and Mary. "Albert Grossman and Milt Okun had an idea to put together a trio," he remembers. "Albert handled Mary Travers and Peter Yarrow as solo performers and they needed a third. They wanted someone that could carry a tune, sing harmony and be reasonably strong as an instrumentalist. Peter wasn't that facile on the guitar and Mary didn't play at all. They encouraged me but I didn't want to do it."

Van Ronk befriended Bob Dylan in the early 1960's. "I met Bobby within a few days after he had been in New York," he recalls. "We continued to be pretty close until well after his second album. When I first heard him, he wasn't singing too many of his own songs. He was doing some talking blues, but mostly, he was doing songs by Woody Guthrie and Hank Williams. He was extraordinary. That he was going to be well-known was pretty much the consensus of everybody that heard him."

The phenomenal success of Dylan, however, had a damaging impact on the folk song movement. "It pretty much put a stop to the folksong revival," Van Ronk claims. "Before Bobby, everybody was singing folksongs. Afterwards, everyone was doing their own stuff." Van Ronk reunited with Dylan at a benefit for Chilean political prisoners in May 1974. "It was sort of the last gathering of the clan," he remembers.

TOM PAXTON

Greenwich Village became a haven for folk-style topical performers including Dylan, Phil Ochs and Tom Paxton. Paxton has used tradition-rooted music to chronicle and satirize American Society. Folk music is, however, only one of several influences. "I've always loved early twentieth century American music," he explains from his home on Long Island. "I spent a summer working in a theater in Colorado. I got to hear (pianist and ragtime enthusiast) Max Morath play twice a day."

Paxton's Background

Born in Chicago in 1937, Paxton spent the first decade of his life living in the city's tough South Side. "It was a real neighborhood kind of life," he remembers. "My horizons took in only one block. It was a big deal to be able to walk to school by myself." Shortly after his tenth birthday, Paxton moved to a small town in Oklahoma. "It was very traumatic," he recalls. "Within three months after we moved, my father died. It was a nasty thing. It's hard to lose a father at such a young age." The loss of his father left a void in the youngster's life. Paxton found solace, however, after becoming involved with drama in school. "I enjoyed doing plays," he says. "I loved the applause, the attention. I didn't get much attention otherwise."

Although he continued to study theater in college, he had already been pulled towards music. "I wanted to be an actor," he explains, "until I discovered that I could sing. It was like finding gold. It was too good to be true." Paxton began playing string instruments after receiving a ukelele in his early teens. Switching to guitar, he developed a repertoire of traditional folk songs. "Folk music meant something special to me," he reflects. "They were songs that had something of interest to say. It fed into my love of history. They were like little time capsules."

After graduating from college, Paxton joined the Army Reserves. Sent to the Army Information School in New Rochelle, New York (and later to Fort Dix in New Jersey), he found it a short ride into Manhattan and Greenwich Village. "(The Village) was where it was going on," Paxton recalls. "I liked the excitement, the poetry, the flamenco guitars." Before long, Paxton was performing guest sets in the folk music coffeehouses that were scattered throughout The Village. "I was always careful not to overstep my welcome," he says. "I would play two or three songs and be out of there." By the time that he had finished his six months in the Army and had moved, "officially," to The Village, he knew his way around and found it an easy transition from military life to full-time performing.

In the fall of 1960, Paxton auditioned for the popular collegiate folk group, The Chad Mitchell Trio. Passing the audition, Paxton was invited to join the trio. However, after a week of rehearsals, it was decided that his voice didn't blend with the voices of the other group members and he was asked to leave. Despite missing his chance to sing with the group, the experience proved to be important to Paxton's career. "I caught the ear of their music director, Milt Okun," Paxton says. Impressed by Paxton's abilities as a songwriter, Okun agreed to publish his songs.

Good Breaks Lead to Recording Career

Paxton's biggest break came when his song "Rambling Boy" was performed at Carnegie Hall by Pete Seeger and The Weavers during their well-publicized reunion in 1963. When the album version of the concert was released, it proved to be the turning point of Paxton's career.

Tom Paxton

Paxton's manager, Harold Leventhal (who also managed The Weavers and Pete Seeger) set up an audition with Jac Holzman who ran Elektra records. "(Holzman) offered me his standard contract," Paxton remembers. "He let me do a three hour recording session and told me that if it didn't pan out, then, I would be given the tapes to do whatever I could with them." The completed tapes were accepted. Over the next six years, Paxton released seven albums on the label.

Paxton's second album (and first Elektra release) *Rambling Boy* featured warm, romantic songs (such as "The Last Thing On My Mind" and "Outward Bound"). His third album *Ain't That News* established him as a leading writer of topical political songs. "It was a very tumultuous time," he recalls. "The Vietnam War was kicking off, the civil rights movement was moving past passive non-violent resistance."

Since 1979, Paxton's albums have been released and/or distributed by the Chicago-based independent label, Flying Fish. Paxton formed his own record label, Pax Records, in 1986. Although the label's first release, *Folk Song Festival,* was a collection of traditional folk songs, subsequent releases (*Balloon-alloon-alloon* and *A Child's Christmas*) have been aimed at children. "I like to write songs that they'll enjoy," Paxton explains. "Songs that'll let them know that imagination and fantasy are OK."

"I wanted to be an actor until I discovered that I could sing. It was like finding gold."

Joan Baez

JOAN BAEZ

Joan Baez was the most important performer to come out of the Harvard Square folk music scene. Although she was best known as a ballad singer, Baez was influenced by a variety of musical styles. "My first musical love was the Sons of The Pioneers," she recalls from her California home. "I had a crush on them when I was eight years old. I loved the way they sang. They had vibratos that I thought were the end of the earth. I loved that."

"Next was Frankie Laine's 'Last Night I Heard The Wild Geese Cry,'" she continues. "Then, in Junior High School, I listened to a lot of rhythm & blues—Johnny Ace, 'Eddie, My Love' and all that schmaltzy stuff."

Folk music, however, became the dominant influence on Baez's style. "My aunt says that when I was sixteen, she convinced me to go to a Pete Seeger concert," Baez says. "I don't remember the concert but I remember that it was just about that time that I was realizing that there was a world outside my little plastic radio by the bed. I started listening to Pete Seeger, Odetta and Harry Belafonte."

After graduating high school, Baez moved with her family to Boston. "The

"I just want to exploit this gift that I have, which is my voice."

scene in 1958 and '59 was the coffeeshops," she remembers. "I found an extraordinary freedom there. I started hanging out. I was supposed to be going to Boston University but I didn't go much and flunked out. I hung out at Tullane's Coffeeshop and then, Club 47. That's where I was first paid to sing for people."

Throughout the 1960's, Baez's songs became increasingly political. "Because I had been known for this pure folk stuff," she recalls, "I went into the songwriters and much more socially conscious songs. That really was me as much as the ballads in the beginning were me." Baez no longer feels obligated to make a political statement. "I love the concerts now because I've freed myself from having to think this or say that," she explains. "I just want to exploit this gift that I have, which is my voice."

Baez has written two autobiographies, *Daybreak* and *And A Voice To Sing With*. "The first one is much lighter and sweeter," she reflects. "I didn't want to deal with music in the first one. The book publisher said, 'Please, write something about music.' So, I finally wrote a paragraph, but I wouldn't write about my career. I dealt much more with it in the second book. It was twenty years later and a lot more had happened."

Baez Aids Dylan's Career

Baez helped Bob Dylan to get his career started when she featured him during her concerts in the early 1960's. "I was very moved by his youth," she says, "and by his brilliance. The fact that he was a rebel was wonderful." Baez continued to work with Dylan through the 1970's. In addition to touring with Dylan's Rolling Thunder Revue, she was featured in Dylan's 1978 film *Reynaldo And Clara.* "He's changed less than I have," she says, "probably less than most people."

Baez is preparing a three CD collection covering her career. "My voice is really not the voice from back then," she says. "The high notes don't stay for anybody. It's darker now and lower. But it's more interesting now and more exciting, more flexible."

TOM RUSH

Tom Rush has helped to revive the spirit of Club 47, producing several concerts under the late Harvard Square folk music coffeehouse's name. "Boston and Cambridge was a hotbed for folk music in the 1960's," recalls Rush. "There were a lot of clubs, but Club 47 was the flagship of the fleet. It was the place that brought in legendary figures, like Doc Watson, The Carter Family, Bill Monroe and Sleepy John Estes, as well as local talent like Eric Von Schmidt and The Kweskin Jug Band."

Tom Rush

Rush Influences Pop Music

Besides composing tunes like "No Regrets," "Merrimac County" and "Kids These Days," Rush introduced and helped popularize songwriters such as Joni Mitchell, Jackson Browne and James Taylor. "I met Joni in a club in Detroit," he recalls. "She did a guest set. I first heard Jackson through tapes that arrived from his publisher. I heard James from tapes that were played for me by my record producer. They were taking folk roots another step, articulating tradition in a very literate manner. It sort of defined pop for the next ten years."

The son of a math teacher, Rush began his musical studies as a pianist. "I took the obligatory lessons for twelve years," he says. "That was maybe going a bit too far. Piano lessons didn't have anything to do with music. It was something I did because I was told to do it. I learned to play but I never really enjoyed it."

Music became more enjoyable after a cousin taught him to play folk songs on ukelele. "I wasn't obliged to play a song exactly the same way that it was written," he recalls. "Most of these tunes weren't written by anybody. They had just been around in a dozen different versions. It was fun to learn all the different versions of a song and know that no one of them was the right one. They had equal validity. You could change the words or the tune. You're not allowed to do that with Beethoven."

Arlo Guthrie

ARLO GUTHRIE

Woody Guthrie's legacy has been carried on by his son, Arlo. Best known as the composer of long, rambling ballads such as "Alice's Restaurant Massacre," Arlo Guthrie has developed into a highly-respected interpreter of contemporary folk songs. "I grew up listening to people who did all kinds of music," Guthrie explains from his home in Western Massachusetts. "I thought that was what folksingers were supposed to do."

Guthrie grew up surrounded by music, dancing and playing harmonica for Leadbelly and Pete Seeger at the age of three. Although he attended a variety of private schools in Brooklyn, New York and Stockbridge, Massachusetts (the site of the "Alice's Restaurant Massacre"), music proved much more adaptable to Guthrie's "last of the Brooklyn cowboys" personality than academic pursuit.

By the early 1960's, Guthrie was a regular at Greenwich Village's folk music coffeehouses. In 1965, he toured Japan as opening act for Judy Collins. Guthrie's biggest break came in 1967 after recording "Alice's Restaurant Massacre," a sardonic look at draft registration during the Vietnam era. "There were other versions of 'Alice's Restaurant,'" Guthrie recalls. "The first one was the only one that was recordable." Although the song has been periodically "retired," Guthrie has resurrected it upon special occasions. "I brought it back when Carter brought back the registration," he says. Guthrie continues to feature the song during his performances. "A lot of young people are coming to my shows," he explains. "The kids of my own peers are showing up. One-third of my audience is new. It gives the song a whole new edge."

Another recent feature of Guthrie's performances is a tribute to his father's music. "It's been twenty years since Dad passed away," he says. "I wanted to remind people without having an actual memorial. He would've enjoyed it."

Guthrie's earliest albums marked him as a "shaggy, hippie novelty act." *Running Down The Road*, his third album, proved to be a major turning point. Produced by pop-minded Lenny Waronker, it featured a virtual who's who of southern California folk-pop session players, including Chris Ethridge, Ry Cooder and The Byrds' Clarence White and Gene Parsons. The album featured Guthrie's original tune, "Goin' Down To Los Angeles," which became the theme song of dope smuggling after being featured in the film *Woodstock*.

Although the follow-up album *Washington County* was commercially disappointing, Guthrie rebounded with his most successful project. Released in 1972, *Hobo's Lullaby* was almost entirely composed by other songwriters. In addition to a version of Steve Goodman's "City Of New Orleans" that became Guthrie's only top twenty hit, the album showcased songs by Bob Dylan, Hoyt Axton and others.

"About eight years ago, somebody asked me how many of the songs were mine," Guthrie reflects. "It actually comes within a few songs short of being fifty-fifty. But they've all been songs that I've loved. I don't believe in worrying about whether an album is all original or not," he continues. "I've always believed in doing an album of good songs."

Arlo Guthrie's Albums to be Re-released

Guthrie's most recent album *Someday* was released in 1986. "We put it out ourselves," Guthrie boasts. "We started our own record company—Rising Son Records. For the first time, we made some money. Over the past four years, we've been in the process of re-releasing all the old albums. We're already five or six records into it. We've also gotten permission from Warner Brothers to re-release the albums still in their catalogue. Soon, all my albums will be available again."

Guy Carawan

"My role was to
draw people out
and to get them to
sing together."

GUY CARAWAN

Folk music's involvement with grass-roots political struggle is best exemplified by The Highlander Research And Education Center in Tennessee. "Music has always played an important role," Guy Carawan says from his office at the school. "It was started by young Southerners, including Don West, Hedy West's father, and Myles Horton, to help solve the economic and racial problems in the South. It made a great contribution to the labor movement, and, later, to the civil rights movement."

Carawan first visited the school in 1953. "I met Pete Seeger in California," he recalls, "and he told me about it. He had come to Highlander as a teenager when Woody Guthrie brought him." Carawan returned to live at the school in 1959. "I called Myles Horton and asked if I could come back," he remembers. "My role was to draw people out and to get them to sing together."

Music and Civil Rights

After returning to Highlander, Carawan and his wife, Candie, became active in the early 1960's struggle for Civil Rights. "In April, 1960, we had the first gathering of people that had been involved with the sit-in movement," he recalls. "Sixty students came from all over the south that had sat down at a lunch counter in Nashville. Many had been arrested. I met Candie who had come over from California on an exchange program at Fisk University. A year later, we were married."

Music played an important role. "The whole idea grew from Gandhi and civil disobedience," Carawan reflects. "Music expressed a great deal. A lot of the songs that we used at Highlander were songs that we had picked up from singers like Bessie Jones in the Sea Islands off the coast of North Carolina. Songs like 'Keep Your Eyes On The Prize' were adapted." Among the many songs that were popularized by The Highlander School was the civil rights anthem, "We Shall Overcome." "It was adapted from the old spiritual, "I Will Overcome," Carawan explains. "It had come up with a couple of Black people involved with the food and tobacco worker's union in the low country area. They changed it from 'I' to 'We.' It was picked up as a theme song in the South. Right away, it spread like wild fire. It was on the radio and in the newspapers."

Carawan is known for his work and publications on Sea Islands traditional singers, including the book *Ain't You Got The Right To The Tree Of Life?* He also helped introduce the hammered dulcimer into contemporary folk music.

DAVID BROMBERG

David Bromberg has created a distinctive sound by blending blues and folk music. "I've always liked more than just one kind of music," he says from his home in Chicago. Bromberg made his earliest musical statements as a much-in-demand session guitarist. "A session musician has to be very versatile," he explains, "and has to be able to adapt to whatever is called for."

Born in Tarrytown, New York, Bromberg became an active part of New York's music scene. "There was no one else in Tarrytown that liked the kind of music that I was into," he recalls. "In New York, no matter what your interest is, there's a hundred people into the same thing. I felt very much at home. It was a very exciting time."

Bromberg's first sessions were as a rock 'n' roll electric guitarist. "I played with Chubby Checker for a brief time," he remembers. "I recorded with Jay & The Americans, Freddy Scott and Dion. I didn't get my name on any albums until I started playing acoustic guitar. Not many people had an electric guitar technique that they could apply to the acoustic."

Numerous acoustic-based recordings featured Bromberg's work. "I loved a session with Jim Ringer I did in Vermont," he recalls. "The Dylan sessions were marvelous. They were exciting. A lot of it was just me and Bob, one-on-one."

Bromberg worked with blues legends Mississippi John Hurt and Reverend Gary Davis. "I performed with Mississippi John at the Philadelphia Folk Festival," he says. "He was a very sweet man and his music had a warm, loving attitude. He played in a style that was beautiful in its simplicity. I used to be Reverend Gary Davis's seeing-eye boy," he continues. "He was one of the most gifted technicians. It was difficult to execute. There were a lot of counter-melodies. To me, the best playing he did, he sung over. You couldn't realize what was going on underneath his singing."

Among Bromberg's most influential sessions was his playing on Jerry Jeff Walker's recording of "Mr. Bojangles." "(Walker) was in a band, Circus Maximus, that didn't like a lot of his tunes," he says. "They were too country. We hit it off. I used to drag him along to (New York radio station) WBAI just so I could get to play guitar with him. We'd play all night on the radio."

Bromberg put his own band together in the early 1970's. "I started writing my own songs," he explains. "I met a very fine guitar player, Steve Burgh. We really hit it off. He really liked my songs and told me that he wanted to be my accompanist. He taught himself to play bass so that he could play with me."

Labels and Deals

Bromberg's earliest solo albums were released on the Columbia Record label. "I never got pushed around by the major labels," he says, "but I was never anybody's baby." His relationship with the label began to wane in 1974. "I had a clause in my contract," he explains, "that I'd get a bonus if an album sold over seventy-five thousand copies. They paid the bonus on the first album and discovered that all my albums were about to reach the bonus point. They dropped my contract and saved a lot of money."

Although he signed with Fantasy Records, the relationship was ill-fated. "The President (of the label) became very ill," he remembers. "They hired a guy that thought my music was a joke and told everybody so. It's kind of frustrating to hear that promotion people were told not to waste their time on my records. I owed them another album but I was fed up."

Disenchanted with the music business, Bromberg announced his retirement and enrolled in the Chicago School of Violin Making. "I studied in order to learn about

"I've always liked more than just one kind of music."

Michael Cooney and David Bromberg

who made them, when and where," he says. "I've graduated but I'm still continuing to study that."

Sideman Serenade, Bromberg's return to the recording scene, pays tribute to contemporary music's best studio musicians. "There's a lot of wonderful musicians I've always wanted to play with," he says. The album took many years to complete. "I had it all lined up but I got pneumonia. I had to cancel all the sessions. When I recovered, I was able to put it all back together again and my father died. I fell apart for the better part of a year. When I was in condition to work again, I put it all back together and my mother died. This was not the easist album to complete."

Among the musicians that appear on the album are David Lindley, Jackson Browne and Dr. John. "One of the first people that I thought of working with was David Lindley," Bromberg explains. "It was the first time that we sat and played guitars face to face. We've played mandolin and fiddles and done a lot of old timey stuff together, usually backstage. I accompanied Jackson Browne before he and David began playing together. He's a very talented guy. He really knows his way around the studio. The tune with Dr. John is my favorite track on any album I've ever made. It's the true stuff."

BILL STAINES

Bill Staines is one of folk music's most melodic songwriters. "From the beginning, I've kept protest out of my songs," he says. "When I played music that I really enjoyed, I wasn't angry. I went out and accented the positive instead of protesting the negative." Although Staines grew up in New England, his songs tell of the American West, rivers and open spaces. "I had to find a format that all the songs would fit into," he says. "I had to do a lot of soul searching because the only thread was they were all written by the same person."

Born in Lexington, Massachusetts, Staines made his performing debut as a member of the Green Mountain Boys. "I put the group together with a friend from junior high school (Dick Curtis), and his younger brother, John," he remembers. "John and Dick were into an old timey and bluegrass sound, while I was more into the school of romantic ballads."

Several years later, Staines managed The Barn, Lexington's Saturday Night coffeehouse. The experience led him to hosting the open mike hoots at Harvard Square's premier folk music coffeehouse, Club 47.

Bill Staines

Yodeling

A unique feature of any Bill Staines performance is his championship-winning yodeling. "I've always been fascinated by yodeling," he explains. "I found that although it sometimes happens when I least expect it, I can control the crackling of my voice." I heard some country bands in the late 1960's and found that, if you can control your voice crackling, it's not that hard to yodel." Staines has the ability to get the audience involved and singing along. "When the audience is willing to sing," he says, "it makes me more comfortable. Sometimes, I'll hear an audience singing in three-part harmony and it feels so nice."

As a guitarist, Staines is entirely self-taught. Using a fingerpicking style that he says he learned mostly from "Jackie Washington, a frequent performer at Club 47 and from Tom Paxton's debut album," Staines turns over a righthanded Martin D-18 acoustic guitar and plays lefthanded.

Since 1966, when Randy Burns & The Skydog Band recorded his first original song, "That's The Way It's Going To Go In Time," Staines' songs have been re-recorded by many performers. "It's exciting to hear one of my songs," he explains. "If it's in tune and it's performed well, I'm flattered."

JOHN HARTFORD

Banjo, fiddle and acoustic guitar player John Hartford is best known as the writer of the multimillion selling tune "Gentle On My Mind." The song, which was a hit for Glen Campbell in 1967 and an instrumental hit for Floyd Cramer, has been re-recorded by more than two hundred performers and has sold over fifteen million copies internationally. "It's hard to say what inspires certain songs," Hartford says from his home in Nashville. "They just come out. A lot of people want to know what inspired 'Gentle On My Mind,' but I'm still not sure. It was written in twenty minutes. It just came pouring out."

Hartford has been exciting audiences with his turbocharged performances since the early 1960's. "I make it up as I go along," he explains. "I don't know what I'm going to do until I hit the stage. It's like a poker game. When you play poker, you don't know what you're going to do until you're dealt your hand. And then, you still don't know what you're going to do until you see what everyone else is going to do." A highlight of Hartford's concerts is the clog-dancing (on a three-quarter inch plywood platform) that he uses to accompany his playing. "It started out as a joke," he remembers. "I used to sit down and play. Norman Blake used to kid me. He'd say, 'Boy, if you could learn to play like that and dance at the same time, you would really have something.' I woodshedded it for a year until I could do it on the stage. Now, it feels good. It's how I get my exercise."

Hartford's Background

"Gentle On My Mind" was written in twenty minutes. It just came pouring out."

Hartford was born in New York City and raised in St. Louis. Music played a strong role in the Hartford home. "My mother played," Hartford explains, "and my grandmothers played." His banjo playing was influenced by Earl Scruggs and by David "Stringbean" Akeman. "I saw Flatt And Scruggs in 1953 or '54," he reflects. "They played a show near St. Louis. It absolutely changed my life. The music went straight to my heart. Stringbean played in a frailing or clawhammer style in which he used the back of his fingernails. It's different from Earl Scruggs' two-finger style."

Hartford was taught much of his fiddling technique by Dr. James Gray. "He was an old man that lived near us when I was growing up," he remembers. "He had been a state champion fiddle player. I got to know him and he showed me different tunes and taught me how to bow. I started playing with him when I was real young."

From an early age, Hartford was inspired by the steam boats that traveled along The Mississippi River. "I wanted to be a river boat pilot," he recalls. "The boats had a very strong impression. I've got a first class pilot's license and I've got a one hundred ton operator's license. I pilot The Julie Belle Swain up The Mississippi, and, lately, I've been doing work on The General Jackson. I've always known that I had to get back to the river."

Music, however, continued to play a dominant role. "I started playing at dance halls where they did a lot of square dancing," he remembers. "The next thing I knew, I was in a full band." Hartford's earliest recordings were produced by small St. Louis-based labels. "They were done with a group called 'The Ozark Mountain Trio,'" he says. "We didn't call it bluegrass yet. It was mostly called 'old time mountain music.'"

Hartford's musical career was bolstered after he moved to Nashville. "I grew up listening to The Grand Ole Opry," he explains, "and I knew that all the good musicians were there. I got to thinking about it and said, 'Well, I guess, I'll try Nashville for awhile.' I got lucky and landed a job with a radio station." He also played on numerous recording sessions, including The Byrds' seminal country-rock album *Sweethearts Of The Rodeo.* "The Byrds came to town," he recalls, "and went to the place where I was playing and heard me. They hired me and Junior Huskey. They were a bunch of rock 'n' rollers, some who had been folk musicians. We went and did the sessions. I didn't think a whole lot about it."

Hartford eventually signed a recording contract with RCA. "Felton Jarvis produced the early records," he recalls. "Chet Atkins oversaw them. Felton also did Mickey Newbury and, later on, became Elvis Presley's producer. I was interested in putting the banjo into different settings. I had strings and, even, brass on some of my records."

Hartford's second album *Earthwords And Music* featured his version of "Gentle On My Mind." "(Campbell) heard it on the radio," Hartford says. "He bought a copy of the record and had his secretary copy the words down. He sings it well. It unlocked a lot of doors for me."

Glen Campbell and The Smothers Brothers

The success of "Gentle On My Mind" led to a regular spot on The Smothers Brothers' and Glen Campbell's TV shows. "It was very heady," Hartford remembers. "It was quite an ego trip. I was a writer and a performer. My job became to find a good song for the

John Hartford

finale. For awhile, I was doing both shows. We taped them both on the same day. I'd do one show and, then, go across the hall and do a spot on the other show." Hartford went on to host his own syndicated show, *Something Else*. "It was one of the first shows that used, what we now call, 'Video Clips,'" Hartford says. "We'd take a group of musicians and film them in a setting."

Hartford's 1971 album *Aero-Plain* was produced by the eclectic multi-instrumentalist David Bromberg. Hartford reached his creative peak with the album *Mark Twang*, which received a Grammy Award as "Best Ethnic Or Traditional Recording of 1976." He recorded several albums in the late 1970's with Doug and Rodney Dillard. "We grew up together in Missouri," he says. "We used to take some rock 'n' roll songs and some Black songs and do them in our own style."

Hartford's latest albums, *The Annual Waltz* and *Down On The River*, feature The Hartford String Band. "We put the group together eight or nine years ago," he explains. "I had just learned how to read music. My (twenty-six year old) son, Jamie, taught me. I got to where I could write out fiddle charts. I had some friends that had just moved to Nashville and had learned to play country music. We got together and started playing and it sounded good. We played some show dates, but to haul a band around, was pretty expensive."

Waylon Jennings

WAYLON JENNINGS

Nashville's hold on country music was weakened in the 1970's by the harder-edged sounds of Willie Nelson and Waylon Jennings. "The Nashville sound was very smooth and control-led," Waylon Jennings explains from his home in the Music City. "My thing has always been very ragged."

The son of a sharecropper, Jennings grew up in Littlefield, Texas. He first attracted attention as bass player for Buddy Holly's band, The Crickets. "(Holly) taught me a whole lot about the music business in a very short time," he says.

After recording a series of ineffectual singles, Jennings began using his road band, The Waylors, in the studio in 1972. "I needed to have more creative control," he recalls. This new approach proved successful. His 1974 album *This Time* (co-produced by Willie Nelson) provided the first of sixteen number one singles. A year later, he was named The Music Academy's Male Vocalist of The Year.

The Platinum-Selling Outlaws

In 1976, Jennings was featured on the seminal country-rock album *Wanted: The Outlaws* which also included songs by Willie Nelson, Tompall Glaser and Jenning's wife, Jessi Colter. The album became the first country music recording to be certified platinum (one million copies sold). "We were at the right place at the right time," Jennings reflects. "Rock 'n' roll had self-destructed and everybody was looking for something to listen to. We were just being ourselves but we were doing something that no one else was doing."

Jennings, Nelson, Cash and Kristofferson

Jennings and Nelson have continued to record duets. "We met in Phoenix in 1964," Jennings remembers. "We've been friends since." Jennings also remains a close friend of Johnny Cash. "We lived together for two years," he says. "We were both going through divorces and we both had drug problems. I began to do speed and graduated to cocaine." Recent collaborations with Nelson, Cash and Kris Kristofferson, under the banner of "The Highwaymen," have resulted in two best-selling albums.

Until 1983, Jennings admits he remained addicted to drugs. "My number was just about up," he remembers. "I went to Arizona (in 1983) and kicked. I looked at my wife and son (Waylon 'Shooter' Jennings) and saw that I was destroying someone else's life. I wanted to see my little boy grow up."

JERRY JEFF WALKER

Jerry Jeff Walker is one of the hardest-living songwriters. Walker first attracted attention with the mid-1960's rock band Circus Maximus. Between 1967 and 1968, the band worked regularly in the New York area—including lengthy stints at the Greenwich Village clubs, The Night Owl and The Electric Circus—and built a considerable following. After two albums and a minor FM hit ("The Wind")the group split up.

Mr. Bojangles

Walker's decision to leave the group was made easier after recording an in-studio appearance at New York radio station WBAI-FM with David Bromberg. The duo's version of Walker's "Mr. Bojangles" was played twice a night for the next six months by the station. Besides being subsequently recorded by everyone from Nilsson and The Nitty Gritty Dirt Band to George Burns and Sammy Davis Jr., the song's success resulted in Walker signing a solo contract with Atlantic Records' Atco label. However, his initial solo releases sold very little.

Following an extended booking at the premier New York music club, The Bitter End, Walker left New York

Jerry Jeff Walker

in 1973 and resettled in Austin, Texas. Accompanied by The Four-Man Deaf Cowboy Band, The Lost Gonzo Band and The Bandito Band, Walker became one of the leaders of the mid-70's Austin,Texas music scene. Although four albums recorded by Walker and The Lost Gonzos set the standard for tight, high-energy country-rock, Walker and the group severed their relationship in 1976. "I got them a record deal," Walker recalls. "We assumed that they'd be pretty famous and that I'd have to find another band. Gary Nunn helped me put a band together but it never matched the intensity of The Lost Gonzo Band.

Twenty-eight years after he left school in upstate New York to roam the country as a wandering musician, Walker continues to produce sensitive ballads and energetic country-rock. Walker's personal life began to settle down after he met Susan Walker, a former legislative aide to Texas Congressman Charles Wilson, in 1976. "We met at her house in Austin," Walker remembers. In addition to becoming his wife, Susan became his full-time business manager and helped to set up Tried And True Music. "They sort of fill in for what a management company should do," Walker explains. "They take care of public relations and fan correspondence. We've built up a good network of fans—almost 10,000 names."

Buffy Sainte-Marie

BUFFY SAINTE-MARIE

Buffy Sainte-Marie is best known for the anti-war songs and pro-American Indian anthems she wrote in the 1960's. "People thought it was unusual for an Indian woman to be singing about the war," Sainte-Marie says from her home in Hawaii. "So, I guess it stuck in their minds. But people forget that I wrote 'Until It's Time For You To Go' which was recorded by over two hundred different artists in sixteen languages. I wrote 'Up Where We Belong' which was used in the film *An Officer And A Gentleman* and won the Academy Award for best song of the year."

Born of Cree Indian parents on an Indian reservation in Saskatchewan, Canada, Sainte-Marie was adopted as an infant by a couple from Maine who were part Micmac Indian. Most of her formative years, however, were spent in Wakefield, Massachusetts.

In the 1960's

Although she played an important role in the 1960's folk revival, Sainte-Marie was never comfortable with the label "folksinger." "I felt like a fraud," she reflects. "I wasn't singing folk songs. I was writing my own material." It was as a songwriter that Sainte-Marie felt most at ease. "A love song will sometimes just show up in my head," she claims, "complete with words and music. But a song with a political message takes a lot of craft. You've got to make a point while holding the listener's attention."

Following a guest performance at a hootenany at the Gaslight Café in Greenwich Village, Sainte-Marie signed a management contract with Herb Gart and began performing on the East Coast coffeehouse circuit.

Sainte-Marie's earlist albums were released on the prestigious folk-oriented Vanguard Record label. "I couldn't even sing then," she contends. "In those days, I just wanted to write. I was scared and inexperienced. I couldn't even sing on pitch."

Among Saint-Marie's first songs was "Universal Soldier." Recorded by Donovan in 1966, the song became an international hit and one of the theme songs of the anti-war movement. "I was in an airport in San Francisco," Sainte-Marie says. "and saw some soldiers coming back from Vietnam. They were in horrible shape. I talked with the people that were escorting them. It hit me that it's not enough to yell at the generals or the power structure. Everyone has a responsibility for democracy."

Many of Sainte-Marie's songs, including "Now That The Buffalo's Gone," "My Country Tis Of Thee You're Dying" and "Native North American Child" examine her role as a Native American. "My early protest songs were trying to reach out to everybody," she explains. "Later, they were just for the people on the reservations. They didn't need songs about how terrible conditions were. They need to be able to look around and dig themselves."

Recent Work

Beginning in the late 1970's, Sainte-Marie and her son, Dakota Starblanket Wolfchild were regulars on *Sesame Street*. In addition to teaching about breast feeding, sibling rivalry and American Indians, she composed many children's songs. Sainte-Marie has, subsequently, contributed to the scores of several films, including *Starman*, *Jewel Of The Nile* and *9 1/2 Weeks*. She was featured as the Indian narrator for *Broken Arrow*, which won the Academy Award for Best Feature Length Documentary of 1986.

Sainte-Marie is currently preparing to record her first album in eleven years. "I'm writing a lot about addiction," she says. "Not about drug addiction or alcohol addiction, but addiction to money and power. But it's always from compassion. It's not enough to just stand there and point at the power junkies. That's not dealing with fixing the situation. That's like firing the actors without replacing the script. You've got to reform everything."

"I'm writing a lot about addiction. Not about drug addiction or alcohol addiction, but addiction to money and power."

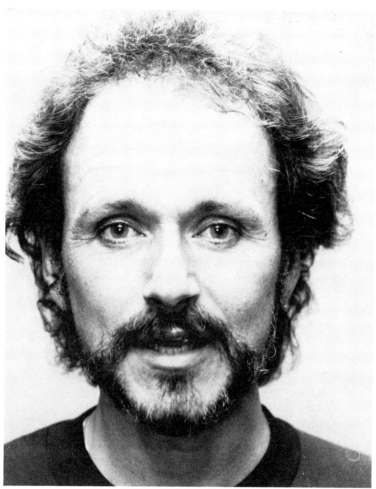

Jesse Colin Young

JESSE COLIN YOUNG

One of the most popular folk-rock bands of the 1960's was The Youngbloods. Led by New York-born and California-based singer-songwriter Jesse Colin Young, the group blended folk music with country and western, blues and rock 'n' roll. "It was difficult to learn how to play as a band," Young recalls from his home in southern California. "We were all very different. (Jerry) Corbitt loved ragtime while I was the only songwriter and a lover of blues and country. I've always listened to everything from T-Bone Walker to Hank Williams."

Gunfighters, Grand Prix and Harvard

The son and nephew of Harvard University teachers, Young was born with the unmusical name, Perry Miller. After recording his debut album *Soul Of A City Boy* in 1962, he renamed himself "Jesse Colin Young" after, what he calls, "a combination of gunfighters and English Grand Prix drivers." "*Soul Of A City Boy* was recorded in four hours," Young recalls. "It's a very innocent-sounding recording. I didn't know too much about performing." In fact, Young hadn't played his first professional gig before he recorded the album.

The Youngbloods

Inspired by The Beatles, Young and Corbitt decided to pool resources and form a band. Together with jazz drummer Joe Bauer and guitarist-keyboardist Lowell "Banana" Levinger, the duo formed The Youngbloods. The group's biggest hit, "Get Together," became one of the theme songs of the late 1960's. Released in 1967, the song remained obscure until being used in a July 1969 TV public service ad. "We weren't getting any radio air play," Young remembers, "except for San Francisco. We walked into a hotel, turned on the radio and there it was. We went back to New York and packed our bags." Despite relocating to California's Marin County, The Youngbloods continued to have problems. When Corbitt left in 1969, The Youngbloods went on as a trio. Although they recorded, what is arguably, their best album (*Elephant Mountain*), the group soon disbanded.

In recent years, Young's performances and recordings have hearkened back to the acoustic sound of his earliest work. Young explains, "I've sensed a rekindling of interest in acoustic music."

LEON REDBONE

Singing 1920's and '30's jazz tunes in his distinctive nasal voice, Leon Redbone has revived the spirit of Jelly Roll Morton, Fats Waller, Jimmie "The Singing Brakeman" Rodgers and other turn-of-the-century jazz and Tin Pan Alley songwriters. Although his earliest performances were as a solo singer-guitarist, Redbone has lately been accompanied by an ever-changing lineup of musicians. "There was a long time before I had anyone playing with me," he says during a recent telephone interview. "There was less noise. Playing by myself, I can do a lot of slow, quiet songs."

The Mystery and the Music

Discreetly hidden behind dark glasses, a bushy mustache and an ever-present white panama hat, Redbone remains one of music's most mysterious characters. "There's not much I want to add at this time," he says.

Questions about music, however, bring a flood of thoughts and observations. "Opera used to be my favorite music," he recalls, "especially tenor arias. I've always listened to Chopin. The sounds of jazz bands were, at first, kind of bizarre."

Leon Redbone

Redbone's debut album *On The Track* introduced him to a cult-like following when it was released in 1972. Four years later, an appearance on *Saturday Night Live* brought him national attention. "It had a positive effect," he claims. "It introduced me to millions of people. A certain percentage reacted favorably. But I didn't like the experience personally."

A starring role in a television commercial for Budweiser beer brought him even greater acclaim. Filmed in 1982, the commercial was repeatedly shown over the next three years. "It wasn't a great acting job," Redbone confesses. "The whole thing was a little too frantic for my taste."

Redbone's 1985 album *Red To Blue* was his first release after a lengthy absence from the studio. "I'd gotten involved with a record label," he explains. "They put out an album, but then, they disappeared. It took a few years before I knew what to do about the situation."

Although Redbone claims that he no longer actively seeks out material ("I've listened to so much over the years, it all remains in my memory"), he continues to research early American music. "I'm really interested in history," he points out. "Especially as it pertains to music—from the turn of the century to now."

John Gorka and Shawn Colvin

Singer-Songwriters

Singer-songwriters comprise the most durable branch of
tradition-rooted music. While an earlier generation referred to themselves as
"Woody's Children," current performers are more closely related to the folk-rock
sounds of Bob Dylan. Although lyrics remain essential, technological advances have
led to a more modern sound complete with drums, electric instruments and well conceived arrangements. "We start by talking about how to realize the potential of each
tune," explains Darlene Wilson, who has produced award-winning albums by Bill
Morrissey and Patty Larkin. "We approach each song as a little gem."

Passim's

Although performers come from areas throughout the United States and the world,
the Boston/Cambridge area remains a hotbed for tradition-rooted music. Passim's,
the Harvard Square folk music coffeehouse owned and operated by Bob and Rae
Ann Donlin, offers music six nights a week. "It's the penultimate place to see nation-
ally-known acoustic acts in an intimate setting," Patty Larkin says from her home on
Massachusetts' Cape Cod. "I've been playing at the club, at least twice a year, since
1983. It's a great place to test new material. For me, it's the real thing."

Passim's is located at 47 Palmer Street, the final site of the legendary coffeehouse,
Club 47. Although it was initially owned by Walter and Renee Juda, the Donlins took
over after a few months. "We started out with classical guitarists and flamenco
guitarists," Bob Donlin recalls. "We thought music was a very risky business but we've
always been interested in folk music. We knew that it would be a good site. It's a prime
location, within walking distance for around 300,000 students."

Folk music's popularity has been, to Donlin, like a roller coaster ride. "It was practically phased out around 1967. People were getting tired of messages," he remembers. "Electricity moved in and pushed acoustic music out of the way. A lot of young
people switched off. It became a hard road." Passim's, however, continued to be successful. "In the 1970's, we had people like John Prine, James Taylor, Steve Goodman,
Jimmy Buffett and Jim Croce," Donlin explains, "and we had to turn people away."

JOHN GORKA

John Gorka was the first artist signed by Windham Hill when the formerly all New Age
instrumental record label expanded to include tradition-rooted singer-songwriters.
"It's a new direction for Windham Hill," Gorka says. "That's a really good thing for
me, since I benefit from all the publicity. They realize that there's a market for this
kind of music. There's an audience for it."

Gorka's writing reflects the painful complexities of modern-day relationships. "I
don't think that all of my albums are going to be dark, depressing records," Gorka explains between sets at the Falcon Ridge Folk Festival.

Born in New Jersey, Gorka has been living in Easton, Pennsylvania since 1976.
"I'm an ear musician," he explains. "In the sixth grade, I studied viola with the Suzuki
method. They taught that talent is not a cause. It's the effect of practicing and working at it."

Gorka was heavily influenced by singer-songwriters such as Stan Rogers, Claudia
Schmidt, Joni Mitchell, Jackson Browne, Judy Collins, Steve Goodman, James Taylor
and John Prine. "It's the personal nature of the songs," he reflects. "It appealed to me
as a whole person rather than just a part of me. It seemed there was music and songs
for my heart and for my head. The range of subjects and different kinds of music was
interesting to me."

Gorka had a natural instinct for songwriting. "It was easier for me to write my own songs," he says, "than for me to learn other people's songs." He was exposed to traditional folk songs when he worked as Assistant Editor of *Sing Out!* magazine. "I did a little bit of everything," he remembers. "I wrote introductions to the songs that appeared in the magazine."

Recordings

The earliest John Gorka recordings were featured on albums issued by *The Fast Folk Musical Magazine.* "I'm fortunate to be sort of an outpatient of the New York folk scene," he says. "I'm able to hang out and be around all these great people but I'm also able to avoid all the politics. I don't know that this person doesn't like that person. I like everybody. I like being part of the scene."

Gorka's albums (*I Know* and *Land Of The Bottom Line*) have been produced by Bill Kollar. "We tried to do things differently this time," Gorka says. "We had some real breakthroughs. Instead of using headphones, which can sometimes distort how you hear things, we used a small speaker in the studio. I also played guitar when I sang, even though I was playing along to an existing guitar track. By playing quietly, without the guitar even being heard, I could sing it exactly as I do when I perform. The phrasing is tied to the way that I play. It's the way that I feel it."

Two songs —"Prom Night In Pig Town" and "I Saw A Stranger With Your Hair"— are featured on both of Gorka's albums. "Will Ackerman (Windham Hill founder and moving spirit) wanted me to re-do half of the songs from the first album," Gorka recalls. "I really like the first album and I'm glad that they liked the songs enough to want to get them to a larger audience, but, I felt that I couldn't do that to the people that bought the first record. I didn't want them to have to buy an album that only had five or six new songs."

Although Gorka usually performs as a soloist, he was accompanied by a band in the recording studio. "When you bring in other musicians," he says, "it changes how you play, especially if you're used to playing by yourself. It's easier for me to play with other people than it is for other people to play with me. It's a careful balance. Sometimes, you can get a more dynamic and varied kind of album if you allow the other musicians to contribute to the arrangements."

> *"It was easier for me to write my own songs than for me to learn other people's songs."*

Fears that Gorka's songs would be obscured by the other musicians proved unfounded. "Some people were afraid that, by going with a bigger record label, my music was, all of a sudden, going to sound overly-produced," Gorka says. "But it's not covered up by the big drum sound of pop music. I think *Land Of The Bottom Line* is an intimate and personal kind of record. It grows on you. It kind of sneaks up on you. People like it more after they listen to it for a while. We took our time doing it and I really like the way that it turned out."

SHAWN COLVIN

Shawn Colvin has sung on albums by Bill Morrissey, Greg Brown, Eric Andersen, John Gorka and Suzanne Vega. Her most satisfying project, however, was singing background vocals on Bruce Hornsby's album *A Night On The Town.* "I think he's great," she says from her hotel room in San Francisco. "I owned his first record and used to sing along. (Singing with him) was very flattering and very beautiful. It wasn't arranged the way that I would've sung it. I like that. It gave me a real push."

Born in Vermillion, North Dakota, Colvin has been playing music since the age of ten, when her father, a "Kingston Trio fanatic," taught her to play guitar. Colvin's earliest break came when she sang background vocals on Suzanne Vega's album *Solitude Standing* and on her European tour. "In one sense, it meant very little," Colvin says.

"But in the long run, it was very important. Suzanne's manager (Ron Fierstein) is now my manager. He's been successful with Suzanne and he's got a lot of influence in the music world."

Stepping onto center stage as a soloist, Colvin is on the threshold of a very promising career. "I'm typical of my generation," she reflects. "I didn't have to rebel against marriage. No one was forcing me to get married. I'm able to pursue what I've always wanted to do. It's time for someone like me to do it," she continues. "The time has come when people want songwriters to express anger and voice concerns."

Colvin initially gave little thought to being a solo singer-songwriter. After performing in the Broadway play *Diamond Studs* and meeting The Red Clay Ramblers, Colvin joined the band. "I thought they were great musicians," she recalls. "They touched on every kind of music—Irish, jazz, bluegrass, blues and folk. We only did one or two of my songs but I like singing harmonies."

Recordings

After playing with a series of pop and rock bands, Colvin attracted attention as a member of the Speakeasy

Shawn Colvin

songwriter cooperative and the *Fast Folk Musical Magazine.* In 1985 she accepted an invitation to perform several concerts with the Fast Folk Music Revue. When her song "I Don't Know Why" was included in the May 1985 album/magazine, *Live At Arlington Town Hall,* it quickly became a modern folk classic. Colvin's debut album *Live Tape* was recorded at the Somerville Theater in Somerville, MA. "I was weary of doing it at all," she explains. "I wanted my first thing to be on a major record label."

Signed by Columbia Records, Colvin's wish for major label success is about to come true. "It's a real good time," she says. "It couldn't have happened five years ago. But when Tracy Chapman's record went to number one, it turned a lot of heads." Colvin's first album for the label, *Steady On,* reflects the vision of John Leventhal, who co-produced the album with Steve Addabo. "He's a great producer," proclaims Colvin. "He has a great sense of sound. He's always been moving and inspiring to me. I've always been able to write lyrics to his music." *Steady On* won a Grammy as the "Best Contemporary Folk Recording" of 1990.

Folk music and major record labels have traditionally differed over creativity and economics. Colvin, however, sees no such conflict. "I don't understand the war between folkies and commerciality," she claims. "I don't mind them being commercial. No one's asked me to change the things that I do."

"The time has come when people want songwriters to express anger and voice concerns."

Patty Larkin

PATTY LARKIN

Patty Larkin is one of the Boston/Cambridge area's most successful performers. When her debut album *Step Into The Light* was released by Rounder/Philo in 1986, it was immediately added to the playlists of folk music-oriented radio programs. "It was a sampler," Larkin says, "of all the different styles of music that I'm into."

Larkin's second album *I'm Fine* received the Boston Music Award for "Best Folk Album of 1987." "We spent a lot more time and money," Larkin says. "It's a lot more produced than the first album."

Larkin's Background

Born in Iowa, Larkin has been surrounded by music throughout her life. "My mother was an artist," she recalls, "and both of my grandmothers taught piano."

Although she performed with a series of bands, Larkin began to be more and more involved with folk and acoustic music. "I met people, like Trapezoid and Claudia Schmidt, on the folk circuit," she recalls. "I realized that it was possible to make a living playing acoustic music. I was getting burnt out on playing rock clubs."

Joining forces with bass player Richard Gates and harmony vocalist Catherine David, Larkin played opening sets for performers such as Loudon Wainwright III and The Persuasions. "Folk music began to really open up," she says. "David Grisman and The New Grass Revival made things really interesting. Joan Armatrading and Steve Forbert had great lyrics, an acoustic background and were being recorded by major labels."

Larkin's dynamic stage show was captured on her 1990 album *Live In The Square*. Recorded during a concert at Harvard University's Sanders Theater, the album ranges from tongue-in-jowl tunes — "Me," "At The Mall" and "I'm White"— to serious social commentary. Larkin's interpretation of Andy Barnes' "The Last Leviathan" is a soul-wrenching tribute to the demise of the great whales, while the original tune "Metal Drums" is a powerful condemnation of chemical waste.

Larkin joined with Christine Lavin, Megan McDonough and Sally Fingerett in the Fall of 1990 to tour and record a live album as *Buy Me, Bring Me, Take Me: Don't Mess My Hair—Life According To Four Bitchin' Babes*.

Larkin's recent performances have been as a soloist. "A band is a lot of fun," she says, "but unless you're able to really rehearse, the music doesn't work. Playing solo is a real challenge. It's a lot harder to feel comfortable when you're on your own."

GREG BROWN

Greg Brown attracted national attention as "house songwriter" for Garrison Keillor's late-and-lamented radio show *A Prairie Home Companion.* "A few acts on the show had done my songs," he recalls from his home in Iowa, "so, the producer finally called me and asked me to appear." Brown spent four years with the show. "I did a lot of tours with them," he says. "It helped me a lot. I could go into any city and they already knew me. It made touring a lot easier. It certainly did help."

Brown's performances on the show, however, gave little indication of his stage persona. "It was different than my shows," he explains. "On the 'Prairie Home Companion' show, I did this thing called 'The Department of Folk Songs.' Kids from all around the country wrote in and requested songs. People thought that I was a lot more traditional than I am." Brown left in 1985. "I got bored with it," he says. "I'd been on it a lot over four years. I told Garrison that I'd do it as long as it was fun."

Brown's early musical influences included gospel music. "My father was an open Bible preacher," he remembers. His musical interests were fur-

Greg Brown

ther influenced by a move to the Ozark Mountain region of Missouri. Although he studied piano and organ, Brown was enchanted by the guitar. "I started playing when I was twelve," he says. "My mother and my uncles played."

Brown's first break came when he was hired as a staff songwriter for the publishing company owned by Buck Ram, former manager of The Platters. "When I was nineteen years old, I was playing in a trio," Brown remembers. "A woman in the band had met (Ram) and had sent him a tape." Working in Ram's Los Angeles office, Brown experienced the assembly-line style of songwriting. "Buck had a lot of bands working for him," he recalls. "I was trying to write stuff for different bands."

Selected Recordings

Brown has released six albums. Brown's debut album *The Iowa Waltz* was written for the Iowa Arts Council. "I tailored it for that audience," he recalls. "It confused a lot of people. They thought I was some kind of a 'folksinger.'" Although his earliest work centered around his acoustic guitar and gritty vocals, his album *One Big Town* features politically-conscious lyrics and fully-conceived, rock-minded arrangements. "I write songs in bunches," he says. "I wrote (most of the album) during a time when I was touring like a maniac. I went to Europe, partly as a vacation and partly to perform. I started thinking about America." The album introduced Brown's music to a much wider following. "It was reviewed in *Rolling Stone*," he explains. "It got a different response than anything I'd ever done before."

Brown's sixth album *Down In There* signaled a return to the acoustic sound of his earlier work. "I had a lot of fun writing those songs," he explains. "There are portraits and short stories about a lot of different characters. The sound is closer to the music that I grew up with—country blues with a little rock 'n' roll thrown in."

Brown's songs have been covered by performers ranging from Bill Staines and Garrison Keillor to Santana and Willie Nelson. An early composition, "They All Went To Mexico," was recorded in 1980 by Santana with guest vocalist Willie Nelson. "It was another typical fluke," Brown explains. "I sent a tape to Muscle Shoals and tried to interest them in a band that I was with. They were recording an album with Santana and decided to do the song. No one in Santana could sing it, so they got Willie Nelson to come in. It was wild."

Songs Of Innocence And Experience

Brown's love of poetry was reflected on his 1986 album-length tribute to William Blake, *Songs Of Innocence And Experience*. "It's one of the nice things about being on a small record label," Brown reflects. "I was a little nervous. I thought I'd bitten more than I could chew. I felt responsible for the poems. I thought everybody played beautifully. A lot of Blake scholars have told me how much they liked it."

Perhaps the biggest compliment paid Brown's music is Prudence Johnson's latest album, *Songs Of Greg Brown*. "She did a really good job," Brown says. "Not only did she do a few favorites, but, she did a few old ones that I've never recorded."

Fast Folk Musical Magazine

The most influential outlet for tradition-rooted singer-songwriters is the monthly audio/magazine *The Fast Folk Musical Magazine,* issued by the Songwriter's Cooperative in Greenwich Village. "I came in a month or two after the thing congealed," Dave Van Ronk says. "The moving spirit was Jack Hardy. He had a songwriter's workshop that would get together once a week. They'd play songs that were new or still in progress and everybody would sit around and critique it and discuss it. They used to meet at the Cornelius Street Cafe, but it got to the point where there was just too many people. The word had gotten around. After a couple of years, they formed the Songwriter's Cooperative and got a deal with a guy that owned a bar, The Speakeasy. They started to book entertainment in the back room. There's no one style that they've been propagandizing," Van Ronk explains, "but, I hear echoes of a style that I think of as the Cornelius Street group sound."

The monthly *Fast Folk Musical Magazine* helped to distribute the early songs of Suzanne Vega, Shawn Colvin, Christine Lavin, John Gorka and Rod MacDonald, among many others. Julie Gold's prayer-like tune "From A Distance," which received a Grammy award as "Best Song of 1990," was first performed in 1988 during the magazine's annual "Fast Folk Musical Revue."

CHRISTINE LAVIN

"I wasn't in *Fast Folk* at the beginning," Christine Lavin recalls from her Manhattan apartment, "but I got involved shortly afterward. I recorded a live album in 1981 but the record company had gone out of business. I wanted to make another record. Someone suggested that I speak with Jack Hardy. He spent a lot of time telling me how to go about making a record." Lavin became the monthly magazine/record's

> *"On the 'Prairie Home Companion' show . . . people thought I was a lot more traditional than I am."*

production coordinator. "It was a real schlep job," she reflects, "but it was a good experience. I learned a lot about the different qualities of vinyl."

Born in Peekskill, New York, Lavin grew up on the campus of a military academy. Appropriately, she sometimes incorporates a baton-twirling bit into her stage act. Lavin learned to play guitar by watching a PBS instruction series. "By the time that I was thirteen," she remembers, "I was performing at school and at girl scout parties. I felt that I could do it for a living."

After moving to New York City in 1976, Lavin began studying under Dave Van Ronk. "He's a stern task master," she explains. "I was working real hard. I took it very seriously. It was costing me a lot of money."

Humorous . . . and Serious

Although she's best known for her humorous songs, such as "Cold Pizza For Breakfast," "Prince Charles" and "Don't Ever Call Your Sweetheart By His Name," comedy is only a by-product of Lavin's deeply insightful vision. "All my songs are based on true things in my life," she explains.

Lavin's most serious project was her album *Good Thing He Can't Read My Mind*, which received the National

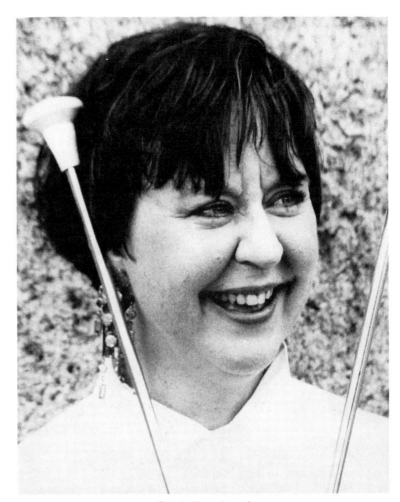

Christine Lavin

Association of Independent Record Distributors' award as "Best Adult Contemporary" album of 1988. "I went more for music than comedy," she explains. "The producer (Bill Kollar) wanted songs that would hold up over time."

Lavin, however, hasn't completely forsaken satire and humor. Her song "Mysterious Woman" pokes fun at fellow singer-songwriter Suzanne Vega. "I wrote it in New Hampshire on my way to a gig at the Folkway," she says. "I wrote half of it in the car. I thought it was really bizarre and shelved it. But when I played it for Andrew Ratshin (of the Seattle-based vocal trio Uncle Bonzai) he told me that I had to record it. Suzanne wrote me a note and told me that she liked it. She was flattered."

Good Thing He Can't Read My Mind also featured a duet with Livingston Taylor of the Petula Clark hit "Downtown." "Folk music gets very little airplay on commercial radio," Lavin explains. "But songs that they know get played. I wanted to take a familiar song and do it in a different way."

Lavin's fifth album *Attainable Love* combines well-crafted Ballads with more satirical songs. "I wanted it to sound like what I sound like on stage," she says. "I sell a lot of records off the stage during my concerts. It's more spontaneous. It's got a more lively sound."

Rod MacDonald

ROD MACDONALD

Poetic vision and journalistic insight are combined in the songs of Rod MacDonald. "A journalist chronicles the times and a poet tells us about his life," the former law student and *Newsweek* reporter explains during lunch in Boston. "I try to do both. The objectivity that I rejected as a journalist, I find now has value to me as a songwriter. There are times when I want to write a song without my opinion in it. I just want to tell people what's going on."

MacDonald's best known songs, "The Sailor's Prayer" and "American Jerusalem" have been covered by many folk performers. "I like Garnet Rogers' version of 'American Jerusalem,'" MacDonald says. Suzie Burke just recorded 'Sailor's Prayer.' Free Hot Lunch, Jean Redpath, Lisa Neustadt, and Gordon Bok and have done it. Everybody does it differently."

MacDonald and The Speakeasy

MacDonald has been at the forefront of Greenwich Village's folk scene since the early 1970's. "I got into the Village around the same time that Jack Hardy and The Roches did," he recalls. "We were the 'new blood.' The Speakeasy was a major thing for me. It really accomplished what it was trying to do. It provided a place for people to play their own songs in a listening environment. Jack Hardy always had a lot of weight with all the singers around town. He declared this meeting and they announced the formation of a cooperative. It seemed like a good idea to me."

MacDonald booked the music for the Speakeasy between 1984 and 1987. "We got better and better performers as time went on," he reflects. "There were always frustrating situations. There were people, that I thought were great, that couldn't draw a crowd. You couldn't do much about it." MacDonald's involvement with the club ended in 1987. "There was a big political struggle," he remembers. "The owner brought in his own person to run it. The cooperative had a vote and decided to leave. The place tried to run as a commercial club—from the owner's pocket into the owner's pocket. That's a different scene. It's not as musically hip."

Although he maintains an apartment in The Village, MacDonald spends much of his time in northern Italy. "The feelings that I've experienced have surfaced in some of my songs," he says. "Sometimes, I believe in reincarnation. When I first went to this part of Italy, I felt like I had been there before. I had such an easy relationship with the people. It's as if we had always known each other. I've even learned to speak the language."

BOB FRANKE

Bob Franke's songs have become standards of contemporary folk music. Franke uses hard hitting and emotionally revealing images. "(The song) 'Hard Love' really moves people," he says from his home in Salem, Massacusetts. "My dad was an alcoholic. As the son of an alcoholic, I see the world differently. The character in the song sees the world in the same way. He's got difficulty seeing the world the way that it is, but goes ahead with living anyway."

Born in Detroit in 1948, Franke began to play guitar at the age of 14 and began writing songs a couple of years later. He eventually became active in Ann Arbor's folk music scene while attending The University Of Michigan. "I paid for part of my college expenses by playing gigs," he recalls.

Franke moved to eastern Massachusetts in 1969. He planned to attend the Episcopal Theological School in Cambridge but was pulled so much by music that he left the school and began to play music full-time. Performances thoughout New England enabled him to build a following for his well-crafted songs.

Bob Franke

Franke and Barbara Smith organized a folk music coffeehouse, Saturday Night In Marblehead, as a ministry of the Church of St. Andrew in 1978. "We approached the church with an eight page proposal. They ok'd six weeks, then increased it to another six weeks. The church tries to be open to different ideas. The pastor is committed to nuclear issues, peace issues and in getting the community together. We were the first in the area to present Stan Rogers, Claudia Schmidt and Cindy Kallet," Franke boasts. "They were hired on the basis of their audition tapes."

A Religious/Spiritual Thread

Many of Franke's songs were written following dreams but other environments have been equally inspiring. "'Beggars To God' was written as a wedding gift. I couldn't be there. When I called the bride, she told me to write a poem. I did it in the middle of the night. I woke at 4 AM in Lansing, Michigan and recorded a cassette. Another friend performed it at the wedding."

A religious/spiritual thread runs throughout Franke's compositions. "I want to state my religious perspective in a form that folk musicians can understand," he explains. "The kingdom of God isn't just life after death. It's the total reality of human life. As an artist, I have to talk about these realities."

Fred Small

FRED SMALL

Although songwriting trends have shifted away from topical songs, several singer-songwriters, including Si Kahn and Fred Small, continue to use tradition-rooted music as the background for their social commentary. "I choose stories that illustrate people at their best," Small explains from his home in Cambridge, Massachusetts. "Stories about people taking charge of their lives. My songs offer lessons on how to take power in our lives without hurting people or being violent. But I'm much more than just a cheerleader. I try to correct the imbalance of the news media. Murder and rape can be expressed easily in a headline. But it's much harder to tell a story about love, courage or community."

Small's Background

Small's musical interests trace back to his parents' collection of Kingston Trio records. "Folk music was very clean-cut," he recalls. "It didn't have the sexuality of rock 'n' roll. At the age of eight, that was very reassuring." Before long, Small began to play guitar. "In those days, you could buy a guitar for $17.95," he remembers. "They were brutal. It was like putting your finger on a slicer."

Friends and baby-sitters introduced Small to the expanding world of folk music. "I heard The Weavers," he says, "and Pete Seeger, Peter, Paul and Mary and early Dylan." His parents also continued to play a role in his musical evolution. "My parents weren't especially musical or political," he says, "but they were extremely supportive. They took us to concerts. I saw Dylan playing a solo acoustic concert at Rutgers in 1964 when I was eleven years old."

Topical songs had an especially potent influence. "I was politicized by music," Small claims. "It was a whole new world reflected through music." A turning point came in 1964 when Small attended performances by Tom Paxton and the late Phil Ochs. "They became major models for me," he explains. "It was a very painless introduction to a liberal perspective (Paxton) and a radical view (Ochs). Paxton's songs are very accessible. They're very clean, very simple, many are political. I love to listen to them. Ochs blew my mind with 'I Ain't A Marchin' Anymore.' By 1965, half the songs that I was singing were by Paxton and another third were by Ochs."

Small's musical aspirations were further encouraged during the summer of 1966 when he attended New York's Indian Hill summer camp. "It was very much in the New York Jewish liberal and socialist tradition," he recalls, "a far cry from the WASP environment in New Jersey. Carly Simon was on the staff. Lorre Wyatt was the guitar teacher. The camp directors were friends with Judy Collins and the Guthrie family. Judy and Arlo used to come and sit under a tree and sing songs."

By the late 1960's, however, folk music was rapidly fading into obscurity. "The folk revival was co-opted by pop music," Small claims. "No one was making the kind of music that I was interested in." With a career in music seemingly out of the question, Small continued his education at Yale University and The University of Michigan. His first original song was written during his first semester of law school. "One morning, after taking a Civil Procedures exam," he remembers, "I wrote a song about land use. Law school was very intellectually rigid," he continues. "My brain was looking for some creative outlet. The songs started to come out."

During the summer of 1975, Small heard that Lorre Wyatt was working on the Sloop Clearwater and paid him a visit. "I hadn't seen him in eight years," he says. "The last time, I was still an adolescent. I played him a few songs. He gave me the contracts for some gigs that he couldn't play. It was exciting to me to be able to sing to an appreciative audience."

Music Wins Out Over Law School

Although Small returned to Law School, he was smitten by the desire to play music. "The last year at school," he recalls, "there was a talent show. I didn't want to participate but they were very persistent. I did a three song set. The place went wild and I won first prize. Afterwards, the Dean of the law school, who had taught me, asked why I wanted to be a lawyer. It gave me pause." After graduation, Small quickly found a high-paying job as an environmental attorney. "It was the perfect job," he claims. "I was thrilled to get it. I walked into Boston Common and threw my new briefcase thirty feet into the air." The job, however, lasted only eighteen months before Small left. "Music was getting more and more exciting."

Most of Small's earliest gigs were at anti-nuclear benefits. "The Three Mile Island accident had occurred," he explains. "Rallies started to draw 50,000 to 100,000 people. Organizers kept me in mind. They knew that I would get people on their feet and singing. They invited me even though they were also inviting Jackson Browne, Bonnie Raitt and Crosby, Stills and Nash. There's a tremendously exhilarating feeling to be able to ignite the energy of a crowd that size. I found it to be intoxicating." Small, however, discovered that a career in folk music was almost impossible. "The folk scene had changed," he reflects. "The folk clubs weren't inclined to welcome new artists."

Small, nonetheless, remained persistent. It wasn't long before his songs were attracting attention. "I had to find places to play," he says. "I did a lot of political gigs. I played rallies on the Common almost every week, meetings, conferences. I played National Social Change conferences and developed a lot of national contacts. Gradually, I developed a following." Small's songs have been covered by Pete and Peggy Seeger, Priscilla Herdman and Steve Gillette.

BILL MORRISSEY

Jug band music and Mississippi John Hurt-style country blues are combined with well-crafted lyrics and arrangements by Bill Morrissey. Although his two earlier albums (*Bill Morrissey* and *North*) focus on ice-fishing, romancing and the working class of the North country, Morrissey's third album *Standing Eight*, which won the Boston Music Award as "Best Folk/Acoustic Album of 1989," deals more with interpersonal relationships. "A lot of it has to do with getting divorced," Morrissey explains from his home in New Hampshire. "You write about what concerns you, so, a lot of songs have that in the background."

> *"I choose stories that illustrate people at their best."*

Bill Morrissey

Standing Eight, whose title comes from the boxing term, features Morrissey's most ambitious musical arrangements. "It's got people like Buskin and Batteau, Patty Larkin, Johnny Cunningham and Cormac McCarthy," Morrissey says. "Shawn Colvin and Suzanne Vega sing harmonies. There are some cuts with a full rhythm section, some that I play solo. It's the first of my albums that I can listen to. It's got a great batch of songs, great arrangements."

Morrissey was featured on Windham Hill's showcase of contemporary singer-songwriters, *Legacy.* "I'm glad to see Windham Hill beginning to discover singer-songwriters," Morrissey says. "They've already signed Pierce Pettis and John Gorka. They're a mid-range label with major label distribution (through A&M). But I don't know why they picked the performers that they did."

Morrissey's Background

Born in Hartford, Connecticut, Morrissey first discovered folk music in the eighth grade. "Every kid could play some kind of instrument," he remembers. "A lot of us had older brothers and sisters who went to the coffeehouses, like Club 47, in Cambridge and came back talking about people like Tim Hardin."

Much of Morrissey's self-taught guitar playing was inspired by Mississippi John Hurt. "I heard a record at a friend's house," he remembers. "It was like discovering The Beatles. He's got the greatest guitar style. He's more of a songster than a bluesman. He'd have the bass line going with his thumb and use his other fingers to pick a melody. At fourteen years old, I could pull off his songs. They had a good-time feel."

Performing solo and, occasionally, with guitarist Russ Washburn, Morrissey became a fixture of New Hampshire's folk music circuit. "There were enough clubs in Newmarket and Portsmouth that I was able to make a living," he explains. Things began to change in 1982. "I got my first press," Morrissey remembers. "The writer had seen me as opening act for Tom Paxton at (a late-and-lamented Cambridge club) The Idler." Moving temporarily to Cambridge, Morrissey joined with Elijah Wald and Dave Van Ronk to form the short-lived Reckless record label. Among the label's three releases was Morrissey's self-titled debut album.

Morrissey has worked closely with the three-year old Falcon Ridge Folk Festival. "I'm kind of a consultant," he says. "Since I'm on the circuit, (Festival promoter) Howard Randall calls me a lot for advice."

CORMAC MCCARTHY

Cormac McCarthy has written about everything from poodles to hereditary madness. His recent songs, however, reflect a much gentler inspiration. "Since the birth of my son," he says from his home in New Hampshire, "I've been able to sing lullabys."

Although he was born in Ohio, McCarthy is firmly rooted in rural New England. "I moved to New Hampshire when I was ten years old," he recalls. "My dad wanted a new start. He had a real pioneer spirit."

Blues and a variety of '60's music influenced McCarthy but acoustic and folk music had the strongest pull. "I gravitated to acoustic music for the lyrical possibilities," McCarthy explains. "I was an English major in college. I had a great love of poetry and fiction. The way that most kids write private poetry, I wrote songs."

McCarthy was encouraged to perform while a student at Plymouth State College. One of the musicians that McCarthy befriended was singer-songwriter Bill Morrissey. "I had heard stories about this guy that played harmonica and wore baggy pants. Eventually, we met and became good friends. He moved into my dorm room and spent the next year and a half trying to get me to flunk out of the college."

Cormac McCarthy

Troubled Sleep

McCarthy's second album *Troubled Sleep* was released in 1990. "It's a fairly dark record," he says. "There's a lot of stories from burnt-out, small-town New England. There's a sea song ('When My Boat Is Built Again') about a guy rebuilding his boat and his life at the same time. Two songs deal directly with dream consciousness. Reality comes in and out, hand in hand with dreams. It's kind of an empathetic record. There's a lot of feelings." *Troubled Sleep* has a much fuller sound than McCarthy's earlier work. "There's a lot of piano and bass," McCarthy says. "Johnny Cunningham plays violin on a couple tunes. There's some Stratocaster-type fills. There's even some sythesizer but it's very much in the background."

The songs span McCarthy's songwriting career. "The title song was written a month before I recorded it," McCarthy reflects. "It's a lullaby for adults, the people that really need them." The oldest song, "Wild Beneath My Window," was written twelve or thirteen years ago. "I was living in a really cheap hotel in east L.A.," McCarthy recalls, "and I felt a little nostalgic for New Hampshire."

"The way that most kids write private poetry, I wrote songs."

David Buskin

DAVID BUSKIN AND ROBIN BATTEAU

David Buskin's songs have been performed by Mary Travers, Tom Rush and Judy Collins. His advertising jingles have promoted Burger King, the United States Postal Service and NBC. His best work, however, has been in collaboration with violin player, guitarist, vocalist and songwriter Robin Batteau. "Robin and I have different ways of approaching a song," he explains from his home in New York. "I'll try to think of a logical story. I craft it so that the story gets revealed measure by measure. Robin will sometimes come up with a line that I hadn't even thought of. Sometimes, I don't like it. But, sometimes, I'm knocked out. That's the essence of the collaboration."

Buskin began his professional career in the late 1960's. "I got out of the army," he remembers, "and decided that I wanted to be a songwriter and a singer. I'd always been in bands. I'd taken piano lessons when I was a kid. I couldn't think of anything that I would rather do. It was tied in with my politics. I was involved in the typical folky liberal causes. Anti-War was a big thing. I got myself a guitar and started working."

His earliest break came when one of his songs was recorded by Mary Travers. "I had written a song that I thought would be great for Peter, Paul and Mary," he recalls. "It was a song called 'When I Needed You Most Of All,' which I eventually put on my first record. They had just broken up. When my manager asked who I would prefer sing it, I said 'Mary.' That's how I ended up meeting her. I wound up being in her band for a couple of years." A solo record deal led him to leave Travers' band.

Pierce Arrow

Buskin & Batteau have been working together since the late 1970's when they met in the rock band Pierce Arrow. Although the group's debut album was a critical success, their second release faltered. "It was obvious that the band wasn't doing well," explains Buskin. "There were a lot of angry scenes." With the breakup of the band, Buskin sought other outlets for his music. "A fellow that I knew needed someone to entertain five thousand kids for an hour and a half. I said that I would do it. I figured that if I got Robin to do a half hour and we worked together for a half hour, I could hold their attention for a half hour. The kids loved us," he continues. "We began to think that, maybe, playing acoustic music could be a lot of fun."

The duo later joined Tom Rush's band. "Tom's piano player had just left and he was looking for another piano player," recalls Buskin. "I went up to his place in New Hampshire. The next night, I played with him."

Batteau was added for shows at (New York City club) The Bottom Line. "I talked to Tom," Buskin explains, "and told him that what he needed was a violin player. It worked great. Tom, Robin and I started going out as a trio. We had a great time. That was one of the most enjoyable gigs I've ever had."

"The Heartbeat of America"

Buskin began writing jingles in 1980. "I was tapped out," he reflects, "and I was looking for a job. I was tired of struggling from week to week. I knew some people that were doing jingles. I thought that I could do it. So, I managed to put together a demo tape and started knocking on doors. Fortunately, I hit the right door. The first one that I sold had quite a bit of success. It was called 'We're NBC, Watch Us Now.' It won a Clio Award, which is like the advertising industry's Oscar."

Batteau also began to write jingles and the duo soon became two of the most in-demand jingle writers. "My favorite is the one that I did for the

Robin Batteau

Postal Service, 'We Deliver, We Deliver,'" Buskin says. "It's a really good example of the form. Of course, no one hears more than just the tag. But it's actually a two minute song. I also wrote one for Burger King called 'This Is A Burger King Town' that I liked very much. I imagine that Robin's favorite is 'The Heartbeat Of America,' which is one of the most popular jingles of all time." Batteau also maintains a busy schedule as a much-in-demand studio musican, including work with Nanci Griffith and Christine Lavin.

Buskin recently disbanded the jingle writing company that he shared with Batteau in order to devote more time to writing songs. "Jingles were taking up all of my time," he explains. "I felt that I needed to back up a little bit. When we started our company, we said that we would get a show together and record another album and all these wonderful things. I want to make some more progress."

Recent collaborations with Judy Collins revived Buskin's interests in songwriting. "We wrote five songs for her new album," he says. "We met her at a benefit at Peter Yarrow's apartment. Judy, Robin and I wrote a song about New York City with a positive outlook called 'City Of Cities.' It ended up on Judy's album. We had such a good time writing that one that we said 'Let's keep on doing this and see what happens.'"

The Indigo Girls

THE INDIGO GIRLS

The Indigo Girls represent the future of folk music. Their self-titled major label debut album, released in September 1989, achieved Gold Record status and led to the duo being awarded a Grammy as "Best Contemporary Folk Group of 1989."

Amy Ray and Emily Saliers met in the sixth grade in Decatur, Georgia. "We were both playing guitar," Ray remembers, "and singing in the playground and the lunch room." They didn't perform together again for several years. "We were in chorus together in high school," Ray says, "and we started to be friends. We decided that it was so much fun that we kept doing it."

Saliers and Ray continued to play together while they attended college in Atlanta. "When we got our name was probably the point where we made a commitment to stay together," Ray reflects. "I found the word 'Indigo' in a dictionary. We liked the way that the word sounded but it wasn't any kind of profound thing."

The duo was absorbed by Atlanta's thriving music scene. "Atlanta's always been really strong musically," Ray says. "But it's never been as noticed as it is now. There's been a lot of great players signed out of Atlanta. When we were going out to hear the music and musicians that inspired us, there were a lot of bands. It ranged from country music to heavy metal rock 'n' roll. There were a lot of punk bands. A lot of people didn't get signed. Some got married and had families. There are a lot of people that influenced us that nobody knows."

Musical Influences

The Indigo Girls mix folk-like melodies with punk rock energy. "The stuff that really inspires me is things like The Jam, The Clash and Elvis Costello," Ray says before a performance in Maryland. "The Replacements have been a big influence. I like singer-songwriters a lot. Dylan is still one of my heroes. But I'm attracted more to singer-songwriters that function in the context of a band. Emily tends to listen more to Joni Mitchell and stuff that's a little more acoustic-oriented."

Saliers and Ray created their own distinctive sound through trial and error. "We've never tried to sound like anybody else," Ray says, "we've taken our weaknesses and turned them into strengths. Emily's developed her own style of guitar playing because she never had a guitar god that she looked up to. She never think's that she's a very good lead player, but I'm astonished, sometimes, by what she does. I could never figure vocal harmonies out by myself, so, I had to learn to sing a harmony by pretending that it was a melody. What that means is that when we sing in harmony, we're both at equal volumes. It's really like two melodies."

Despite their different musical preferences, the duo has grown together as songwriters. "I'm a little more abstract," Ray explains. "Emily's a little more linear. She uses longer words, harder chords. I'm a little more gutteral than she is. But there's a lot of things that I've learned from Emily. As the years go by, our influences become wider apart, our songwriting styles grow closer together."

Recordings

The Indigo Girls recorded their debut single "Crazy Game/Someone To Come Home" in 1985. "The single was kind of funny," Ray recalls. "We had never done anything in a studio except for some demo tapes that were done in a small eight-track studio. We paid a lot of money for this big studio but we could've paid the same money at a smaller studio and recorded a high-quality single." The duo released an EP the following year. "The EP was kind of cool," Ray says, "because we did it in some guy's basement. He was a good friend who was into our music and had all these weird ideas about production. We took a shot. He gave us all this free studio time. It was a great experience."

The Indigo Girls' 1990 release *Nomads, Indians And Saints* continued their collaboration with producer Scott Litt, best known for his work with R.E.M. "When we did the first album," Ray explains, "(Our record company) Epic told us to pick whomever we wanted. We had a few ideas. We were initially drawn to Scott because of his engineering skills. He's got a really great reputation as an engineer. But it ended up that he was really strong as a producer and had a lot of really great ideas. We worked really well together. We don't keep tempo. We just play our guitars. Scott's really good with rhythm and arranging percussion, drums and bass. We did the second album because we still had things that we wanted to explore."

Both of the albums The Indigo Girls have recorded for Epic (*The Indigo Girls* and *Nomads, Indians And Saints*) feature guest musicians and vocalists including Ireland's Hothouse Flowers, Luka Bloom, Jim Keltner, Peter Buck (of R.E.M.) and Benmont Tench (of Tom Petty's Heartbreakers). "We used musicians that we felt could, in a musical sense and a spiritual sense, lend themselves to the songs," Ray says.

Epic has also reissued The Indigo Girls' self-produced 1987 album *Strange Fire*, featuring the original versions of the songs "Blood And Fire" and "Land Of Canaan." "The record company really liked those songs," Ray explains. "We did them in a different way. Emily likes the new versions better but I like the early ones." The Indigo Girls' version of The Youngbloods' "Get Together" was included on the album.

"We've never tried to sound like anybody else . . . we've taken our weaknesses and turned them into strengths."

Wonder Years and Habitat for Humanity

"The *Wonder Years* TV show wanted us to record a song," Ray explains. "One of the songs on their list was 'Get Together.' We'd been doing it since high school. So we said, let's do it. It'll be sentimental.' Then, when they were planning to reissue the album, we said 'Why don't we put it on.'"

A video of "Get Together" was created in cooperation with the Georgia-based housing organization called Habitat For Humanity, who invests in low-cost housing for the economically deprived. "The idea was to make it a single," Ray says, "and give the proceeds to something that we believed in. We decided to do it for Habitat For Humanity. It was more of an awareness thing. Rather than just releasing a song for our benefit, we released it as a kind of public service announcement."

Kate and Anna McGarrigle

THE McGARRIGLE SISTERS

The repertoire of The McGarrigle Sisters includes Stephen Foster parlor songs, Celtic and French Canadian folk songs, gospel and pop standards. Since 1974, when Anna McGarrigle's "Heart Like A Wheel" became a multimillion selling hit for Linda Rondstadt, Kate and Anna have made their most lasting musical statements through their original songs. "I was going through a period of heartbreak when I began to write," Anna says from the Montreal home of her sister and manager, Jane McGarrigle.

Canadian Background

Although they studied classical piano with local nuns and sang French Canadian folk songs in school, a turning point came after hearing Pete Seeger. "When I first saw Pete," Kate says, "I fell madly in love with him. He played a lot of different instruments and was very loose on stage."

Before long, Kate and Anna were listening to American folk songs and teaching themselves to play folk instruments. The sisters formed The Mountain City Four with Pete Weldon and Jack Nissenson. Although they played at Quebec's folk music coffeehouses and universities, little thought was given to making music their livelihood. "There was no music business here," Kate claims. "If anyone wanted to make it in music, they'd have to go to Toronto."

In 1969 Kate graduated from McGill University (with a degree in science) and moved to New York City. She began to perform with guitarist/cellist/vocalist Rosa Baran. "She was into more of a commercial sound," Kate reflected. "Perhaps, she was interested because we had a more esoteric repertoire." Kate later sang background vocals on her then-husband Loudon Wainwright III's album *Attempted Mustache*. He's a very strong leader," she claims, "and a very strong timekeeper. He's nice to work harmonies off of."

In Montreal, Anna was beginning to write songs. "I like songs to be spontaneous," she says. "I need to be inspired by a phrase or an idea. Then, I can build a story around it. It's sort of like finding a pearl in an oyster."

After Linda Ronstadt reached the top of the charts with Anna's "Heart Like A Wheel," Warner Brothers suggested that the sisters join forces. Their debut release *Kate and Anna McGarrigle* was named second best album of the year by *The New York Times* and best album of the year by *Melody Maker*. Their follow-up *Dancer With A Bruised Knee* was an even bigger success. It ranked number twenty-eight on *The Village*

"I need to be inspired by a phrase or an idea. Then, I can build a story around it. It's sort of like finding a pearl in an oyster."

Voice list of the top 50 albums of the 1970's. "We tried things that were pretty adventurous," Kate explains. "It took a lot of people by surprise."

When they attempted to record a more commercial album, the results were disastrous. "(*Pronto Modo*) was a compromise," Kate explains. "Our producer turned out to be too safe." Since leaving Warner Brothers the McGarrigles have released three albums—*French Record* in 1981, *Love Over And Over* two years later and *Heartbeats Accelerating* in 1990. They remain committed to the progress their music. "We've been working in the studio with Rosa (Baran) as producer," Kate explains. "We're trying to get a new sound."

LOUDON WAINWRIGHT III

Humor and social-minded satire has been at the root of Loudon Wainwright III's music. "It's one of the freedoms of being a songwriter," he says from his New York apartment. "I can say intensely personal things but still be protected."

Born in Chapel Hill, North Carolina in 1946, Wainwright grew up in the luxury of New York's Westchester County. His parents met while they were in the Marine Corps. Wainwright remembers his family life as "Disciplined, but my parents weren't maniacs."

Loudon Wainwright III

The Songs Kept Coming

Wainwright's playing is the result of a variety of musical styles. "I like guitars and banjos," he says, "but I'm not a folk musician. My records are found not only in the folk bin, but also in the rock bin and the pop bin. I was influenced by all kinds of these— Rambling Jack Elliott, Mose Allison, Leiber and Stoller, show tunes especially by Frank Loesser and Richard Rodgers."

Wainwright didn't write his first song until 1968. "It was about Edgar, a lobster fisherman. It wasn't very good, but it was enough that I was starting to write songs." From that point, the songs kept coming. Before long, Wainwright began to perform in clubs and coffeehouses in Cambridge and Greenwich Village. "I was lucky," he claims. "It was a time when acoustic guitarists could be signed by a major record label. Everyone was getting signed," he explains. "They (the record companies) were looking for a 'new Bob Dylan.'" After signing with Atlantic Records, Wainwright began to attract a cult-like following.

Michelle Shocked

A more comical side of Wainwright's initially serious persona appeared on his third LP *Album III*. "There was a change," he reflects. "People started to laugh at the songs. My instinct was to get them to laugh more." The change paid off when the song "Dead Skunk" reached the Top Twenty. "('Dead Skunk') had a positive effect on my career," he recalls. "It sold a lot of records and made me a lot of money. But it also had its negative effect. The next time I went into the studio, the record company wanted another funny animal song. I had a real struggle within myself."

Wainwright appeared on TV's "M.A.S.H." "I'm still affected by it," he says. "Although I only did three shows, they're still shown in repeats." He's also played roles in the musical *Pump Boys And Dinettes* and in the Neil Simon film *The Actor's Life*. "Every couple of years," he explains, "I like to venture into other kinds of performance." Music continues to be the best medium for Wainwright's subtle humor. His most recent albums sparkle with brilliant full-band arrangements and also feature guitarist Richard Thompson.

MICHELLE SHOCKED

Ever since the release of her 1986 debut album *The Texas Campfire Tapes,* which was recorded at the Kerrville Folk Festival on a Sony Walkman by British producer Pete Lawrence, Michelle Shocked has consistently broken every musical stereotype.

Born in rural East Texas, Shocked is the daughter of a part-time carnival ride operator. She stayed with her mother after her parent's divorce in 1963 but never felt comfortable with homelife. Following her mother's remarriage and conversion to the Mormon religion, Shocked felt so ill at ease that she ran away and moved in with her father in Dallas. He introduced her to blues and country music. Her mother, subsequently, had her twice committed to mental hospitals. She was released when her mother's insurance coverage ran out.

Leaving home and school at the age of sixteen, Shocked squatted in empty buildings in New York's East Village, San Francisco and Amsterdam. Raped in Italy, Shocked moved, temporarily, into an Italian "women's separatist community."

Shocked recorded her debut album shortly after returning to Texas. It reached number one on the British chart of independent records and caught the ear of several American record labels. Although she signed a recording contract with

Polygram, she accepted less than half of the company's proposed $130,000 advance. "I figured they could take the money and record some of the other people doing this music," she explained to *People Weekly* magazine.

Shocked's subsequent albums, *Short Sharp Shocked* and *Captain Swing* have been fully realized studio albums. Her unique mixture of folk, country and protest music, however, has remained intact. She currently lives in Los Angeles.

CONNIE KALDOR

"Canada has a rich folk scene," Connie Kaldor says from her home in Vancouver. "A lot of people are folksingers, especially women."

Kaldor was born in Regina, a small town in the Saskatchewan prairie. "(Regina) has the most beautiful sky in the world," she reflects. Her earliest musical training was on piano. "I was forced to play piano," she claims. "My parents told me that they'd buy me a guitar if I took piano lessons."

Before long, Kaldor was composing her own songs. "I started writing to amuse myself while practicing," she says. Songwriting has remained Kaldor's greatest asset. "I'm really happy when I write," she explains. "I get the same adrenaline from writing a song as I get from performing."

Connie Kaldor

Kaldor's songs reflect a variety of musical influences. "I grew up in the teenage years of the 60's and early 70's," she explains. "So, I listened to a lot of The Beatles, Joni Mitchell and Carole King. But I've got a very eclectic background. I've listened to a lot of country music. I've always had a soft place for show music. Of course, I've been influenced by gospel and church music."

Theater and Music

Kaldor's effervescent stage presence stems from her experience as an actress. "I love to perform," she explains. "I went to theater school. It taught me a lot about my culture. When I didn't have work in the theater," she says, "I'd do music. Eventually, I had to choose. So, I quit the theater and played everywhere I could."

Kaldor's persistence paid off, culminating in her nomination for a Juno Award (Canada's version of The Grammy Award) as "Most Promising Female Vocalist" in 1985. "The nomination was amazing," she remembers. "I'm on an independent label and not on the pop circuit. I don't have a record company behind me. But the nomination brought me in touch with a lot of people in the music business."

Cheryl Wheeler

CHERYL WHEELER

Cheryl Wheeler's songs have been recorded by performers such as Juice Newton, Linda Thompson and Sawyer Brown. Dan Seals' recording of her tune "Addicted" reached the top slot of country music's hit parade in 1988. "Nothing that has happened to me has been more significant," Wheeler reflects from her home in southern Massachusetts. "It opened doors that would still be closed."

Wheeler's Career Development

Wheeler was born in Baltimore and grew up in Timonium, Maryland. She began her musical career in 1972. "I did a lot of stuff from Graham Nash's album *Songs For Beginners*," she remembers "and songs from (Neil Young's) *After The Gold Rush.* I loved folk songs and Ian & Sylvia songs. I played some of my own stuff, too. After some time, more and more of my own stuff got in there."

A turning point came when Wheeler met folk-pop performer Jonathan Edwards. "I met Jon at the Salt Theater in Newport," she recalls. "I opened for him. During the concert, he asked me onto the stage to sing with him."

Wheeler joined Edwards for several tours. "It was like going from third grade to college," she remembers. "The gigs were intense. Millions of people were there. It was completely different."

Recordings

Wheeler released her first solo recording, an EP entitled *Newport Songs*, shortly after moving to Rhode Island in 1976. Wheeler's 1985 debut album was produced by Jonathan Edwards. "It was more serious (than the EP)," she remembers. "I went down to Virginia to record it. The only one I knew in the studio was Jon."

Wheeler's 1990 album *Circles And Arrows* was produced by Kyle Lehning. Although it was recorded in Nashville the emphasis remains on a laid-back folk-oriented sound. "I told Kyle that I didn't want to make a country record," Wheeler explains, "and he said that he didn't either. That's all there was to it."

Circles And Arrows reprises Wheeler's tune "Arrow" which first appeared on her self-titled debut album. "We did another recording of it," she says, "but didn't like it as much as the original. So we used the original track and added Mark O'Connor's wonderful violin and a little mandolin. There's also a synthesizer on it that we used to give it ground cover."

NANCI GRIFFITH

The folk roots of Woody Guthrie and the country vocals of Loretta Lynn are combined in the "folkabilly" of Austin, Texas-born Nanci Griffith. She also performs many original compositions. "If a song doesn't come in twenty minutes," she claims, "then it's not worth doing. Lyrics and music come at the same time. It's a very quick thing, an immediate release."

Griffith has always been surrounded by music. "My dad sang with a barbershop quartet," she says from her hotel room in Los Angeles, "and had me singing harmony almost from the time that I could speak." Griffith sang in honky tonk saloons from the age of fourteen and recorded her debut album *There's A Light Beyond These Woods* in 1978.

She remained relatively unknown outside of songwriting circles until her third album *Once In A Very Blue Moon* was released in 1984. Besides a memorable interpretation of the Pat Alger-composed title track, the album included Griffith's original tune "Love At The Five And Dime" which was later recorded by Kathy Mattea and became a Top 5 country hit.

Nanci Griffith

Everly Brothers and Overseas Hits

Griffith has toured several times as opening act for The Everly Brothers. "They're great heroes of mine," she confesses. "They treat me so well. They've helped to expose my music to a lot of people that hadn't heard me before."

Griffith initially attracted attention while recording for the independent Rounder/Philo label. Beginning with her 1986 outing *Lone Star State Of Mind* Griffith has recorded for the much larger MCA label. "Tony Brown was the deciding factor behind signing with MCA," she explains. "I dearly respect his work. He's produced Steve Earle and all of the MCA master series. He also played keyboards for Elvis Presley for many years."

Lone Star State Of Mind was a major hit overseas. "It reached number seven on the charts in the United Kingdom," Griffith boasts, "before crossing over to the pop charts. In Ireland, 'Trouble In The Fields' became an economic anthem and was recorded by Mary Black and Maura O'Connell of DeDanaan."

Griffith has written one novel (*Two Of A Kind Heart*) and is currently working on her second (*Love Wore A Halo Before The War*). "The songs that I play are short stories in themselves," she explains. "If I can't find something to write about, I can pull characters out of my novels."

"The songs that I play are short stories in themselves."

AZTEC TWO-STEP

The early 1970's was a heyday for pop-folk performers. Aztec Two-Step, featuring the vocals and guitar playing of Rex Fowler and Neil Shulman, is one of the few acts that continue to perform. "We're the duo that wouldn't die," Shulman jokes from his New York home. "I attribute it to our own stubbornness. But I mostly attribute it to the fact that, on one level, it works. There's always been an audience (for us). They've imparted to us their enthusiasm."

On their most recent album *See It Was Like This . . .* the New York-based duo put a twist on all the singer-songwriters that have arranged their folk-like songs for a commercial, full-band sound. Armed solely with their acoustic guitars and harmonica, Fowler and Shulman rerecorded their best-known (and mostly out-of-print) songs. The result was not only a scaled-down greatest hits album but also a testament to two musicians' continued growth.

The duo formed in the spring of 1971. "Rex was living in Boston, down from his home in Maine," Shulman recalls. "I was also in Boston. I was supposed to be going to music school but I was mostly sleeping late." Shulman was primarily attracted to Fowler's songwriting. "Rex is a very personal writer," he explains. "He had ambitions

Aztec Two-Step

and really stretched. I see him as a true writer." Shulman's strongest asset is his melodic guitar playing.

Aztec Two-Step recorded five albums for Elektra and RCA. "Seals and Crofts had had a string of successful albums," Shulman remembers. "It was a time when you could have a successful album without a hit single."

Their earliest recordings were marked by pop-minded arrangements featuring a lengthy list of guest musicians. "I was a little resistant," Shulman says, "especially by the second record." The duo made a successful artistic comeback with their sixth album, *Living In America*, in 1986.

LIVINGSTON TAYLOR

Many of the most successful performers have blended tradition rooted music with more pop-conscious formulas. "I'm a pop musician," Livingston Taylor says from his home in Massachusetts. "I'm not a sensitive folksinger." Taylor, however, is one of acoustic music's most in-demand performers. His self-described "scratchy baritone vocals" have been featured on albums by Rory Block and Christine Lavin.

Although he was exposed to the R&B that his older brother Alex played and the show tunes his parents loved, Taylor's strongest influence came from AM Top 40 radio. "When I hear a great record," he claims, "it knocks me out. It doesn't matter if it's Mike & The Mechanics or Dolly Parton—if it's got a great kick and it's got a hook, it comes right at you."

Livingston Taylor

"When I walk out on the stage and look at the audience, that's my canvas."

Taylor's performances combine acoustic music with a deep sense of entertainment. "My shows are very much an exchange between the audience and myself," he explains. "I've got all these colors in my brain, and when I walk out on the stage and look at the audience, that's my canvas."

In the twenty years since he signed his first record contract Taylor has recorded only six albums. "The world doesn't need another mediocre album," he says. "There's plenty of them out there already. What the world needs is better records. Frankly, I think everyone would be better served if musicians took the time to make better records. The longer you wait, the better the album."

Taylor's brother James became an internationally-known performer, while his older brother Alex and sister Kate recorded albums in the 1970s. "We lived in a very close-knit family," Taylor reflects. "Music was an accepted form of expression. There were other forms but they weren't accepted. Perhaps if they had, music wouldn't have been so important."

FERRON

Deeply emotional lyrics and highly syncopated melodies have contributed to Ferron's success. "I feel like somebody who woke up in a dream," she says from her adopted home in Seattle. "I value that I live in a culture where I can go from being a waitress to playing music. But I also feel, sometimes, that the economic structure is laid out to keep a lot of people down. It's required. I got to the next rung in my life and I feel inclined to yell down 'It's not too hard.' My writing and my music is always being thrown like a rope. It comes to me that way, too."

Since her earliest performances in the mid-1970's, Ferron has cultivated a personal relationship with her audiences. "I'm very conscious of the audience," she explains. "It's very hard for me to be in an audience. It's hard for me to go somewhere and sit for an hour and a half or two hours. I'm always happier when I'm involved or entertained. Those are the two key words—involved and entertained. There used to be a time when I would tease the audience and say 'Of all the places that you could've been, you're here. Is it going to be a fun time or did you waste your money? Are the friends that you brought going to feel OK?' They'd all laugh. But through the laughter I'd see that some of this was quite true. I'm aware of the audience and that a moment is good if you're in it."

The oldest of seven children, Ferron was born in Toronto and raised in a semi-rural suburb of Vancouver, British Columbia. She dropped her last name, Foisy, at the beginning of her career. "No one knew how to spell it," she explains. "If I was going to be known, it was because of my music and not my last name."

"My writing and my music is always being thrown like a rope. It comes to me that way, too."

Ferron's Career Background

Ferron's career began in 1975. "A friend submitted a tape of my songs to a benefit concert," Ferron explains, "and I was accepted. That was the push that got me up on a stage. I was just terrified. I played in front of five hundred people. You could've heard a pin drop. I guess they liked it."

Before long, she was performing in Canadian folk music coffeehouses. Her first two albums, *Ferron* and *Ferron Backed Up* were self-produced recordings that were available only in Canada. "The first album was recorded two-track live in a TV studio," she remembers. "It's got a young kid's voice. We only made one thousand copies. It was done with money that was given to me by friends. It started being distributed through Ladyslipper, which is now quite a big distribution company. Then we did another album that sounds even worse. But, we were just trying to get the music out. It was just passion. I was young. I was only twenty-four and lost on my own."

The turning point came in 1978 when Ferron met Gayle Scott, an American photographer working on a Canadian film production, who became her manager. "She was absolutely the first person that said 'You can do this. You just have to pay the price,'" Ferron says. "I had no idea what the price would be, but I knew that I wanted to play music. She guided me and still does." Together, Ferron and Scott formed a record label, Lucy Records/Penknife Productions Ltd. In 1980, they borrowed $27,000 to produce and press Ferron's first real studio album, *Testimony*. The following year, Ferron gave up her blue-collar day job and began playing music full-time.

Testimony was distributed in The United States by Redwood Records, the label founded by Holly Near. "We went with Philo for a moment," Ferron explains, "and they went bankrupt. The album was just floating around. In order to distribute it through Ladyslipper, we had to press it ourselves and ship it down to the States. Then, the next conversation that occured was how we could get a company in The United States to manufacture it. Ladyslipper gave us a proposal and Redwood gave us a proposal. It seemed that Redwood was more than a distribution company but less than a record company for us. So we went with them. It was still on the Lucy/Penknife label, but distributed and manufactured by Redwood. So, that alleviated a lot of the problems." Ferron's *Shadows On A Dime* was also distributed by Redwood.

The association with Redwood gave Ferron a connection with Women's music. "It's women's music," she says, "But it's also leftist music. (Redwood) does a lot more than just women's music. Women's music, in my mind, means much more than just women. It's a sensibility that's often going to be just a little to the left. I most certainly would wind up falling into that category."

Recent Work

Ferron's latest album *Phantom Center*, her first release in six years, is on the Capitol-distributed Chameleon label. "Redwood introduced us to Chameleon," she explains. "They knew that they weren't playing big enough ball to do the next step with us. It was something that I wanted to get out for a long time," she says. "I felt more joy and celebration in my heart and I wanted to get it out through my music. This was the time to do it."

Ferron

Ferron has lived in The United States since January 1988. "Crossing the border trying to do shows was getting to be problematic," she explains. "I had been living on a small island (in British Columbia) and felt it was time to walk around a little bit and see what was going on. I now live in Seattle, which is like a sister city to Vancouver."

Ferron has toured both solo and with a band. "Playing with a band is a celebration kind of thing that we do when an album comes out," she says. "People like it. Some people prefer me alone because it gets inside me more. I like that and I live for that, but I also want to be able to do a knock-out, drag-down, show." She took a year off from performing in 1987. "I needed a break," she recalls. "I needed to be really normal, with friends and kids around. I gave myself that for a year."

The year-long retreat served to revive Ferron's performances. "Road life is very trying. You're not following any pattern. The other thing that happened over time was I felt I had the right to reevaluate what I'm doing and whether it's useful to me. I came to this gentle place of seeing that performing was something that I did well enough. It was something that other people missed when I wasn't going to their towns to sing. I had to respect that. I felt like I really had to respect the position that was given to me. So, I went back with a renewed tenderness and confidence."

Holly Near

HOLLY NEAR

The women's music movement has attracted a loyal following. "The new feminism created a need for music," Holly Near explains from the office of Redwood Records, the Oakland, California-based company she formed in the mid-1970's.

"Women started to take an active role in music. There was a rowdiness, at first. There were more outspoken songs needed to help us to have courage. But the songs have become sophisticated. So has the network."

Near studied drama at UCLA in the late 1960's and landed roles in films such as *Slaughterhouse Five* and on TV shoes such as *All In The Family, Room 222* and *Mod Squad.* In 1971, she joined Jane Fonda and Donald Sutherland in a tour of Vietnam, entertaining troops. The tour became a consciousness-raising experience, inspiring Near to voice her political beliefs through music.

Since then, Near has recorded nine solo albums and has collaborated on albums with Ronnie Gilbert, Inti-Illimani and H.A.R.P. (which featured Gilbert and Near with Arlo Guthrie and Pete Seeger). Near recently released her autobiography *Fire In The Rain . . . Singer In The Storm,* published by William Morrow & Sons.

Redwood Records

Redwood Records, which began as a small mail order company that distributed Near's records, has grown into a powerful organization with international distributors and a full roster of performers. The label was formed in response to Near's frustrations at getting a recording contract with a major label. "There was some resistance," she says, "to some of the more outspoken songs that I was doing. I thought that I would go off and record my anti-war songs independently, and then, record my love songs for a major label."

Near's debut album was recorded in a small home studio and distributed in front of stages after concerts and through the mail order company run by her parents. "We thought that sales would be slow," she says, "but the album really started to sell. Distributors were asking for it." Near was persistent in her attempts to bring attention to her music. "I would tear the page with record stores out of the telephone books at airports," she recalls, "and send postcards telling them that I had just been in their town and had an album to sell. I was a real entrepreneur."

THE WASHINGTON SQUARES

Although The Washington Squares reflect the pop-folk vocal harmonies of Peter, Paul and Mary, their music also has more contemporary influences. "Some people are curators of traditional folk music," explains Bruce Jay Paskow, ex-guitarist/singer-songwriter for the band. "But we're into taking a folk melody, blending it with the energy of the Punk movement and saying something in a clear, distinct way."

The Washington Squares were formed in 1983 as a reaction to the "purity" of American folk music. "When we first started," Paskow remembers, "the folk scene was a bunch of purists. We called ourselves a folk band. We were a parody, but people were kind of threatened by us." The group has downplayed their tongue-in-cheek approach. "As we went on," Paskow says, "being a parody was not as much fun." Living in New York plays a major influence on the band's sound. "Being in New York gives us a sense of up-to-the-minuteness," Paskow says. "It's being plugged into the pulse."

The Washington Squares have not given up all association with the beatnik days of the late 1950s. I grew up in the '50s," Paskow explains. "I would've liked to have hung around with Jack Kerouac and Neil Cassady. In those days, it was a daring act to be bohemian. It took bravery."

The Washington Squares

John Duffey

Bluegrass

Bluegrass continues to evolve from the string band-oriented
sounds of founding fathers such as Bill Monroe and The Stanley Brothers. Performers
such as Ron Thomason uphold traditional styles and values. At the same time, recent
groups like Northern Lights create a distinctive contemporary sound.

Another branch of bluegrass is the "new acoustic music" that fuses bluegrass with
jazz—both big band and small ensemble swing and classical music. "Dawg Music"
pioneer David Grisman has participated with and influenced many performers, alter-
nating between new acoustic music and the traditional Bill Monroe/Flatt & Scruggs
style. Musicians such as Matt Glaser, The Nashville Bluegrass Band, Alison Krauss and
others have continued to bring the music of the hill country up to date.

THE SELDOM SCENE

The Seldom Scene was one of the first bands to add an up-to-date flavor to bluegrass
music. "We've never thought of ourselves as a progressive band," says dobro player
Mike Auldridge. "A lot of progressive musicians are only interested in playing for other
progressive musicians. David Grisman and New Grass Revival and other groups doing
jazz and rock 'n' roll on acoustic instruments are really pushing things to the limit.
We've always considered ourselves to be a contemporary acoustic music band," he
continues. "We're trying to do what's happening today—in step with today. We'd like
to bring our music into the mainstream. But do it with more respect for the roots."

The Washington, D.C.-based band has been at the forefront of contemporary
bluegrass since 1969 and recently released a two-album set, *15th Anniversary Celebration,* featuring guest appearances by Emmylou Harris, Linda Ronstadt, Jonathan Edwards and Ricky Skaggs, among others. "The philosophy of this band," Auldridge
suggests, "is that we never rehearse. We used to play (Washington D.C. bluegrass club)
The Red Fox every week. That was our rehearsal space. We're still doing things the
same way. Now we play every Thursday night at The Birchmire (in Fredericksberg, Virginia)."

The Seldom Scene's 1988 album *A Change Of Scenery* introduced a new lead
vocalist/guitarist (Lou Reid—no relation to the New York-based rocker Lou Reed), a
new bassist (ex-Doc Watson electric bassist T. Michael Coleman) and a new sound.
"Basically, it's still The Seldom Scene," Auldridge explains. "But to me, it's a much
more contemporary sound. Who ever the lead singer is—even when John Stalling and
Phil Rosenthal were with us—is a big influence on how we sound. Lou gives us more of
an edge."

Reid initially attracted Auldridge's attention while performing with the South
Carolina-based bluegrass band, Southbend. "They were the opening act at a Dolly Parton concert that I went to," Auldridge recalls. "I was completely knocked out."

T. Michael Coleman, who joined The Seldom Scene in February 1988 after spend-
ing fifteen years accompanying Doc Watson, represents the group's first use of electric
instruments. "It was awkward at first," Auldridge admits. "A lot of fans would come to
shows and not like it. It was a big deal that Michael was playing electric bass. It took a
while. Luckily, we didn't have to go into the studio right away and could take the time
to get it to jell."

The presence of Reid and Coleman gives Auldridge another outlet for his playing.
As a trio, the group has already recorded an album, *Auldridge-Reid-Coleman.* "We got
carried away and it snowballed into something very exciting," says Auldridge. "It's two
or three steps ahead of The Scene. The drums are real outfront. The material is very
contemporary sounding. There's some hit record on this thing."

Mike Auldridge

The core of The Seldom Scene's sound continues to be original members John Duffey (also a founding member of The Country Gentlemen) on mandolin and tenor vocals; Ben Eldridge on five-string banjo; and Auldridge.

"Ben has always been underrated as a banjo player," Auldridge points out, "It's usually a hard-edged instrument. But we've always reflected the softer side of that kind of music."

"Duffey's always been weird," Auldridge continues, "to the extent of really being out there. Duffey is Duffey. There's nobody like him. It's reflected in how he plays. He's always been leaning towards the modern camps—he hasn't changed much."

RON THOMASON

Although more and more bands are emphasizing a more progressive edge, traditional bluegrass continues to thrive. "We get a lot of songs from Fiddlin' John Carson and others of that era," Ron Thomason, mandolin player, lead vocalist and monologist of The Dry Branch Fire Squad, explains from his horse farm in Ohio. "I pick out all the material, so, I pick stuff I really like a lot—George Jones, The Stanley Brothers and The Blue Sky Boys. I like Uncle Dave Macon and Tommy Jarrell. A lot of it is even more obscure. Some of it has never been done before—stuff from my great Aunt and my grandmother, a lot of Church material."

Thomason's Background

Thomason combines the philosophies of the hill country with a working man's sense of contemporary society. "My mother and father felt that being a musician was shameful and not any kind of work," Thomason recalls. "We were all taught not to play music, and, if we did, it was only for the church. To this day, the only reason that my mother tolerates the fact that I play music is that I do honest work (as a farmer and ninth grade English teacher) in addition."

Thomason continues to follow his parents' beliefs. "I've got to agree," he explains. "I certainly don't want my son to think of me as a musician. I've never met many people with respect for musicians, least of all, other musicians. It's just not real work. Music *is* hard work. It's tiring. But, as far as some guy that goes out and plays on weekends and comes back and practices all week, he'd ought'a get himself an honest job."

Born in Russell County, Virginia, Thomason was raised on his grandparents' farm. "When I was very young, we lived with my grandparents," he says. "They were dairy farmers and grew tobacco and corn. My grandmother chopped coal out of the hills."

Although on stage, Thomasson personifies a backwoods, hillbilly-like character, he's no country bumpkin. "My father brought us north (to Ohio) so that I could go to a decent school," he explains. "The irony is that, eventually, I ended up going to college. My mother went for nurse's training. After I finished college, my father decided to finish high school and went to college. He ended up as president of one of the largest local unions and the chief negotiator for several unions."

Thomason fell in love with bluegrass at an early age. "I was four or five years old," he remembers, "and I was in my dad's old Chevy. He had 'Farmer Fun Time' on the radio. It was The Stanley Brothers. It just blew my socks off. I was real little but it just made me feel like I was grown up. I've never quit loving it."

Thomason's biggest break as a performer came in 1969 when he joined Ralph Stanley And The Clinch Mountain Boys. "It was the biggest job I've ever had," he reflects. "That was the very reason that I quit it. It was the second best mandolin job in the whole world but it wasn't what I wanted. I thought, if this is it, then, I'm gonna have to find something else to do. I loved the music but I played more

Ron Thomason

music before I went with Ralph. He had fifteen songs that he'd do every show. I love Ralph and I respect him, but even at that time, he'd grown kind of jaded."

The Dry Branch Fire Squad

Thomason left The Clinch Mountain Boys in 1970 and was replaced by Ricky Skaggs. Determined to play his own music, Thomason formed The Dry Branch Fire Squad. "I decided that I hadn't liked any of the bands that I had played with," he recalls. "There were some things that I thought were missing from bluegrass music. The obvious cure was to start my own band."

The Dry Branch Fire Squad is rooted in the Brother Duets of the 1930's and '40's. "It started with just me and John Baker," Thomason says. "We went on a tour for the National Council for Traditional Arts." The group has recently expanded its sound. "Now, we're going to be even more far ranging," Thomason predicts. "(Former Hot Mud Family vocalist) Suzanne Edmundson is singing with us now."

Thomason and The Dry Branch Fire Squad have hosted the Winterhawk Bluegrass Festival since 1985. The band's involvement stems from a late-night discussion between Mary Doud and Thomason's wife, Eugenia Snyder. "They decided that having a

"As far as some guy that goes out and plays on weekends and comes back and practices all week, he'd ought'a get himself an honest job."

bluegrass festival might be a good idea," Thomason recalls. "They wanted to know if I had any ideas. The next day, when I woke up, I remembered that I must've said 'yes.'"

The Winterhawk Bluegrass Festival is the product of many hard-working people. "One of the things that the Winterhawk partnership is specialized in is that we have more than one partner and each does what he does best," Thomason says. "It's not any big secret. We don't necessarily fence off areas. We take our end and go. My end has to do with partially putting together the line-up, the scheduling of the acts and workshops, coordinating the workshop stage, the mailing list, getting the flyers printed. We work on it all year long and really work hard at the festival."

ARTHEL "DOC" WATSON

"Bluegrass is only one segment of the country music I play."

Traditional sounds are brilliantly displayed through the singing and playing of flat-picking guitarist Arthel "Doc" Watson. "A lot of people think I play bluegrass," Watson says from his home in Deep Gap, North Carolina, "but, I play so much more. Bluegrass is only one segment of the country music that I play."

Watson's Background

Unlike many so-called "folk revivalists," Watson learned most of his repertoire first-hand. Born in 1923, Watson grew up in a musical family. His father led the choir at the local Baptist church. His mother sang the children to sleep and led the family in Bible reading and hymn singing. "My father wasn't a professional musician," Watson says, "but he played old time banjo. When I was eleven, he made me a banjo (out of hickory, maple and catskin) and taught me frailing." A couple of years later, Watson got his first guitar. "One of my cousins had a guitar," he remembers. "My father said that if I could learn to play a song, he'd take me downtown to get a guitar. I knew a few chords a friend (at the Raleigh School For The Blind, which Watson attended) had shown me. So, he had to keep his promise." Much of Watson's early playing was self-taught. "I listened to old seventy-eights and to an old battery radio," he recalls.

Watson's earliest performances were with his older brother, Linny, singing old timey and bluegrass tunes. At the age of seventeen, Watson cut wood to earn enough money to buy a guitar from Sears/Roebuck. His first stage appearance was at the fiddler's convention in Boone, North Carolina, where he performed Bill Monroe's "Muleskinner Blues."

In 1941, Watson joined a band that occasionally performed on radio. During a broadcast the following year, the announcer didn't like the name "Arthel" and suggested that Watson change it. According to legend, some women overheard the discussion and shouted "Call him Doc." The name stuck and Watson has since been known affectionately as "Doc" Watson.

Watson temporarily switched to electric guitar in 1954 and formed a band with Jack Williams of Johnson City, Tennessee. For the next eight years, Watson and Williams performed a mixture of rock 'n' roll, country & western, pop standards and square dance tunes at VFW clubs throughout eastern Tennessee and North Carolina.

At the same time, Watson continued to play old-time music with the traditional folk musician, Clarence Ashley. When Ralph Rinzler came to record Ashley in 1960, he was introduced to Watson. "(Rinzler) is the key to my being on the road," Watson reflects. "He did the discovering. Ralph's a very modest fellow. But without him, I couldn't have done it."

When Ashley's group came to New York to play a Friends of Old-Time Music concert at Town Hall in early 1961, Watson came along. His solo spots were so impressive that he was booked to play Gerde's Folk City in December, 1962 and at the Newport

Folk Festival in 1963. Watson later returned to Town Hall as opening act for Bill Monroe & The Bluegrass Boys.

In 1965, Watson added his then-fifteen year old son, Merle, on second guitar. Until his death, Merle Watson continued to grow as a guitarist and record producer. He was especially respected for his distinctive slide guitar playing. Much of Merle's playing was influenced by blues guitarist "Mississippi" John Hurt. "Merle met John Hurt at the Newport Folk Festival," Watson recalls. "He really enjoyed John Hurt's music and often played in that style." The benefits of Merle's presence, however, were more than just musical. "Without Merle, I would've quit," Watson admits. "The road was too hard without him. He wanted to leave in 1967. I offered him half the profits if he stayed."

The road proved difficult for Merle. Towards the end of his life, he often stayed home on the farm when his father toured. Jack Lawrence, a North Carolina-based guitarist, was called on as a substitute. "I hired Jack two years before Merle died," Watson says. "He's very versatile. He can play a lot of different styles."

Doc Watson

From the beginning, Watson maintained a steady flow of recordings. Among his early albums are *Jean And Doc At Folk City*, recorded with folk dulcimer player Jean Ritchie, and *The Watson Family, Volume I and II*, featuring Doc's mother, Annie, his brother, Arnold and Arnold's brother-in-law, Gaither Carlton. Watson's most recent albums have been thematic, paying musical tribute to bluegrass (*Ridin' The Midnight Train*); country blues (*Pickin' The Blues*); the American South (*Down South*); and instrumental flat-picking (*Doc & Merle Watson's Guitar Album*).

Watson's Brilliant Career Marred By Tragedy

Watson's career has been marred by tragedy. His son and long-time musical partner, Merle, died in a tragic accident in late 1985. Although he planned to retire, recent situations have caused him to alter his plans. According to Watson's manager, Mitch Greenhill, Watson's wife, Rosa Lee, "had open heart surgery a year ago and an infection developed. They operated in January but it hasn't healed properly." "I talked about retiring," Watson says, "but I can't for financial reasons. If my wife has surgery tomorrow, it'll be the eighth time in nine months. I don't know how she's able to do it." Watson's personal grief is best expressed through his music. His album *On Praying Ground*, a tribute to gospel music, won the 1991 Grammy award as "Best Traditional Folk Recording."

Northern Lights

NORTHERN LIGHTS

Although many of the best "progressive" bluegrass bands, including New Grass Revival and Hot Rize, have recently broken up, other groups continue to fill the void.

"We don't want to be identified as a traditional Southern band," Taylor Amerding of New England's premier bluegrass band, Northern Lights, says from his office in Salem, Massachusetts. "We try to project somewhat of an urban image."

Amerding joined Northern Lights when they were known as "How Banks Fail." "I saw an advertisement for a mandolin player," he recalls. "I had learned fifteen fiddle tunes, but they were all on the guitar. After I saw the ad, I went out and bought a mandolin. It looked like it was made out of plywood." Three months after Amerding joined, the group changed its name to Northern Lights.

Take You To The Sky

Northern Lights' fourth album *Take You To The Sky* was light years ahead of their earlier work. "I've heard from DJs all over the country," Amerding says. "They've been playing the socks off of the record. I was thrilled. They were playing the songs that made the charts—'Winterhawk' and 'Northern Rail.' But, I've heard from bluegrass people that like our version of (Jimmy Martin's) 'Hold What You've Got.' I've heard from folk music radio stations that have been playing (John Prine's) 'Souvenirs' and (Bill Staines') 'Roseville Fair.'"

Take You To The Sky is strengthened by the presence of guest fiddlers Matt Glaser and Alison Krauss. "As young as Alison is," Amerding says, "she's a very traditional bluegrass player. Matt has an endless knowledge of the jazz language. Both did wonderful jobs."

Amerding's mandolin playing and high tenor vocals and Bill Henry's guitar playing and baritone vocals remain at the band's core. But it was Mike Kropp's banjo playing and ex-band member Oz Barron's electric bass playing that gave *Take You To The Sky* much of it's potency. "Mike's been a friend of Billy's since they were kids in Connecticut," Amerding explains. "He's been with us since the summer of '84. Oz really helped us to solidify our sound."

A Transition

The band recently underwent a transition. "We've got a new bass player (Jeff Horton)," Amerding says. "He's a gret player. He was a founding member of The Neon Valley Boys. He played with them for just as long as they were together. But it's going to take two or three months to start jelling. A band has its own internal rhythm and it takes a lot of playing together to get it."

Former bass player Guy "Oz" Barron related some cogent insights about Northern Lights' relation to bluegrass. "There's a feel to it that it must be bluegrass. But bluegrass has always been a fusion of different music. Bill Monroe fused old blues, R&B, swing and country music into the acoustic fusion of its time."

Northern Lights' Work With Peter Rowan

Peter Rowan, whose vocals can be heard on one verse of "Winterhawk," has used Northern Lights as his band for a few recent shows. "Playing with Peter is alternately uplifting and maddening," Amerding reflects. "He doesn't like to rehearse. You've got to have a working knowledge of his music. It can be frightening. But, his rhythm guitar playing is so strong that the whole band gets locked in. There's a feeling of confidence. Of course, he's got a great set of vocal chords. It's a joy to sing with him. It's like being in a band that's really well known."

"Bluegrass has always been a fusion of different music."

PETER ROWAN

Peter Rowan has performed with Bill Monroe's Bluegrass Boys, Earth Opera, Sea Train, Old And In The Way, Muleskinner, and as leader of his own band, Free Mexican Air Force. Rowan is currently performing solo. "I've been doing solo performances in Europe for the last ten years," he says from his home in Nashville. "There's a real empty feeling of loss before a new project. But I decided after being in Nashville for five years, that instead of going the usual route and cutting a record, I'd face the songs as honestly as I could and just do it on my own."

Rowan's Background

Rowan's quest for what he calls "the simplicity of music" goes back to Earth Opera, the short-lived folk-rock band that he formed with David Grisman in the mid-1960's. It was just David and me at first," Rowan remembers. "It had a real sparse sound. When we started to bring other people in, there were all kinds of problems."

Rowan, along with Richard Greene, was a founding member of the late 1960's band Seatrain. Although the group showed early promise, internal conflicts prevented their success. "It was egos," Rowan admits, "probably my ego. We were six young guys tied up in a project not knowing what we were doing. Some people tried forcing their musical directions. But if we'd been mature enough to take some time off, and then regroup, we'd still be together."

Born and raised in Wayland, Massachusetts, Rowan's earliest musical interests were sparked by the country music he heard on the radio. "There was a show called 'Hayloft Jamboree,'" he says, "that played a lot of country music. Jack Clements was (a regular) on the show. He produced all of Jerry Lee Lewis' early hits, and, later, produced U2."

Rowan's musical inspiration came from a variety of sources. "In Wayland, there was a real cosmopolitan mix of country music and rock 'n' roll," he says. "I was always playing rock 'n' roll as a teenager. The first band that I played with was with Bob Emery (former member of Northern Lights)—The Cupids. We played a lot of record hops."

Peter Rowan

Blues, Monroe, Grisman and Others

Bluegrass and blues were important influences on Rowan's music. "I heard bluegrass for the first time at (legendary Boston nightclub) Hillbilly Ranch," he explains. "(Texas bluesman) Lightnin' Hopkins was a big influence."

An active folk music session player in the early 1960's, Rowan's earliest break came when he was invited to join Bill Monroe's Bluegrass Boys. Performing with the band until 1967, Rowan found the experience invaluable. "To play (bluegrass) right," Rowan claims, "you've got to learn it from someone like Bill Monroe, who has it in his genes. Bill's a very strong leader. He wouldn't stand for any messing with his music. After he goes, very few people will be able to do anything but a fast or slow tune. (Bluegrass) isn't a dance style anymore. All the old steps are being forgotten."

David Grisman has played an ongoing role throughout Rowan's career. "From David, I've learned how to listen to music," Rowan says. "He's got tremendous ears. The first time I heard him was in North Carolina at Union Grove. He was with The New York Ramblers. They won the band contest. I thought the band was excellent in its execution but played too many notes."

Old And In The Way

In addition to the above-mentioned Earth Opera, Grisman and Rowan worked together with fiddler Richard Greene in Muleskinner, with Jerry Garcia of The Grateful Dead and with Vassar Clements in Old And In The Way. "Richard was with The Bluegrass Boys," Rowan says. "Old And In The Way represents a time in Jerry's life when he was willing to be in a band without being in the spotlight. The direction came from David and me. But everyone was comfortable with each other. The band sounded different than any one person's trip. That's why it has such an enduring quality."

Old And In The Way's self-titled 1973 album, their sole recording, featured Rowan's anthem-like tune "Panama Red." "I wrote it in 1969 in Cambridge," Rowan recalls. "It's now at the front of my set. It may date me but it's a good, fun song, and a good finger-picking song."

HOT RIZE

Hot Rize won the International Bluegrass Music Association's award as "Best Act of 1990." Even though the Boulder, Colorado-based band recently broke up, they deserve mention because of their impact on contemporary bluegrass. The group featured Tim O'Brien, Nick Forster and Pete Wernick. Earl Scruggs' banjo playing was important to the band. "I really like Earl Scruggs," banjo player Pete "Dr. Banjo" Wernick explains. "I try to play as appropriate a banjo part as possible. I emphasize less of the banjo's uptempo, happy sound. There are more emotional overtones. It's a real good sound—clean, driving and interesting."

The turning point in Hot Rize's evolution came when Forster joined in May 1978. "Everybody got better," Wernick remembers. "Tim began writing songs. Nick was never a singer before but he can match Tim's sound very well. When they're singing harmony, it's hard to tell who's who." A highlight of Hot Rize's performances was the set by the group's alter-egos, "Red Knuckles & The Trailblazers." "Whenever I speak to newspapers, I explain that we met Red Knuckles and The Trailblazers when we were passing through Wyoming, Montana," Wernick says. "It's really like they're separate people. There's really eight of us on the bus."

Hot Rize
Pete Wernick, Nick Forster and Tim O'Brien

The recent break-up of Hot Rize signalled the end of Red Knuckles And The Trailblazers. "They're saying that they'd like to stay together," Wernick claims, "but, I don't really see how. Hot Rize pays all their travel expenses." Nevertheless, Red Knuckles And The Trailblazers recently reunited to perform at the Winterhawk Bluegrass Festival in Hillsdale, New York.

Demise of Hot Rize

Hot Rize's demise reflects lead vocalist, fiddler and mandolin player Tim O'Brien's decision to pursue a solo career as a country singer. "A year ago, Tim got an offer to sign with Columbia," Wernick explains. "A lot of people think that they signed him to replace (late country music singer-songwriter) Keith Whitley, but the process was well in place when Keith died. The idea didn't start there. It just happened that the day that they planned to showcase Tim was the day that Keith died. It was a strange coincidence. " The final blow, however, came when bassist Nick Forster agreed to be a sideman in O'Brien's new band. "It put an end to the group," Wernick claims. "We wouldn't be able to do it without them."

Hot Rize recently put the finishing touches on their final album. "Everybody's aware that we want to be really good for our last album," Wernick says. "But we've always set a high standard for ourselves. We've wanted to sound really good on all of our albums. We've really agonized over records. They've taken a long time." Hot Rize initially came together in 1977. "Tim and I were working on solo albums," Wernick recalls, "and we planned on touring with a band to promote the albums. I called (guitarist) Charles Sawtelle and a guy that was only in the band for a short while. We knew each other from working at the Denver Folklore Center."

Banjo player Wernick's future promises to be as busy as ever. "I'm going to be gigging with (multi-instrumentalist) Jody Stecher and (banjoist) Tony Trischka," he explains. "I've known Tony for twenty years. We take turns playing solo and backup for each other. When he's given a license to fly, he flies hard. I'm more on the down to earth side but I occasionally display flights of fancy." Wernick also plans to continue teaching. "I conduct five banjo camps during the summer," he says. "People come from as far as Singapore and Austria."

THE NASHVILLE BLUEGRASS BAND

The Nashville Bluegrass Band, who recently received the International Bluegrass Music Association's award as "Best Bluegrass Vocal Band Of 1990," has managed to avoid the stereotypes of Nashville scene. "All kinds of acoustic musicians have moved here recently," guitarist-vocalist Pat Enright says during a recent telephone interview. "The opportunity is here to be able to get up in the morning and get involved with some kind of music. It's always there. I've never found that in any other place that I've lived in."

Nashville Bluegrass Band Pays Their Dues

The Nashville Bluegrass Band originally came together to perform as a part of a country music show that was headlined by Minnie Pearl. "There was a western swing band," Enright recalls, "a country-rock band and square dancers. We were the bluegrass band. We went out on the road and did about nine thousand miles of one-nighters. We only played three songs a night. But there was enough money so that the tour was worthwhile."

After the tour, the band agreed to stay together. "We started from scratch," Enright says. "We decided that if we were going to do it, then, we would do it full-time."

Although they initially began as a quartet, the band was expanded with the addition of fiddler Stuart Duncan, The IBMA's "Best Fiddle Player Of 1990." "I met Stuart a long time ago," Enright says, "when he was ten years old. We met him in Ohio at a benefit for Don Reno. We picked a little. When he moved into town, he wanted to get into something. We were more than willing to let him get into what we were doing."

The group remains centered, however, around the playing and singing of Enright and banjo player Alan O'Bryant. "Alan and I came to Nashville about the same time in 1974," Enright says. "He was one of the first people that I met. We used to play informally at a place called 'The Station Inn.' We're both into singing. We could both sing lead or tenor."

Enright and White also played together in the mid-80's bluegrass 'super-group,' Dreadful Snakes. "It was a band for people to play in when they weren't doing anything else," Enright says. "The band never toured. It was less a band than something for people to do for fun. But it worked well enough for Rounder to want to make a record. It just turned out that we were having such a good time that it was a good record."

Recent Work

The Nashville Bluegrass Band has gone through a number of recent changes. Their 1990 album *The Boys Are Back In Town* features a new mandolin player, Roland White, formerly with The Kentucky Colonels and Country Gazette, and a new bass player, Gene Libbea. "(White) brings many years of experience," Enright explains. "He's someone who we've always looked up to, someone we've always tried to emulate. He's got a wonderful sense of music. Gene is from California. We played some shows with him when we needed a bass player. After we finished the tour, he said that he wanted to join the band. We were all for it. He's an excellent musician and he knows his way around the bass. He's great on stage. He's got a lot of energy. He's been a real asset."

"We ran into the back of a Semi—and didn't miss a gig."

The Boys Are Back In Town comes two years after a bus accident nearly put the group out of commission. "We ran

Pat Enright

into the back of a semi," Enright recalls. "It was a rainy night. There was an accident at the bottom of a hill. We were at the top and couldn't stop. There was no place to go. There was traffic in the left lane. So, we ran into the back of a semi, which was stopped. (Former bassist) Mark Hembree was hurt very bad. All of us sustained some injuries— lacerations, cuts. Nobody broke any bones but there were some terrific sprains."

The group, however, remained persistent in their quest for musical success. "We didn't miss a gig," Enright says. "We went out the next weekend and played at the National Folk Festival in Lowell, Massachusetts. We kind of hobbled for a while but we just kept going."

The Nashville Bluegrass Band collaborated with singer-songwriter Peter Rowan on the album *New Moon Rising*. "Originally, the concept was that he would just join the band for the record," Enright recalls. "He would sing some songs and we would sing some songs. It was supposed to be a real collaboration. As it went along, we ended up doing a lot of original material. Peter started writing stuff for it. So, when it came time to go into the studio, we ended up doing, with the exception of two songs, all of Peter's songs. It worked well. We went into the studio and it was up to us to put our sound on his songs."

Matt Glaser

"I reflect my personality traits through my playing."

MATT GLASER

Violinist/fiddler Matt Glaser has incorporated a plethora of influences into his playing. "In whatever idiom I play," Glaser says from his home in Cambridge, "I reflect my personality traits through my playing. I've got a strong sense of humor. I can be inventive. I incorporate a fairly wide range—versatility and humor."

Glaser's Background

Born in Brooklyn, New York, Glaser's earliest musical memories are of his mother, a former opera singer, playing piano. Although he studied classical piano from the age of nine and took up Dylan-style guitar and harmonica the following year, his musical leanings were altered after hearing a TV commercial that featured, what he remembers as, "a scratchy old timey fiddle."

This budding interest was enhanced by a radio show that was broadcast over New York's WBAI-FM. "They played a lot of bluegrass and old timey tunes," he remembers. He was hooked by the excitement of southern and Appalachian music. He began to plead with his parents to get him a fiddle. Finally, they bought him a violin for his 13th birthday. "I tried picking things out by myself," he says, "but I wasn't very successful."

After deciding to find a teacher that could show him how to play, he enrolled at the Fretted Instrument School in Greenwich Village and began to study under John Burke. "He was a banjo player who also played fiddle," Glaser recalls. Burke showed him the basic rudiments of playing bluegrass fiddle.

Glaser's studies, however, took a sharp turn when he moved with his parents to Katonah, New York (about an hour north from New York City) and began studying classical violin with Paul Ehrlich. "He was very open minded to me playing other kinds of music," he says. "He turned me on to Byron Berline. One summer, he took me to the fiddler's convention at Union Grove. He took me to hear Stephane Grappelli at a club in New York. I was very inspired by this teacher."

For a while, Glaser entertained thoughts of becoming a professional classical violinist. "I played a lot of chamber music," he recalls. His flirtation with classical music, however, was drastically affected after hearing Vassar Clements for the first time. "I was amazed," he says. "It put me into the gear that I'm still in. I was proficient in the student classical violin manner but I didn't know how to begin to sound like Vassar. It was like hearing a completely new language."

His interests in bluegrass were cemented during his senior year in high school. He met fiddler-mandolinist Jay Ungar, Sam Bush and Tex Logan. However, his parents convinced him to apply to several music-oriented colleges and universities. Although he says he "squeaked" into The Eastman Conservatory, he soon grew disenchanted with his studies. "I went crazy," he explains, "and formed bluegrass bands." After his freshman year, it was obvious that the academic world wasn't suited for him. Dropping out, he headed straight to New York City. "I wanted to play bluegrass for a living," he says. Before long, he hooked up with the seminal bluegrass/swing band The Central Park Sheiks. "It was my first exposure to jazz," he remembers. "Richard Lieberson, the guitarist who led the band, very patiently taught me standard tunes."

Glaser's listening habits also began to change. "I started listening to Stephane Grappelli, the great western swing fiddler Johnny Gimble and a lot of jazz violinists— Svend Asmussen, Stuff Smith, Eddie South and Joe Venuti." Together with the Sheiks, Glaser experienced his first recording sessions when the group recorded the album "Honeysuckle Rose" for Rounder. "It's still in print," he boasts. "It was a great experience to play and record at such an early age. I was pretty precocious. I played well for a 19 year old."

The New York All Stars and Other Collaborations

Acoustic music was going through a period of transition at the time. Although many groups eventually emerged, there weren't a lot of people playing jazz-influenced string band music in New York in 1975. Consequently, a sense of community began to develop among the few musicians pioneering the musical style. "It was a creative time," Glaser recalls. "Tony Trischka, Kenny Kosek and Russ Barenberg were real active. I remember Bela Fleck as a youngster, studying with Trischka. There was a real scene." Kosek and Glaser practically formed a musical partnership. "Once a week," Glaser explains, "we sat around trying to play a lot of different things. We played in a lot of brain-damaged avant-garde bluegrass bands and did a lot of recordings together. We even did a McDonald's commercial in Spanish."

The "partnership" culminated in the group The New York All Stars which brought Glaser and Kosek together with Statman, Trischka, Barenberg and bass player Roger Mason. "(The group) evolved out of (seminal bluegrass band) Breakfast Special," Glaser reflects. Although the group was short-lived, Glaser has continued to work with the other musicians in the band. Together with Barenberg and Trischka, Glaser formed Heartlands in 1977. Despite an abundance of talent, this group never made it onto vinyl. However, when Barenberg recorded his debut solo album *Cowboy Calypso*, the group backed him on several tunes.

Glaser continued to work with Barenberg in the traditional folk-rooted band Fiddle Fever. The group, which has recorded two albums for Flying Fish—*Fiddle Fever* and *Waltz Of The Wind*—is notable for its use of three fiddlers (Jay Ungar and Evan Stover in addition to Glaser). "Jay is the strongest old timey player," Glaser explains, "and usually plays melody. Evan is a very distinctive musician. He's amazing. He plays very weird but he thinks he's playing straight bluegrass. With the three fiddles, we try to get a wall of sound."

Although the group has developed its own unique sound, each band member is active in a variety of projects apart from the group. "There's been a geographical diffusion," Glaser reflects. "In the beginning, we were very New York based. Now that I'm in Boston and Russ is in Nashville, it precludes extensive rehearsing."

Fiddle Fever's recording of Jay Unger's tune "Ashokan Farewell" was used as a theme song for Ken Burns' PBS documentary on the Civil War and has brought a renewed attention to the group. "It looks like we're going to get back together to do another PBS documentary called 'Songs of The Civil War,'" Glaser says. "Various people (including Judy Collins and Paul Simon) are going to sing these songs. We're going to get together and play 'Ashokan Farewell' as a group."

For a while, Glaser and Barenberg also played with Andy Statman in the more experimental group, Laughing Hands. "The three of us had an interest in playing different idioms," he remembers. "We were good improvisers and there was a very good musical interaction between us." The group gathered critical acclaim for its all-original material, however, they eventually disbanded before recording together.

With Stephane Grapelli

Among Glaser's memorable collaborations is his work with Stephane Grappelli. He first met the influential French violinist while appearing in the film *King Of The Gypsies*. "Grisman was in New York," he explains, "writing the score for the film. He asked me to be Grappelli's stand-in and I immediately said 'yes.' I was the fiddler in the opening scene. I sat around with Grappelli for hours during the filming. He wanted to do nothing else but play. He's 70 years old but he's got such a child-like joy for music."

The collaboration between Glaser and Grappelli continued after the filming was finished. Oak Publishing (who had published Glaser's two books—*Teach Yourself Bluegrass Fiddle* and *Vassar Clements Fiddle*) had commissioned a book on jazz fiddling to be written by Grappelli with Richard Greene and Robin Williamson. However, getting the three potential authors together had proven so futile, that Glaser was asked to replace Greene and Williamson and complete the project with Grappelli. "It took three years to complete," Glaser reflects. "It's a major work. I really wanted to thoroughly chronicle jazz violin. I spent hours and hours talking with Grappelli. I interviewed Jean-Luc Ponty and Joe Venuti. Venuti died right before the book came out."

Glaser went to Boston when he and Barenberg were asked to conduct a visiting artists clinic at the Berklee College of Music. "When I got back to New York," he recalls, "I got a letter from the school that said that they wanted to revamp their string department." Glaser accepted a position as chairman of the department. "It's a very small department in a very large school," he says. "Although the school emphasizes jazz, we try to embrace all the idioms that violin, viola and cello players can play. I've met a lot of people, it's been very stimulating. My playing has grown as a result."

Glaser released his debut solo album *Play, Fiddle, Play* in 1991. His recent projects include an appearance on David Grisman's album *Dawg '90* and a performance with Jerry Lee Lewis on the soundtrack of the film *Dick Tracy*. Perhaps his most commercial work has been in association with Maurice Starr and New Kids On The Block. "I play concertmaster," he says, "and I contract the musicians for the string section. That's been very lucrative and fun."

ALISON KRAUSS

Emotional depth and infectious charm have placed vocalist-fiddler Alison Krauss at the forefront of contemporary bluegrass. Although she's only nineteen years old, Krauss has repeatedly garnered the respect of her peers and ever-growing following. At the recent International Bluegrass Music Association's award ceremonies, Krauss was named "Best Female Vocalist of 1990."

Krauss's Background

Krauss has been a favorite of bluegrass fans since 1983. "I played in fiddle contests since I was eight," she recalls during a recent telephone interview. "A lot of them were at bluegrass festivals."

Krauss was born in Champaign, Illinois in 1971. Her father, a real estate broker, sang with the amateur opera society at the University of Illinois. "My parents encouraged me to do just about anything," Krauss recalls. "They owned a Flatt and Scruggs album but it wasn't what I listened to. I listened to J.D. Crowe And The New South."

Although she initially expressed a desire to play piano, Krauss was persuaded to study a different instrument. "My brother was already playing piano," she recalls. "I took classical music lessons on violin for six years but I taught myself how to play bluegrass."

Krauss's playing was greatly influenced by the fiddling of Kenny Baker, formerly of Bill Monroe And The Bluegrass Boys, and Stuart Duncan. "Kenny's tone is so great," she explains. "His songs are amazing. When Stuart plays a break, you can't ever imagine it being played any other way."

It didn't take long for Krauss to attract attention. In 1983 and 1984, she was voted "Most Promising Fiddler in The Midwest" by the SPGMA (Society For The Preservation Of Bluegrass Music In America). At the age of thirteen, she won the fiddle contest at the National Flatpicking Championship at Winfield, Kansas. "I had a lot of real good people to listen to," she says, "a lot of really great records."

Alison Krauss

A Turning Point at Newport

The turning point for Krauss came when she and her band, Union Station, performed at the Newport Folk Festival in 1986. "It was incredible," she remembers. "We'd never played anything like that before. The amount of money we got really freaked us out. It was a huge help. We got other festivals because we could say that we played there. A lot of people that hired us had seen us there. It was such a prestigious thing to play that it helped us tremendously." The same summer, Union Station was named "Best New Bluegrass Band" at the Kentucky Fried Chicken Bluegrass Festival in Louisville, Kentucky. "It was really good for us," Krauss explains. "It enabled us to do the band record."

Krauss has performed as a guest on a number of albums. "You'd better know the songs," she explains. "There's a lot of money being spent."

Krauss's status as one of the most significant rising stars in bluegrass music was cemented when her song "I've Got That Old Feeling" won a Grammy as "Best Bluegrass Recording" of 1990.

Cathy Fink and Marcy Marxer

CATHY FINK AND MARCY MARXER

The string band tradition is at the root of Cathy Fink and Marcy Marxer's music but their songs reflect a singer-songwriter connection. "We still play string band music," Fink explains between sets at The Philadelphia Folk Festival, "but we've evolved from those skills and have applied lyrical content. String band music is for dancing but we wanted to express ourselves more." Marxer adds, "String band music is only one aspect of what we do."

Marxer, who grew up in Michigan, is the fourth generation of women musicians in her family. "I had no choice," she reflects. "I was raised to be a musician."

Fink grew up in Baltimore and started playing piano and singing at the age of four. "I took formal piano lessons," she says, "but dropped the piano for a guitar when I was in high school. When I was nineteen, I took up Appalachian dulcimer and, eventually, added fiddle and banjo." After performing in a duo with Duck Donald, Fink moved to Washington, D.C. and began a solo career. "There's a big scene in Washington," she says. "It's a wonderful movement with a lot of songs coming out of our own homes and lives."

Fink Meets Marxer

Fink and Marxer have been playing together since 1980. "We met at a folk festival in Toronto," Fink recalls. "Marcy was with a group, The Bosom Buddies. We hit it off big and toured together. Marcy and I got to know each other. When she moved to Washington, D.C., it gave us an opportunity to do things together. We realized that what we wanted to do was to play together. She brings out a lot of flexibility in my music. Marcy is an excellent lead player. She helps to broaden the style of music that we can play."

"I really love to play eclectic styles," Marxer continues. "In the past, I've had to play in a bunch of different bands. Cathy does it all. There's also a real quality in her singing. I love to back-up singers. She does it really well. There's an emotional depth to her singing."

Recent Work

In addition to her work with Marxer, Fink has produced recordings by such performers as The Rude Girls, Patsy Montana, Magpie, The Children Of Selma, Blue Rose and The Critton Hollow String Band. "As a producer, I've got to be an organizer," she explains. "I've got to be an arranger and a support system. I've got to offer encouragement and make decisions. It's a stressful situation. I'm a real perfectionist."

The duo recently completed an album with Si Kahn. "A lot of Si's songs seem traditional," Fink reflects. "Many people don't even realize that he wrote such tunes as 'Aragon Mill.' He's such a prolific songwriter, he deserves a lot of attention."

Fink and Marxer have also been actively involved with children's music. "Children's music has gotten more respect in the past few years," Marxer explains. "It's a more family-oriented generation. A children's event has a built-in novelty factor." Their album *Help Yourself!* won the 1990 Washington Area Music Awards honor as "Best Children's Recording." The record has received attention for its sensitive handling of children's issues such as abuse and neglect.

BRYAN BOWERS

The string band tradition is reflected through the music of autoharp player Bryan Bowers. "I grew up on a farm in rural Virginia," he says from his home in Seattle. "I heard field chants on a daily basis. They were doing the call and response thing. I heard the dancers as they walked up the railroad line laying down the track. Across the street was a Catholic Church that had a string band. They played old time dance music but they also played a lot of Czechoslovakian fiddle tunes. My parents were Presbyterian. Their music was pretty stiff and boring. At the Baptist and Black Churches, the walls would be shaking. That was the kind of stuff that I heard without even turning on the radio."

Bowers is also heavily influenced by the Ballad tradition of stories set to music. "All my songs have to tell a story," he says. "It's got to be a real story. Don't give me something complex. Just give me a good story line."

Five-Finger Style

Bowers' distinctive five-finger style was developed as a defense mechanism. "I was a street singer," he explains. "People asked me if I could play louder but I didn't want to get an amp. Eventually, I worked out a way to get a little something out of each finger. It's got a real dense sound and I'm able to get a lot of volume out of it."

Bowers heard the autoharp for the first time while attending grade school. "The teacher couldn't tune it," he remembers. "There was a string missing. Bowers' opinion of the instrument changed after he heard a more professional autoharp player. "He

Bryan Bowers

"It's got to be a real story. Don't give me something complex. Just give me a good story line."

really got it in tune," he recalls. "That made all the difference. I bought one and started to play eight to twelve hours a day."

Bowers began his professional career in Washington, D.C. "My first gig was opening for Emmylou Harris," he remembers. "No one knew her then. She was playing in a little bar with a guy from Colorado, Mike Williams. She was playing purely acoustic. I opened for her for six months. I made five dollars and all the cheeseburgers I could eat."

Career Break

Bowers' first career break came when he was heard by Mike Seeger of The New Lost City Ramblers. "He got me to play at the Chicago Folk Festival," he explains. "I got three major reviews in Chicago newspapers. The next thing I knew, I had a following."

Bowers' music was introduced to bluegrass audiences by The Dillards. "They took me to festivals," he says. "When they got an encore, they would do it. If they got a second encore, they would send me out. I still play at a lot of bluegrass festivals. I play a lot of Carter Family songs and the old time songs."

The Washington, D.C.-based duo, Bill and Taffy Danoff, also helped to promote Bowers' playing. "They helped me to get my song 'Berklee Women' to John Denver," Bowers explains. "He liked it and said that he'd like to record it." Denver's recording provided a major boost for Bowers' career. "It was amazing," Bowers reflects. "I got royalty checks every six months that were the equivalent of what I made as a street singer in a year. That went on for eight or ten years. Then, he did a 'Best Of' album and recorded a rock version of the tune. It was a ballad but he rocked it out."

The windfall from Denver's recordings changed Bowers' life. "The life of a street singer is very close to the vest," he says. "You don't make much money. As soon as I started making more than I needed, I started to save for a down payment on a house. I had been living in my panel truck for seven years."

Bowers has been living in Seattle since 1975. "It's a real healthy music scene," he says. "It's a melting pot with a wide diversity of things happening. People from the East Coast brought their music, while, people from French Canada added their sounds. Old time music has been big for years. There's Cajun players and a lot of western swing. The folk society is real active, from concerts to some really fine teachers. There's Monday night Old Timey jam sessions."

ROBIN AND LINDA WILLIAMS

Robin and Linda Williams have been collaborating since 1973. "We met in Myrtle Beach, South Carolina," Williams recalls. "The marriage and the partnership came at the same time. The relationship had gotten to the point where we had to do something about it. We decided that if we were going to get married, then, we'd better figure out a way to make a living. So, we teamed up."

Williams' own songs have been recorded by performers such as Emmylou Harris and the Minneapolis-based Celtic-rock group Boiled In Lead. "Linda has some great ideas lyrically," Williams says from his home in Virginia. "I have some great ideas musically."

Both husband and wife bring different things into their collaboration. "There's no one that keeps me honest anymore than she does," Williams reflects. "When I was performing as a soloist, I'd be on the stage in front of a good crowd and, sometimes, pull some stunt or say something that wasn't me. I'd get off the stage all full of myself and look at Linda for encouragement and she'd say something like 'Well, that's good. But what was that all about?' On the other hand, I bring to her music a sense of looseness and relaxation. I try not to take things quite so seriously."

Robin and Linda Williams

A Prairie Home Companion

The duo attracted their widest attention as semi-regulars on Garrison Keillor's radio show *A Prairie Home Companion*. "We were working with (multi-instrumentalist) Peter Ostrouchko," Williams recalls. "He said that we ought'a call Garrison. So, we did. He drove over to see us. He was his own talent scout then. Things were different."

"Once the show went national," he continues, "we started playing on it quite a bit more. It was a great experience. It constantly challenged us and we were forced to come up with good, quality material. We worked things up with the other musicians that were going to be on the show. It really made us better musicians."

The Williams' home in the Shenandoah Valley region of Virginia has inspired much of the duo's recent work. "It's a great place," Williams says. "We've gotten a lot of songs from the people around us. It's beautiful. We've got some of the best friends that anyone could ever hope to find."

John Lee Hooker

Blues

When Czechoslovakian composer Antonín Dvorák came to
the United States to research his Symphony in E minor, *From The New World,* he observed that the only true American folk music was being produced on plantations
throughout the South. Since the mid-nineteenth century the outgrowth of that plantation music, the blues, has affected every form of popular and traditional music in the
United States.

W.C. Handy, who titled his autobiography *The Father Of The Blues,* is credited with
publishing the first blues. Handy's *The Memphis Blues* appeared in 1909 but the blues
go back much further. The *Rolling Stone Encyclopedia Of Rock & Roll* explains,

> The blues arose sometime after the Civil War as a distillate of the African music brought
> over by slaves. From field hollers, ballads, church music and rhythmic dance tunes called
> jump-ups evolved a music for a singer who would engage in call-and-response with his
> guitar; he would sing a line and the guitar would answer it. In the Thirties and Forties, the
> blues spread northward with the black migration from the South and filtered into big-band
> jazz; they also became electrified as the electric guitar became popular.

"A lot of people say that if you play the blues, that's all there is to it," guitarist Eddie
Kirkland explains during a recent interview. "But that's a lie. You've got all kinds of
blues. There's smiling blues. There's twenty-four bar blues, eight bar blues, twelve bar
blues, rhythm & blues and Delta blues."

Although acoustic country blues originated in the Mississippi Delta, the most influential post-World War II forms have come from Detroit, Chicago and Texas. We represent these styles here, repectively, with John Lee Hooker, James Cotton and
Clarence "Gatemouth" Brown, along with some of the other finest representatives of
the Black tradition and the blues as it branched out to other musicians.

JOHN LEE HOOKER

The blues produced in Detroit reflect the boogie-influenced rhythms of Mississippi-
born and former Motor City resident John Lee Hooker. Hooker is known for his
raucous, folk-rooted guitar playing. "Nobody plays like John Lee Hooker," the bluesman boasts from his home in California. "There's a lot of good guitar players who try
to play in my style, but after a while, they all begin to sound the same."

"My stepfather, Will Martin, taught me to play," Hooker reflects. "It's a very good
lead style. A very sad music—very lonesome, deep and blue." By the late 1920's,
Hooker was performing with his stepfather at local fish fries and dances.

Country blues guitarists Blind Lemon Jefferson, Blind Blake and Charley Patton
were early influences, while the music of T-Bone Walker inspired Hooker's move to
electric guitar. "(Walker) was the first bluesman to play electric," Hooker explains. "He
was my idol. I followed him everywhere."

After leaving Mississippi in 1941, Hooker played blues with B.B. King and Bobby
"Blue" Bland in Memphis and sang with gospel groups in Cincinnati. His career really
got under way, however, after moving to Detroit in 1943.

Hooker worked during the day as a hospital attendant and, later, at an auto plant.
Playing in the Motor City clubs at night, Hooker began to attract attention for his
highly-charged music. His debut single "Boogie Chillun" was the best-selling blues
record of 1948. "It happened in the studio," Hooker remembers. "The boogie's been
around for a long time. It's almost an instinct—you just start to play and it comes out."

Prolific Recordings

From the beginning, Hooker was one of blues music's most prolific recording artists.
Besides the records that he produced under his own name, he used a lengthy list of

James Cotton

pseudonyms (including Texas Slim, The Boogie Man, Delta John, Sam & His Magic Guitar and John Lee Booker) to record for as many record labels as he could.

Although he had subsequent hit singles (including "Crawling King Snake," "Serves You Right To Suffer," and "I'm In The Mood"), only "Boom Boom" placed on the national pop charts. Beginning in 1959, when he recorded his first full-length album and performed at the Newport Folk Festival, Hooker began to exert a much wider influence. During the mid-1960's British blues revival, Hooker was acknowledged as one of the "founding fathers" of the blues. When he toured England in 1965, The Rolling Stones were his opening act. "They had just been organized," Hooker remembers. "I had John Mayall backing me—with Eric Clapton and Peter Green. It was a great tour." Hooker's songs have been performed by The Animals, The Doors, Canned Heat, George Thorogood, Mick Jagger and many others.

His albums have featured guest appearances by many of rock 'n' roll's best-known musicians (including Van Morrison and Bonnie Raitt). In 1970, Hooker collaborated with blues-rockers Canned Heat for a double album, *Hooker 'n' Heat*, that was on the national charts for months. Hooker's latest album *The Healer* featured Charlie Musselwhite, Robert Cray, Huey Lewis and Carlos Santana, and received the Grammy Award as "Best Blues Album of 1989." Hooker received another honor in 1991 as he was inducted into the Rock & Roll Hall of Fame.

JAMES COTTON

"Chicago has never had the blues. It's people who've had them—people like Memphis Slim, Muddy Waters, Big Bill Broonzy and James Cotton."

James Cotton has been one of the prime movers of the Chicago blues scene. "I am Chicago blues," claims Cotton. "Chicago has never had the blues. It's people who've had them—people like Memphis Slim, Muddy Waters, Big Bill Broonzy and James Cotton."

Although he recently celebrated his fifty-fourth birthday, Cotton is in no danger of slowing down. "I've got nothing else to do," he explains. "I'm going to get a bus and travel from city to city. I'll get off, sing the blues and get right back on to the bus."

The son of a Baptist minister, Cotton was introduced to the harmonica by his mother. "She made noises on the harmonica," he remembers. "She imitated the sound of a train whistle, the cackling of hens."

Inspired By Sonny Boy Williamson

Cotton's main inspiration was blues harpist Sonny Boy Williamson (Alex "Rice" Miller). After hearing Williamson's radio show "King Biscuit Time" over an Arkansas radio station he was hooked. "There was a local guy that played blues," he recalls, "but Sonny Boy really knocked me out." Before long, Cotton met his hero. "I had an uncle that knew Sonny Boy," he explains. "One day, I sat on the porch and blew my harmonica. I made forty-eight dollars in a couple of hours. My uncle saw that I had a talent for music so he asked Sonny Boy if he could help me out a little."

Not only did Williamson agree to help the nine year old boy, but also, for the next six years, Cotton was taken in as a member of the Williamson family. "(Sonny Boy) was a sweet cat," Cotton reflects, "but whatever he believed in was the way that it was."

Cotton's apprenticeship ended when he inherited Williamson's band. "Sonny Boy's wife split," he says, "he gave me the band and went off to look for her." The group managed to stay together for only another six months. "We were only fifteen years old," Cotton explains. "You know, young cats sometimes get a little crazy."

Howlin' Wolf, Muddy Waters and An Optimistic Future

Cotton wasn't out of work for long. Besides leading his own band, James Cotton And His Rhythm Playmates, he played with the historic Howlin' Wolf Band of the early 1950's. His biggest break came in 1954 when he joined Muddy Waters' band. "Junior Wells had just left," he remembers, "and they needed a harp player."

Cotton's harmonica was a fixture of Waters' band for the next twelve years. Although they separated in 1966 ("I figured it was time to do my own thing," he says), they continued to record together until Waters' death in 1983. "We were used to playing together," he reflects.

Cotton remains optimistic about the future of the blues. "I think the blues are coming back," he says. "People are beginning to listen again. When I was with Muddy in the 1950's, rock 'n' roll broke and people stopped listening to the blues. But, they're coming back."

CLARENCE "GATEMOUTH" BROWN

Clarence "Gatemouth" Brown is one of the most influential Texas blues guitarists. The blues, however, represent only a small slice of Brown's music. Brown's recordings and playing have attracted an increasingly wider following. His album *Alright Again* won a Grammy Award as "Best Blues Recording of 1982" and was named "Album of The Year" by a German Record Critics' Poll. A multiple Handy Award winner, Brown was named "Instrumentalist of The Year" in 1982 and 1986 and "Entertainer Of The Year" in 1983.

Brown's Background

Born in Vinton, Louisiana in 1924 and raised in Orance, Texas, Brown plays a host of different instruments, including fiddle, drums, piano, viola and harmonica in addition to guitar. His earliest break came in 1947 when he filled in for an ailing T-Bone Walker at the Golden Peacock nightclub in Houston. The club's owner, a Houston businessman named Don Robey, was so impressed that he eventually became his manager. "(Robey) was a smart businessman," Brown remembers. "He formed Peacock Records around me. I was playing drums and singing. No one knew that I played guitar and fiddle."

Under Robey's guidance, Brown assembled a twenty-three piece band. "I was the youngest big band leader," he claims. Unfortunately, the era of the Big Bands was near-

Clarence "Gatemouth" Brown

ing its conclusion. "Economics broke up the big band," Brown explains. "It became too hard to support a band on the road. We played all over America but there weren't many big venues for Black musicians."

In the 1960's, Brown moved to Nashville to lead the house band for the syndicated R&B television show *The Beat.* Throughout the 1970's, Brown was a major star in Europe, recording nine European-released albums. His first American album *Blackjack* was released in 1978.

Brown has collaborated with many other musicians including country music performer Roy Clark, and the late New Orleans pianist, Professor Longhair. "They respected me," Brown recalls. "They knew that when I got up there to play that I knew what I was doing."

Recent Work

Brown's latest release *Standing My Ground* showcases his eclectic repertoire and includes jazz, blues, swing, ballads, funk and zydeco. "I wrote most of it myself," Brown points out. Although the album features a version of Muddy Waters' "Got My Mojo Workin'" Brown gives the classic tune a distinctive twist. "I thought it was a good tune," Brown recalls, "but I had to change the lyrics a little. I don't like negative music. I want people to feel good about themselves. If you go with your wife to listen to music, you want to be uplifted."

The album also includes an original zydeco tune, "Louisiana Zydeco," that features Terrance Simien on accordion and Earl Salley on rubboard. "I can remember my father playing zydeco and Cajun music," Brown says. *Standing My Ground* is marked by Bill Samuel's horn arrangements. "I like the sound of horns and pianos," Brown explains. "I get a big band kick with my guitar. I've always tried to copy the horn sound." Brown has brought his music to every corner of the globe. "It's very easy for people to listen to me," he says. "The music does the talking."

MOSES RASCOE

Moses Rascoe is keeping alive the tradition of country blues. For most of his seventy-three years, however, making a living at music was the furthest thing from his mind. "I heard tell of so many people that had got beat out of their money," Rascoe explains, "that I said 'forget it.' They weren't going to beat me out of anything."

Instead, Rascoe spent most of his adult life as a coast to coast truck driver. "I always carried my guitar with me," he explains. "Every time I got the chance, I'd pluck on it. I had seen this old man about thirty-five or forty years ago. I knew that he used to pluck a guitar and was very good at it. He told me that he wanted to see my guitar, so I showed it to him. His fingers had gotten stiff so he couldn't do it anymore. I didn't want to get where I couldn't play. But I never thought about performing out."

Rascoe's Background

Rascoe was born in a North Carolina town that was so small that he says, "we weren't big enough to even be a one-horse town." From earliest memory, blues captured Rascoe's attention. "My daddy used to have his own business," he recalls. "On Saturdays, I used to go with him to work. These fellers would be outside in the back playing the blues. I just loved the sound. It got inside me and stayed there. I was just a young kid—eight or nine years old. I didn't know what the blues were about. It was just something that had an effect on me."

Rascoe ordered his first instruments from Montgomery Ward on the installment plan. "They sent some country & western stuff," he remembers. "I learned to play it by the book. They had the chords drawn out. Most of it was in (the key of) G and C anyhow. I just learned to play it. I knew the songs so I could sing them."

Moses Rascoe

Rascoe's love of the blues was not completely accepted at home. "My daddy was alright with the blues," Rascoe recalls, "but my mother just didn't care for them. We had a piano and an organ in the house but my parents liked gospel music or the country music that they heard on the radio."

Influenced By Big Bill Broonzy

Rascoe's guitar playing reflects the same roots as Big Bill Broonzy and Brownie McGhee. "Very seldom do you hear Big Bill run strings together, strumming down over it," Rascoe explains. "He just picked a solid tune out. Brownie McGhee is very similar. When I found that they were playing that way, I just loved it. I played the same way but I didn't know that I was backtracking nobody."

Rascoe's material comes from three weather-beaten books of old time blues songs. "I like the old stuff," Rascoe says, "and I play it. I've got a camper that I put in back of a van. At night, my wife likes to look at television. I like music, so I go out to the camper so I'm not disturbing her and the television don't be bothering me."

Rascoe gave his first professional performances in 1982 in Pennsylvania. "People liked what I was doing," he reflects. His debut album *Blues* was released in 1987.

"I heard tell of so many people that had got beat out of their money, that I said 'forget it.' They weren't going to beat me out of anything."

JOHN HAMMOND

Beginning primarily in the mid-1960's, blues have been played by white, middle class musicians. John Hammond's music is rooted in country and Delta blues and in the R&B of the 1950's. "The first music that I was exposed to," he remembers from his home in New York, "was the music that I heard on the radio in the early 50's. People like Ray Charles, Chuck Berry, Bo Diddley, Jimmy Reed."

Although Hammond is the son of late record producer John Hammond (who "discovered" many jazz, blues and folk musicians including Bob Dylan and Bruce Springsteen), his father's tastes in music played a very small role in his musical development. "I didn't grow up with my father," he explains. The senior Hammond's influence throughout the music industry was sometimes a problem. "There have been difficult times," states Hammond. "It's been hard for some producers to see me for what I am."

Jimmy Reed Inspires Research

"There have been difficult times. It's been hard for some producers to see me for what I am."

An album by Jimmy Reed that Hammond bought in 1955 inspired him to research earlier blues. "The liner notes suggested other recordings," Hammond recalls. "It led me to people like Blind Boy Fuller and Robert Johnson. It flipped me out." From that point, Hammond's love for the blues continued to grow. At seventeen years old, Hammond bought his first guitar. Two years later, he had taught himself enough to be able to begin playing professionally.

Many of Hammond's earliest gigs were in the coffeehouses that were scattered throughout New York's Greenwich Village. "It was a street basket house scene," Hammond remembers. "You could make twenty dollars a night if you had a good night. I remember playing at the Gaslight and at Gerde's Folk City for one hundred dollars a week."

By 1965, however, things were a lot different. The success of the Newport Folk Festival had placed a new focus on folk styles. Bob Dylan made a great impact by using electric instruments. Folk-rock bands came out en masse. Before long, almost every one-time Folky was switching to electric instruments and forming bands.

Together with Robbie Robertson (then, with The Band) on guitar and Bill Wyman (of The Rolling Stones) on bass, Hammond recorded his debut album for the small Red Bird label. "The owner (of the record company) said that I wasn't promotable," Hammond claims. "The album had been produced by Leiber and Stoller. But the LP was shelved." When Red Bird decided not to release the album, Hammond was temporarily disillusioned. "I took some time to get away," he recalls.

Collaborations—Jimi Hendrix, Duane Allman and Others

Music had too strong a pull for Hammond to stay away for long. When he returned to New York, he put together a band. For a brief while, late guitarist Jimi Hendrix was a member. "I met Jimi in New York," Hammond reflects. "He was playing at the Cafe Wha!. A friend of mine had told me that I had to hear this guy, so I went. After the show, we met and got this thing together. Jimi was just playing the blues. He was a real good guitar player. I don't think he had even taken acid yet."

Hammond also worked with many other influential musicians. In 1963, he met rockabilly singer Ronnie Hawkins' band, The Hawks (who later changed their name to "The Band") in a Toronto club and lured them away to back him up in New York. "Robbie (Robertson) was the best natural guitar player I've ever heard," Hammond says. "I made the mistake of introducing him to Bob Dylan. That was the last I heard of him."

Although he continued to work with other musicians, Hammond began to perform more and more as a soloist. In 1972, he finally decided to go it alone. "I signed with Capricorn and recorded an album," he explains. "One side was solo. I decided that, rather than putting another band together, I was going to run my own life. So, I became a solo artist."

Subsequent albums have alternated between solo recordings and collaborations. Playing with veteran Bluesmen Roosevelt Sykes (on the 1978 album *Factwork*) and Larry Johnson (on the 1970 album *Southern Fried*) allowed Hammond to work with pioneers of early blues. "Larry had a problem communicating with people that wanted to book him. So, he never got the momentum that, I think, his music deserved. Roosevelt Sykes, on the other hand, was very easy to work with." The *Southern Fried* album also featured Duane Allman. "We played a lot of shows together," Hammond recalls. "Duane was, unfortunately, killed just as he was becoming a star."

Hammond, with Dr. John and Mike Bloomfield, formed the short-lived supergroup Triumvirate in 1973. The group's self-titled album was Hammond's attempt at recording a

John Hammond

hit record. "We thought it was good," he reflects. "A week after the album was released, it was already on the charts. We were featured on the TV show 'In Concert.' But there was an FBI investigation into Columbia records. Clive Davis (the label's president) resigned. Every penny for promotion was frozen."

Soundtracks and Solo Work

Hammond has provided the soundtracks for two films—Arthur Penn's *Little Big Man* and Mason Daring's *Matewan*. "I auditioned for Arthur Penn," Hammond remembers. "I had gotten a phone call saying that they'd like to hear me play. So, I flipped a coin in my mind and decided to do it. When they showed me the film, I was completely overwhelmed. I didn't think that I could do it but Penn told me that I could do anything. It was pretty scary. I was flown to Los Angeles and worked for a month in a sound studio."

Although the full-band sound is custom-made for Hammond's high energy acoustic blues, he continues to perform solo. "It all boils down to money," he claims. "I can't get paid any more if I have a band than I get paid to play by myself. I don't like being a psychiatrist or a roadie. I'm not just starting up. I don't want to have to pay my dues all over again."

Bonnie Raitt

BONNIE RAITT

A unique mixture of blues, R&B, pop and folk have made Bonnie Raitt one of contemporary music's most popular performers. Raitt's 1988 album *Nick Of Time* marked the peak of her musical career. Her amazing Grammy coup included awards for "Album Of The Year," "Best Female Pop Vocalist" and "Best Female Rock Vocalist," and "Best Traditional Blues Recording" for her duet of "I'm In The Mood" with John Lee Hooker.

A Major Comeback

The album's success represented a major comeback for the red-haired, Los Angeles-born guitarist-vocalist. Two years earlier, the Warner Brothers record label refused to release Raitt's proposed ninth album, "Tongue In Groove." At the time, Raitt was beset with her well-publicized addiction problems, which she has since conquered.

Born in Los Angeles, Raitt hails from a Quaker-activist background. Her mother was a preacher's daughter who played the piano. Her father, John Raitt, was a highly successful Broadway actor.

Beginning to play guitar at the age of twelve, Raitt developed a fondness for the blues. After attending Radcliffe University for two years, as an African studies major, she left school to pursue a musical career. Her early performances made her a favorite of the folk and blues communities in Boston and Philadelphia.

Raitt's self-titled debut album included tunes by Sippie Wallace and Robert Johnson and featured Chicago blues session players Junior Wells and A.C. Reed. Her second album *Give It Up* featured more songs by Wallace and helped to introduce the songs of Jackson Browne and Eric Kaz.

Recent Work

Raitt has been involved with many politically active groups. As a member of M.U.S.E. (Musicians United for Safe Energy) in 1979, she performed five shows at New York's Madison Square Garden and was featured in the concert film and album *No Nukes*. She also sang on the 1985 Steve Van Zandt-written and produced anti-apartheid record, "Sun City."

Raitt performs over one hundred shows a year, split between "acoustic shows" with bass guitarist Johnny Lee Schell and R&B/rock-oriented shows with her band. Her vocals and distinctive slide guitar playing have been featured on numerous albums including John Lee Hooker's *The Healer* and A.C. Reed's *I'm In The Wrong Business*.

RORY BLOCK

Greenwich Village-born singer-guitarist Rory Block blends blues and folk music to create a very personal style. "My thing has always been a lot of variety," Block explains. "Even back in the days when I was with major labels. It confused a lot of record executives. They said you have to have only one theme. Either you're a Disco Queen or you're a folksinger. You can't blend jazz, folk, R&B, blues and gospel on one album."

Block's Background

Block grew up in a musical environment. "A lot of people became interested in roots music at the same time," she recalls. "I was exposed to it in my early teens. This surge of energy was very inspiring to me." Block's father, Allan, played an important role in her musical growth. My father started to play country fiddle," she remembers, "and I backed him up." The senior Block provided an entry into New York's folk music circles. "When the folk revival started happening," Block says, "my father's sandal shop became a sort of central meeting place for musicians. I was exposed to a lot of really great music, people like John Sebastian, John Herald of The Greenbrier Boys, Maria Muldaur and Bob Dylan."

Rory Block

Block initially attracted attention as a member of The Woodstock Mountain Review, a mid-1970's folk music "supergroup." "It was a great bunch of old friends," she recalls. "It was a communal situation with organization."

Block recorded several disappointing albums in the late 1970's. "I've always been way off the trends of the music industry," she explains. "Ten years ago, I started as a rhythm & blues singer. I wrote funky, uptempo R&B. But, it was pre-Bee Gees and they couldn't relate to it. They asked 'why can't she just sing rock 'n' roll?'"

Stunning Reviews

Turning her back on the established record industry, Block signed with the Cambridge-based independent label Rounder Records and recorded the ground-breaking acoustic blues album *High Heel Blues*. "It got stunning reviews," Block remembers. I was suddenly in demand as a blues singer."

Although Block's album *Best Blues And Originals*, released on the Holland-based Munich record label, sold enough copies to be certified gold and her latest release, *Turning Point*, placed number three during a critic's poll in Germany she continues to play in small, folk music coffeehouses in The United States. "The fans (in The United

States) are easily as loving," Block says. "They're just not able to get my records as easily. In Holland, my albums have had excellent distribution. Every record store has my product. People could get the records. In the United States, if I counted all the people who've told me that they can't find my records, it would add up to a gold record."

Block, nonetheless, has remained true to her music. "What I've learned is doing my own thing is all I can do," she says. "If I buckle under and try to make a disco album because a major label is going to make me a star and it doesn't make me a star, I'm going to be left with a feeling of being used and raped. It's going to be a dreadful feeling to have to live with."

Block's subsequent albums have continued to showcase the diversity of her music. Her latest American release *House Of Hearts* ranks among contemporary music's most personal statements. "It was a memorial to my son, Thiele (who died in an auto accident)," Block reflects. "People say it's very moving, (that listening to it was) so intense that they cried all the way through. I get loving, personal, letters saying that it was part of the healing process. A record producer used the album as a model for a band whose road manager had died. I feel very honored."

GEOFF BARTLEY

"I'm learning ways to let go and give myself to the audience."

Geoff Bartley is a master of the acoustic guitar. A two-time winner of the New Hampshire Acoustic Guitar Contest and a four-time Second Place winner at the National Fingerpicking Championships in Winfield, Kansas, Bartley combines urban blues with a classical and rock touch to create a deeply personal sound. "I'm not a solo guitarist," he says during breakfast at his home in Cambridge, Massachusetts. "I'm more of a rhythm player who can play some hot licks. Much of what I play is blues-tinged."

Bartley has recently been experimenting with electric guitar. "The electric guitar is much more delicate," he explains. "With an acoustic guitar, you've got to hit the strings with more force. The controls on an electric guitar are more sensitive. They're designed to reflect a player's smallest nuances. It's like going from a one ton pick-up truck without power steering to a Honda civic."

Bartley has also been incorporating a variety of sound effects into his music. "I've been using a volume pedal," he says. "It allows for really beautiful swells. It makes it sound orchestral. I've also been using an E-bow. It's a small electromagnet run by a battery that you hold in your right hand and vibrate the guitar strings without touching them. You don't hear the attack. The sound swells out of nowhere. The sounds are suggestive of a range of instruments."

The musical experiments have influenced Bartley's approach to playing the acoustic guitar. "I've had to be much lighter," he says. "I've learned that I play more musically when I'm relaxed. It's like learning a new lesson."

Influences

Born in New York City and raised in a small town on the eastern shore of Maryland—where he spent the first fifteen years of his life—Bartley has subsequently lived in Nevada, Colorado, Connecticut, New Hampshire and Pennsylvania. He first moved to Boston to attend Boston University in 1967.

Bob Dylan's music influenced him to begin playing guitar in 1963. His discovery of Lightnin' Hopkins was a major turning point. "(Hopkins) is the missing link," he explains, "between the Black blues singers of the 1920's and '30's and the very slick, much more commercial, high powered blues of Chicago. I've listened to a lot of those riffs." Other influences include Bessie Smith, Son House and Robert Johnson.

Songwriting

Bartley has no easy prescription for writing songs. "Songs don't come easy to me," he explains. "Sometimes I get a germ of an idea but I have to really work at putting together a finished song. I've been mainly concerned with writing lyrics. It's easier for me to come up with chords and a rhythm. More and more, I've been writing about the world. I've been reading about what's going on in India, Africa, Central America and The Mideast and I've been addressing those issues."

Two of Bartley's songs, "Who Should Know" and "Leaving Soweto," have been featured in performances by The Fast Folk Music Revue. For the past three years, Bartley has shared his love of songwriting with members of his songwriting group. "Constructive criticism has helped to strengthen all of our songs," he reflects. "Jack Hardy and The Fast Folk Music Cooperative have been a real inspiration."

Bartley has increasingly focused on expanding his capabilities as a vocalist. "I've quit smoking," he says, "and I've taken voice lessons from Sonia Savig in Avon-On-Hudson, and Phyllis Capana and Walter Dixon in Cambridge. He's a trained operatic tenor who's on the faculty at the University of Massachusetts. I've been playing guitar for twenty-five years but I want to really be a singer and let my feelings out. I'm learning ways to let go and give myself to the audience. I want to really open up my skills and grow."

Geoff Bartley

Recent Work

Bartley continues to create significant new material. "Pipes And Drums" pays tribute to the creative muse, while "My Daughter, This Mirage" reflects changes in Bartley's life. "It's about a young girl going to her first prom," he explains. "It was a dangerous subject. It's about an underaged girl becoming a woman, but it's also about my increased interest in fatherhood. I really care about this kid. She's the daughter of a woman that I've been seeing. The song means a lot to me."

Bartley's new songs, which also include "The Language Of Stones," "Up Here With The Moon" and "Muscle For The Wing," continue to reflect his involvement with human issues. "I've written a song ('The Wreck Valdez') about the Exxon oil spill of March, 1989," he says. "It's political, but I've tried to maintain the sense of poetry. *Sing Out!* magazine has published this song complete with footnotes."

Recordings

Bartley has recorded three albums, *Blues Beneath The Surface, Interstates* and *I Am The Heart,* for his own independent record label, Magic Crow Records. "(*Interstates*) has more instruments than the first album," he says, "and more singers. Anne Weiss, Shawn Colvin and Patty Larkin sing background vocals. I think they did a great job. I was looking for a special kind of sound. There's a lot of drums. I wanted the drums to be an extension of the guitar. There's also a lot of vocal harmonies. It adds a human element."

I Am The Heart captures Bartley during a solo, studio performance. Many of the songs tackle difficult issues. During "Bullets And Canned Goods," he focuses on the possibilties of a nuclear winter and the need to go to "the iron cold of Vermont" to build "a shelter underground of earth and rock and wood." "Modern Valentine (Rubber Love)," co-written with John Gorka, is a tongue-in-cheek tribute to prophylactics ("They come in every color/not just black and white/so you can see a rainbow/on a Saturday night"). "City Of Faith" satirizes television evangelists ("I've heard His voice/this is what he said/you'd better raise eight million/or I'll strike you dead").

THE DIXIE HUMMINGBIRDS

"It surprises them when we dance—we move and glide across the stage."

One cannot write about blues without mentioning gospel, the more spiritual side of Black American music. Blues and gospel have long been intertwined genres. One of the most influential gospel vocal groups is The Dixie Hummingbirds. Although the group has been singing for over sixty years, tenor vocalist Beechie Thompson demonstrates that they are in no danger of slowing down. "We surprise a lot of people. They expect us to be old people with white hair and canes. It surprises them when we dance—we move and glide across the stage."

The Hummingbird's History

The Dixie Hummingbirds trace back to 1928 when James Davis (who retired in 1983) assembled a quartet of fellow Sterling High School students in South Carolina. "The group was derived from the glee club," explains Thompson, who joined in 1943. "They used to sing in Church. That was the only singing they did until they started traveling."

Throughout the 1930's, the group toured throughout the Carolinas. Shortly after recording their first record in 1939, The Hummingbirds were joined by lead vocalist Ira Tucker (formerly of The Gospel Carriers) and bass singer William Bobo. "Ira was only fourteen when he started," Thompson claims. "We picked up (Bobo) in New York."

In 1942, The Dixie Hummingbirds moved to Philadelphia and began broadcasting regularly over the radio. After John Hammond Sr. had them booked into New York cafés and nightclubs, The Dixie Hummingbirds became one of the first gospel groups to reach out to a wider audience. "It was the beginning of something new," Thompson remembers. "People reacted very favorably." Throughout the late 1940's and 1950's , The Dixie Hummingbirds produced influential gospel records including "Jesus Walked On The Water" and "I Can't Help It."

Although they originally sang a capella, guitar (currently played by Howard Carroll) has been an important element of their sound since the late 1950's. "It's like having an additional singer," Thompson says.

In 1966, the group performed at the Newport Folk Festival. "It was a real cross-section of people," Thompson recalls. "It was an anything goes audience. If you put your best into it, they knew it."

A Million-Seller With Paul Simon

The Dixie Hummingbirds are perhaps best known for their background harmonies on Paul Simon's 1973 hit "Loves Me Like A Rock." "It opened a lot of doors," Thompson reflects. "We became better known to the other race. We had always been from the other side of the tracks. We tried to break through. But nobody listened."

Although Simon's recording of "Loves Me Like A Rock" reached number two on the pop charts and won the Grammy for "Best Gospel Performance," The Dixie Hummingbirds' version initially met with opposition. "A lot of Black people thought we were singing rock 'n' roll," Thompson says. "They'd never heard a record played so much. It really threw them for a loop. The Black D.J.s had to break it down and explain what the song really meant. Then, people started jumping on the bandwagon. It sold over a million copies."

The Dixie Hummingbirds

Michael Doucet

Louisiana

Louisiana is possibly the richest musical state in America.
The roots of jazz, Dixieland, rhythm & blues and rock 'n' roll can all be traced to the Pelican State. The state's French-speaking southwest triangle, stretching from Lafayette to St. Charles has been the traditional home of Cajun and zydeco music. Long associated with the increasingly popular Cajun food, including Gumbo and Jambalaya, the area's music can be traced back to the late eighteenth century when the formerly French-held Canadian territory known presently as Nova Scotia and New Brunswick was taken over by the British. When the French-descended landholders were given the opportunity to swear allegiance to the British crown, those who refused were placed on boats and dispersed throughout the American colonies. Permitted to bring only what they could hold in their hands, they brought their fiddles, which were easiest to carry. Many eventually settled in the French-speaking bayous of Louisiana.

In the mid-eighteenth century, when the first railroads were being built, German workers introduced the accordion to the area. Until the early twentieth century, the area was cut off from the rest of the country. There were very few roads and, until the 1920's, no English-speaking radio stations. As a result, the Cajuns, whose name was derived from "Acadians" in the same way that "Injins" was derived from "Indians," produced their own indigenous music.

Joe Falcon recorded the first Cajun tunes in the late 1920's. It wasn't until 1964, when Dewey Balfa performed at the Newport Folk Festival, that the rest of the country heard Cajun music. In recent years, Cajun two-steps and waltzes have been brought up to date by performers such as Michael Doucet, Zachary Richard and Filé.

MICHAEL DOUCET

"Cajun music is the folk music of the Acadian people that settled in southwest Louisiana," fiddler-vocalist Doucet says from his home in Lafayette, Louisiana. "The basic things don't change. We still play acoustic instruments. But there's a definite evolution of the music. We play the older, forgotten, songs—the blues, ballads and jazzier songs. But Louisiana is where rock 'n' roll started. Everyone was affected."

Doucet's fiddling was heavily influenced by legendary Cajun fiddlers Hector Duhan, Canray Fontenot and Dennis McGee. "Everyone was so different," Doucet recalls. "Each was able to convey their individual feelings. My style comes from all these people."

Beausoleil

Formed in 1976, Beausoleil represents what Doucet jokingly calls "the sleazy roots of Cajun music, the wild side of Cajun music." Doucet and Beausoleil incorporate a variety of musical styles. "It runs the gamut," Doucet says, "from traditional songs of the zydeco tradition to American fiddle tunes by Tommy Jarrell."

Beausoleil's latest release is a live in-concert recording, *Live From The Left Coast*. "We recorded it at The Great American Music Hall in San Francisco," Doucet says. "It gives us a chance to finally hear for ourselves what we sound like. We're a really good dance band. Performing live gives us an opportunity to really stretch out. Most of the songs have never been recorded by us before. There's no overdubbing. There's a mixture of old tunes, such as Nathan Abshire's 'Pine Grove Blues,' and new songs. I wrote a tune about the first Cajun video star, Aldous Roger."

Much of Beausoleil's current sound reflects the accordion playing of Jimmy Breux, whose grandfather wrote the Cajun classic "Jolie Blonde." "Jimmy is the best accordionist we've ever had," Doucet claims. "He's very young, only twenty-one. But he's a master. The accordion is truly his instrument." David Doucet also contributes much to

Zachary Richard

Beausoleil's sound. "(David) has his own ideas about music," Doucet explains. "He listens to a lot of American folk music, people like Doc Watson and Leo Kottke. He also incorporates the sound of Cajun steel guitar into his playing."

Doucet's Work Outside Beausoleil

Doucet released a solo album, *Beau Solo.* "It's mostly me on fiddle and (my brother) David on guitar," Doucet explains. "Chris Strachwitz (of Arhoolie Records) followed me around my house and recorded me playing accordion. I play mostly in the old-time style." Doucet is also co-leader (with Ann and Mark Savoy) of The Savoy-Doucet Band. "We take a house band or back porch approach," he says.

Besides performing and touring with Beausoleil, Doucet is active as a session player. His fiddling was featured on Keith Richards' *Talk Is Cheap* and on Greg Brown's tribute to the songs of William Blake, *Songs Of Innocence And Experience.* "It was quite an experience to play with Keith," Doucet reflects. "It was a neat thing to be able to meet the guy. Greg and I share a love of William Blake's poetry. In college, I was going to go for a Master's degree in comparative literature. But I went to France instead. Greg and I met on 'A Prairie Home Companion' and spoke about our mutual appreciation of Blake. He approached me, later, about putting Blake's words to music. The first day, we listened to the songs and, on the second day, we recorded them. Greg's a wonderful writer. I still can't listen to the album without crying."

ZACHARY RICHARD

Zachary Richard is more than a Cajun performer. Although the Scott, Louisiana-born vocalist/multi-instrumentalist is deeply rooted in the sounds of Southwest Louisiana, he's added contemporary rock 'n' roll, funk, New Orleans-style R&B, African, Afro-Cuban, Caribbean and even rap influences to the Cajun and zydeco traditions. The result is a potent gumbo of Louisiana-flavored dance music.

"I've never pretended to be a traditional musician," Richard claims from his home in Lafayette. "A lot of my influence comes from outside of the Cajun culture."

Playing guitar since a youngster, Richard bought his first accordion with the money that he received from signing a contract (as a solo performer) with Elektra Records in 1973. "I listened to (zydeco accordionist) Clifton (Chernier) late at night," he remembers. "Iry LeJeune was very important. He died tragically in 1955. Up until him, the assimilation was going full-tilt. The music was all being done in an anglo style. He brought back the popularity of the accordion."

A Cult-like Following

Although relatively unknown in the United States, Richard is a major star in Canada, where two of his seven albums achieved gold status (500,000 copies sold). His 1979 single "L'Arbre est dans ses Feuilles" was number one on the Canadian charts for three months in 1979.

In France, Richard has enjoyed a cult-like following. He was the recipient of the prestigious Le Prix du Premier Ministre as "outstanding young French language singer of 1980." "We spent two years living in Paris," he says, "cementing our status in France. Craig (Lage) was with me as orchestra leader. We used a French rhythm section."

When the album he recorded for Elektra went unreleased, Richard returned to Louisiana and formed The Bayou Drifter Band with high school friend, Michael Doucet (later the fiddler and leader of Beausoleil). Although short-lived, the group was the first Cajun band to perform in Louisiana's rock 'n' roll clubs.

A trip to the Acadian area of New Brunswick and Nova Scotia led Richard to undergo a political transformation. "I'd go into bars," he recalls, "and insult people that didn't speak French. A number of people my age are too lazy. Shame was my father's generation but there's no reason why we shouldn't speak French. It's just laziness." Richard quickly acquired a reputation for his militant views. He was called "The Bad Boy of Cajun Music." "When I go home," he says, "I laugh my head off. It's a big country and there's room for a lot of different things."

BOOZOO CHAVIS

Wilson "Boozoo" Chavis is one of the founding fathers of zydeco music. A thirty year hiatus from recording (1955-1984) and a fear of flying have made the sixty year old accordionist one of Louisiana's best-kept secrets. "What I'm doing now, I should've been doing thirty years back," Chavis says from his home in Lake Charles, Louisiana.

"I got soul with my music. I got a beat that the rest don't have."

Chavis' style of zydeco differs from other zydeco bands. "I got different beats from them," he says. "I got soul with my music. I got a beat that the rest don't have. They're trying to get it now but they're messing it up. I have a beat that they can't get. It's a gift that came to me. I've always had it in me. You keep hearing 'Zydeco this' and 'Zydeco that.' But they're not zydeco and they're making me mad."

Chavis' style of zydeco traces back over one hundred years. "Zydeco goes way back to my grandfather's time," he explains. "It comes down from slavery time. People were on the plantations in the cotton fields or in the sugar fields. On Saturday, they'd go to house dances. They had an accordion and a triangle. Sometimes, they had a scrub board. Whether they call it 'zydeco' or 'Cajun' music, it's all the same thing. The only difference is that a Black person dances different than a White person. The Black person holds their partner close and they dance. You can't pass a needle between them. The man puts his hands around the lady's waist. She's got her arm right on his shoulder. They're together when they turn around."

Chavis had his biggest success in 1954 with his zydeco tune "Paper In My Shoe." "I got it from Joe Jackson," he remembers. "He used to play dances around here. He sang 'Paper In My Shoe' and I played washboard behind it. I learned it. I kept messing with an accordion and I picked it up. I was the only one that could play it." Although the song remains one of the staples of most zydeco bands' repertoire, it was a bitter memory for Chavis. "I got gypped out of my record," he says. "I get frustrated, some-

Boozoo Chavis

times. I love to play, but when I get to thinking about 1955 . . . They stole my record. They said that it only sold 135,000 copies. But my cousin, who used to live in Boston, checked it out. It sold over a million copies. I was supposed to have a gold record."

The dispute caused Chavis to get out of the music business. "I got disgusted," he remembers. "I said, 'Well, I don't have to do this and I don't have to do that.'"

Peak of Popularity

Chavis was at the peak of his popularity. "These people came from California looking for me," he remembers, "and Eddie Schuster (who owned the Goldband record label and Chavis' contract) turned them back. If it hadn't been for that, I would've been as big as Clifton (Chenier). He was running first (in the popularity polls) and I was running second. He played in more of a blues style on the piano accordion. He played some zydeco but he played it fast. He took a lot of the same songs that I used to play. I quit and he kept going. "

After "retiring" from music, Chavis pursued his second love—training race horses. "I went from place to place," he says. "I trained horses in Shreveport, Lafayette and Texas."

A Second Musical Career

Chavis began his second musical career in 1984. "My wife said that I should start thinking about playing again," he recalls. "But I was already thinking about it." Since his return Chavis has recorded two albums, one for Rounder Records and one for Maison De Soul. "They got better equipment than they had in the 1950's," he explains. "The sound system is better. It looks like it's easier than it was before. It doesn't take as long to record anymore."

Chavis recorded several songs with the New York-based rockers, N.R.B.Q. (New Rhythm & Blues Quartet). With a reputation as "the world's greatest bar band," N.R.B.Q. had an interest in seeking out the infectious Cajun rhythms and performers. "(Keyboardist) Terry Adams was trying to find me for years," he explains. "He saw me at The New Orleans Jazz And Heritage Festival and got in touch. He came to my house and heard me play. A bunch of them came to hear me play in Waikiki. They got in touch with me. They're very fine people. They showed me something that I didn't know and they helped me to see the light."

BUCKWHEAT ZYDECO

An offshoot of Cajun music, zydeco (which translates as "Snap beans") originated in the mid-1940's as a blend of traditional Cajun music, Caribbean rhythms, Texas-style blues and New Orleans-style rhythm & blues. "I used to listen to a lot of Fats Domino," Clifton Chenier, the late "King of Zydeco," said during a 1985 interview.

Among zydeco's best-known players are Buckwheat Zydeco, Queen Ida and Terrance Simien. Accordionist/organist Stanley "Buckwheat Zydeco" Dural and his band, The Ils Sont Partis Band, have added elements of funk, soul, blues, rock 'n' roll and jazz to create a sizzling hot contemporary music. "My music is for all generations," Dural says from his home in Lafayette, Louisiana. "I want to modify the music, bring it up to date."

Early Influences and Clifton Chenier

Although his father played accordion in the traditional zydeco style, Dural initially rebelled against the instrument. "I was running away from it," he recalls. "No one was speaking French or playing the accordion until 1979." Despite his aversion to the squeeze

Buckwheat Zydeco

"My music is for all generations. I want to modify the music, bring it up to date."

box, Dural began playing piano before his fifth birthday. "I started real early," he says. "By the time that I was nine, I was already on the bandstands playing organ." Eventually, Dural left school to play music full-time. After serving apprenticeships with Sammy And The Untouchables and Little Buck And The Topcats, he formed his first band, Buckwheat And The Hitchhikers, in 1971. "It was a large band," he remembers. "There were five singers and sixteen musicians. We played a little bit of everything: James Brown, Al Green, Earth, Wind and Fire."

In the early 1970's, Louisiana underwent a grassroots cultural resurgence. Like many others, Duval began to rediscover his Creole heritage. When he was invited by Clifton Chenier to join his Red Hot Louisiana Band, Duval disbanded The Hithchikers and accepted the offer. "(Chenier's) a good friend of my dad's," Dural explains. "He's one of a kind. He's such a dynamic musician. He's not working as much anymore because of his illnesses but I knew him when he was at full strength. He's one of the main influences on my music." Chenier recently passed away.

Performing with Chenier was the turning point for the budding young musician. In addition to playing on world tours and recording sessions, Duval was reintroduced to the accordion. "Clifton could get so many sounds on his accordion," he says. "It was amazing. It was the music that I had grown up with but people were getting really ex-

Queen Ida Guillory

cited about it. I couldn't believe it." After leaving Chenier in 1978, Duval bought an accordion of his own and formed The Ils Sonts Partis Band. "Before I started playing accordion," Duval claims, "no one of my generation did anything like this. They thought Buck had gone crazy. The band thought I had gone wacky. But there's a lot more accordion players in Louisiana now."

Although Dural initially had some doubts about playing tradition-rooted music, they were soon forgotten. "I was going to give it two years," he says. "But within six months, we were attracting over two thousand people a night. Before the year was finished, we recorded our single— 'I Bought A Raccoon.' The next thing we knew, we were packing the place. It surprised me. But it's been getting better all the time."

Buckwheat Zydeco And The Ils Sont Partis Band released eight albums on Blues Unlimited, Black Top and Rounder before signing with Island Records. Their latest albums have featured guest appearances by Eric Clapton and Dwight Yoakam.

QUEEN IDA GUILLORY

"The music is earthy—simple, but happy. It gets right into their soul."

Queen Ida Guillory is one of the few women playing Cajun or zydeco music. "Men didn't want us," she explains from her home in San Francisco. "It's the same way with reggae. Women have very rarely played instruments."

Guillory's music has consistently received critical acclaim. She received a Grammy Award (for *Queen Ida—On Tour* in 1983) and two Grammy nominations (for *Queen Ida In New Orleans* in 1980 and for *On A Saturday Night* in 1984). An appearance in the Francis Ford Coppola film *Rumble Fish* brought her to an even larger audience. "We were heard by people that wouldn't have come out to hear the band," Guillory says.

Guillory's Background

Born in Lake Charles, Louisiana, Guillory hails from a musical family. "My dad played the harmonica," she recalls, "and my mom's two brothers played accordion with Cajun bands." Guillory initially gave little thought to music as a profession. "I put the accordion into the closet," she says. "I was the mother of three children and I had no time for anything else."

The situation began to change, however, after the kids left to attend school. "It was very lonely," Guillory reflects. "I suddenly had a lot of free time, so, I took out the accordion and started to play along to old records." Before long, Guillory was yearning to perform with a band. "My brother (Al Lewis, who's since changed his name to Al Rapone) played with a rock band," she remembers. "When they would finish rehearsing, I would ask them to back me on a few songs."

A turning point came when Guillory was asked to perform at a charity Mardi Gras party. "I didn't want to do it," she says, "but my brother and my husband encouraged me." The performance was attended by a San Francisco Chronicle writer. "At the party, I was crowned 'Queen Ida,'" Guillory recalls. "There's always a Queen of the Mardi Gras. So, when the article came out, I became Queen Ida."

Fighting For The Accordion

Guillory has continuously fought to have the accordion accepted as a legitimate instrument. "The American people weren't ready to accept the accordion as a lead instrument," she says. "The only thing that they'd heard was polkas and, if that turned them

Terrance Simien

off, they were turned off by the accordion. But once they get a chance to hear zydeco," she continues, "they change. The music is earthy—simple, but happy. It gets right into their soul."

Performances have increasingly featured the accordion playing and lead vocals of Guillory's thirty-five year old son, Myrock "Freeze" Guillory. "(Myrock's) been in the band for four or five years," she explains. "Zydeco music is traditionally passed down from generation to generation. I told him that it was time for him to step forward and do something. At my age, I don't have too many more years."

TERRANCE SIMIEN AND THE MALLET PLAYBOYS

Flawless musicianship and well-executed theatrics are combined with an understanding of Cajun and zydeco traditions by twenty-three year old accordion player and vocalist Terrance Simien and his band, The Mallet Playboys.

Musical Influences

Born in Mallet, Louisiana (a small town of 500 people about 70 miles from Baton Rouge), Simien was first attracted to the accordion after seeing a band at a local dance hall. "The band was playing," he remembers during a recent telephone interview, "and everyone was having a good time. It seemed like something that I could do." Simien put together the current Mallet Playboys—Earl Salley (rubboard); Pop Espree (bass); Gene Chambers (guitar); and Rudy Chambers (drums)—after auditioning twenty-six other musicians. "I looked for the best musicians," he says. "I looked for guys my own age. I'm lucky. The guys that I've got are really good musicians. They're dedicated to me and to my music."

Earl Salley has been instrumental to Simien's music from the earliest days, supplying uptempo rhythms on the rubboard that he wears like a vest. "When I was getting the band together," Simien recalls, "he came to a dance that I was playing and sat in. He's got a lot of energy. People are amazed by the rubboard. It's a unique instrument, used only for zydeco. He's a master."

Shortly after Simien put the group together, they were encouraged by a gig at the World's Fair in New Orleans. "My ex-drummer's father had played at the fair," Simien explains, "and told the head of the folklife pavilion about us. It was a turning point. It was the first time that we played in front of a big audience."

Paul Simon Helps The Playboys

Word about the band's highly charged performances spread. When Paul Simon came to Cajun country in search of zydeco bands to back him on *Graceland* he was steered to Simien and The Mallet Playboys. "A local sax player told him about us," Simien says. Although Simon chose Good Rockin' Dopsie & The Twisters to perform on the album, he was so taken by the Mallet Playboys that he helped finance and sang background vocals on a recording of Simien's tune "You Used To Call Me."

The group performed to a club filled with influential musicians at New York's Lone Star Cafe in 1985. "It was the night before Live Aid," Simien explains. "We opened for Lonnie Mack. All kinds of musicians showed up to hear us. Keith Richard and Ron Wood got on stage and played. Paul Simon came down to hear us, Mick Jagger, Bob Dylan."

Simien and The Mallet Playboys made their cinematic debut in Jim McBride's film *The Big Easy*, starring Dennis Quaid and Ellen Barkin. "We did two tunes in a nightclub scene," Simien says. "and a song that I co-wrote with Dennis Quaid, 'Close To You,' was used in the love scene. The Neville Brothers and Dickey Landry back us up."

Unlike most zydeco accordionists, Simien prefers the one-key Cajun accordion over the more flexible piano accordion. "It lets you hit your notes much faster," he says. "I fell in love with the smaller instrument." Simien and The Mallet Playboys released their debut album *Zydeco On The Bayou* in 1990.

FILÉ AND THE NEW GENERATION OF CAJUN MUSIC

"We respect the tradition but we try to take it a step further."

Groups like Filé (pronounced Fee-Lay) represent the new generation of Cajun music. Although their sound is based on the traditional two-steps and waltzes and the playing of Ward Lormand on accordion and Darren Wallace on fiddle, the influence of contemporary music is obvious. "We've become more eclectic," Lormand says during a recent interview. "We've tried to keep the Cajun stuff but we've taken a few different steps. We've got some new influences in the band and we've been trying to expand our sound. We respect the tradition but we try to take it a step further. We're trying to make our own sound."

Much of the band's sound reflects the presence of new musicians. "Darren Lawless comes from a bluegrass background," Lormand explains. "He's a master stringman. He plays just about anything with strings on it. His influences are real wide. We've also added another guitar player, Brian Langlinia, who comes from a Swamp/pop background," Lormand continues. "His father was in several popular Swamp/pop bands. He also grew up in Lafayette."

Filé began as an offshoot of another band, Cush Cush. "The bass player (Kevin Shearin) and I have been together since 1979," Lormand says. "When Cush Cush broke up in 1983, we agreed to continue playing together. We knew a fiddle player and we got the guitar player from Cush Cush."

The band's earliest gigs were at the World's Fair in New Orleans in 1984. "I grew up on Cajun music," Lormand reflects. "I never had to learn any songs. They were already ingrained inside me." Nevertheless, it took years before Lormand was comfortable with his roots in Cajun music. "I didn't like the music when I was growing up," he recalls. "It wasn't the cool thing to do. I was a rock 'n' roll drummer in garage bands."

A Switch—To Accordion

A revival of traditional Cajun music in the mid-1980's influenced Lormand to rediscover his musical past. "When I was eighteen or nineteen, I started to really listen to it," he remembers. "A couple of younger players, like Zachary Richard and Michael

Filé

Doucet, had started their own bands. They really put things in a different light. It started making sense to me." Lormand switched to accordion shortly afterwards. "A friend had bought an accordion," he says, "but he couldn't play. I started messing around with it. I had a couple old teachers. I haven't strayed too far from the traditional styles. My main influence is Mark Savoy. I've been listening to David Hidalgo (of Los Lobos) a lot."

Cajun music is essentially a dance music. "We try to make people dance," Lormand says. "I've heard one analogy that a Cajun band without a dance is like an orchestra without a conductor."

DR. JOHN

Much of Louisiana's music remains centered in New Orleans. The city's second-line rhythms and boogie woogie piano playing have been at the root of Malcolm John Rebennack Jr.'s music. Better known as the voodoo-inspired "Dr. John, The Nighttripper," Rebennack has broadened the musical vision of the Crescent City as a much-in-demand session player and producer.

From New Orleans to L.A. and Back

The son of a professional model and an appliance store owner who sold records, Rebennack began his career at an early age. His baby picture was featured as the Ivory Soap Baby in company ads. By the time he was fifteen, Rebennack was already working as a session musician at Cosimo Matessa's recording studio in New Orleans. "When I was coming up, it was a whole different scene," he recalls from his home in New York. "I got to work with my heroes. Two of my guitar teachers (Walter "Papoose" Nelson and Ray Montrell) were professional musicians and played with Fats Domino's band. It was a real wild way to learn the trade. I was totally blessed as a kid. I worked with all the great piano players in New Orleans. When I played guitar, I'd be looking over their shoulders and learning stuff."

Things started to change in 1963. "Jim Garrison started padlocking all the clubs," Rebennack remembers. "At the same time, the music union was chasing a lot of musicians away from New Orleans. Musicians were forced out of town." Although Rebennack moved to Los Angeles to work with Sam Cooke's band, his plans were tragically altered. "By the time I got there," he says, "(Cooke) was dead."

Sonny and Cher, Voodoo and Psychedelia

Rebennack was quickly absorbed into L.A.'s music scene, working with Sonny and Cher and legendary record producer, Phil Spector, among others. "My business partner, Harold Battiste, did some early sessions with Spector," Rebennack says. "(Spector) was really into New Orleans music and wanted us to put that kind of flavoring in. I couldn't understand where he was coming from, but musically, I really respect him."

Inspired by stories that he had read about voodoo, Rebennack developed the musical character Dr. John Creaux the Nighttripper. "I had a concept for an album in mind," he explains. "I had read some stories about 'Dr. John, the Voodoo King.' Voodoo is still active in New Orleans. I developed the concept from a mixture of being in New Orleans and from what I'd read."

Rebennack initially planned to produce the album with Ronnie Barron as vocalist. "I figured that I'd just produce it," he recalls, "but when I tried shopping it to a label, no one was too interested." Rebennack recorded the planned concept album, *Gris*

Gris, during sessions for a Sonny and Cher album. "While Sonny and Cher were blowing studio time, I did the album," Rebennack says.

Rebennack's portrayal of Dr. John was so intense that he fit in with rock's most psychedelic acts. "Battiste booked me into Psychedelic venues," he recalls. "Instantly, instead of a Voodoo band from New Orleans, I was a psychedelic performer. It helped to make *Gris Gris* a large cult record. It's sold a lot of copies over a long period of time. Atlantic kept it in the catalogue for years. Alligator rereleased it last year."

Although early albums (*Babylon, Remedies* and *The Sun, Moon & Herbs*) were underground favorites, Dr. John didn't break into the musical mainstream until his tribute to New Orleans' R&B, *Gumbo*, was released in 1972. "One night, when we were recording *Remedies*, a group of people came to the studio," Rebennack remembers. "Jerry Wexler learned that I could play the piano and that I knew Professor Longhair's tunes. He said that he wanted to do a record of this stuff. We got all the original guys together that we could."

Dr. John

Top 40 Hits

The album marked the peak of Dr. John's popularity, with all three of his Top 40 hits ("Iko Iko," "Such A Night" and "Right Place, Wrong Time") coming over a two year period. "It was a real fun time," he recalls. "Atlantic had really great promotion. It's how I look at Warner Brothers today. They're really into the music, not just trying to hustle a record."

Rebennack has appeared in two films. He performed "Such A Night" in The Band's 1978 film, *The Last Waltz*. The cult film *Candy Mountain* features his only non-musical performance. "It showed me that acting wasn't my thing," he says. "But it opened a lot of doors for me. It led to my scoring a lot of films (including *Bull Durham, St. Elmo's Fire* and *Cannery Row*)."

Rebennack has also provided voiceovers for a number of television commercials. "I've been doing it for the past ten or fifteen years," he says. "Not only is it a good way of making money but it's a good way of keeping your voice in front of the public."

Dr. John's latest album *In A Sentimental Mood* pays tribute to the Tin Pan Alley pop tunes of the 1930's and '40's. "It was meant as a real surprise," Rebennack says. "I

Gregory Davis

wanted to try a different kind of thing for my first album on a new record label (Warner Brothers). But it was real exciting. I hope every record is different."

Rebennack recently toured with Ringo Starr's All-Stars. "Ringo was great," he says. "He's got a great personality. Not only is he a classic drummer, but, he's a natural comedian—a real unique character."

THE DIRTY DOZEN BRASS BAND

Jazz, rhythm & blues and pop are blended with the traditional second line rhythms of New Orleans marching bands by The Dirty Dozen Brass Band. "All of us listen to different things," Gregory Davis, the band's trumpet player, vocalist and leader, says from his home in the Crescent City. "I bring my love for gospel and R&B. The tenor player (Kevin Harris) and the bass drum player (Lionel Batiste) listen to a lot of fusion. (Baritone and soprano saxophonist) Roger Lewis played with Fats Domino's band, so, I guess, he came up with rock 'n' roll. Everyone brings their own thing into the band."

The band's recently released fourth album *The New Orleans Album* is a tribute to the sounds of the Crescent City. "We didn't realize that we were doing mostly music produced in New Orleans until after we had recorded it," Davis claims. The songs were chosen because The Dirty Dozen Brass Band had "developed a good feel for these songs. "We rehearse a lot of material," Davis explains. "We're always trying to add something new to our shows."

The Fats Domino Connection

The New Orleans Album reunites Lewis with Dave Bartholomew, best known as Fats Domino's bandleader and arranger. "Dave's still a musician," Davis says. "He still writes and performs with a Big Band and a small combo. Roger and I both worked with him. I worked with him for two years. Roger worked with him in Fats Domino's band for fifteen or twenty years. We had started doing that song, 'The Monkey.' It just didn't have that fullness without Dave doing the vocals himself."

Danny Barker, who helped to initiate the Brass Band revival, makes a rare guest appearance on two songs. "We had to pay homage to him," Davis says. "I was going to sing (Barker's tune 'Don't You Feel My Leg'), but then, I had the idea to call and ask him to do it. He not only came and play on that one, but he wanted to do the guitar strumming on 'That's How You Got Killed Before.'"

The biggest surprise on the album is the piano playing of Eddie Bo. "I knew him from songs like 'Check Out Mr. Popeye,'" Davis says, "but I didn't know he was an accomplished pianist. He could really, really play. I didn't know that. After he had a string of Rhythm & Blues successes in the 1960's and early 1970's, he just dropped out of sight."

The album's best known guest, Elvis Costello, sings lead on the Bartholomew-composed tune "That's How You Got Killed Before." "We had done the *Spike* album with him," Davis explains, "so, we had gotten to know him a couple of weeks prior to doing this record. He actually initiated the contact. It was a blessing. It's good to be liked by your peers."

Richard Thompson

British Isles

The traditional music of the British Isles is at the root of

American folk music. "There was a collection of jigs, reels and strathspeys published in New England in the 1840's," Mary Drouin, of the Rhode Island-based Celtic band Pendragon, says before a performance at Johnny D's in Somerville, Massachusetts. "It was published many years prior to the well-known O'Neill Collection of Irish Traditional Music in America. There were one thousand and fifty tunes. But it practically disappeared. I have one of only two known copies. There's some feeling that they headed west and south with the pioneers and that the tunes became southern music as we know it."

Paradoxically, traditional music in the British Isles itself was in danger of being lost due to pressures of 21st Century modernization. "After the second World War, people in Ireland and Scotland were looking to catch up," says Johnny Cunningham, a Scottish fiddler who helped spark a revival in Scottish music. "It was like, 'Let's bring this country up to the twentieth century.' When I started going to folk clubs, everyone was singing American songs."

The revival of traditional British Isles music began in the late 1950's. "Ewan MacColl and Alan Lomax had gone out collecting, laying a lot of ground work for the revival," Guy Carawan explains. "The young people had gotten to hear the old timers. There were a lot of young people discovering all this rich Irish and Scottish and British music. They were digging back into their roots. But it had a real political edge to it. They were active in the anti-Polaris Missile movement and were against the English domination of Scotland."

Richard Thompson, the influential singer/guitarist and former Fairport Convention member, has been a leading figure in keeping the spirit of Birtish Isles music alive in contemporary pop music. A number of other performers and groups are continuing, renewing and experimenting with this branch of musical tradition.

TOMMY MAKEM AND THE CLANCY BROTHERS

Tommy Makem, along with The Clancy Brothers, was instrumental to both America's folk boom and the revival of Irish music. "People were turning their back on folk music," he says from his adopted home in New Hampshire. "Most people thought that it was just the music of the poor people. I remember going with a band and they didn't want to have anything to do with the music at the dances. But if they went to a house party and any of them was asked to sing, then, inevitably, they would sing a folk song."

The Clancy Brothers and Tommy Makem were among the first groups to introduce traditional Irish ballads in The United States. "When we were starting," Makem remembers, "the folk boom was going on. Here we were, four guys, with a large repertoire of songs that none of the folksingers knew."

The group had a great impact on Bob Dylan. "Dylan would come in and listen to what we were doing," Makem recalls. "Then, he'd make up songs with the same tunes. We'd meet him at Sixth Avenue at 3 o'clock in the morning and he'd stop us to sing a song that he had written. He wrote 'With God On Our Side' to the tune of 'The Patriot Game.' The funny thing was that it had originally been an American pop tune, 'Hear The Nightingale Sing,' which had been recorded by Patti Page or Jo Stafford. It had gone over to the other side and had been adapted by Dominic Behan. It was a lovely tune."

The Clancys' unparalleled American success was an important factor behind the revival of traditional ballads in Ireland. "When we went home in 1962 for our first tour of Ireland," Makem recalls, "we had already been playing in The United States for a number of years. The national radio station started playing our records incessantly.

Tommy Makem

People started thinking 'This is our music. These four fellows took it over to America and the Americans are listening to it. There must be some good to it.'"

Makem's Background

Makem was born in the occupied territories of Northern Ireland. "I had a wonderful childhood," he reflects. "There was a lot music. I came from a very small town of only two thousand people. But there were five dance bands, a pipe band and an accordion band."

Folk music played an important role in Makem's family. "My mother was known as a source of folk songs," Makem says. "A lot of people came to collect from her. The BBC used hundreds and hundreds of songs that they got from my mother. The first folk music radio show that I can remember was on the BBC World service, which went out to all the English-speaking countries. It was called 'As I Roved Out' and was on every Sunday morning at 10 o'clock. The show's signature song came from my mother."

Makem's biggest break came after he met Tom, Paddy and Liam Clancy. "Diane Hamilton had come over to Ireland," he explains. "She knew Paddy and Tom Clancy in New York. She was going to record my mother after visiting their mother in Carrick-on-Shuir in county Tipperary. She didn't have a tidy little recording machine like they have now. It was a big, heavy, chunky, clumsy, box. Liam Clancy came along to carry her recording equipment. When Liam and I met, we hit it off. We were both going off to The United States to seek fame and fortune as actors. When I came over, I met up with him again. Then, I met his brothers. Someone had asked them to do a recording of Irish Rebel songs. They asked me if I would sing a few songs. A year later, we did an album of Irish drinking songs."

None of the five musicians had given thought to becoming singers. "I was out in Chicago doing repertory theater," Makem says. "We were at The University Of Chicago doing three plays. The run was over and I was supposed to be going back to New York. The full cast went out, one night, to a place called 'The Gate Of Horn,' which was a folk music haven. Some of the cast urged the owners to get me up to sing. I had never been in a nightclub before. After I sang, the owners asked me to stay on for another two weeks."

Shortly after returning to New York, Makem began singing with Liam Clancy. "I got a part in a play," he recalls, "and Liam was in the play, too. Three men came to the play one night, and asked Liam and me to come and sing at a little folk music club called 'Gerde's Fifth Peg.' It was later renamed 'Gerde's Folk City.' We were each getting forty-five dollars a week acting off-Broadway and these guys offered us one hundred and twenty five dollars each to sing every night."

Although they began to sing as a duo, Makem and Clancy were often joined by the two older Clancy brothers. "Once in a while," Makem recalls, "Tom and Paddy would wander in around midnight. We'd get them up to sing a couple of songs with us."

The 60's Folk Boom and Ed Sullivan Put The Clancys and Makem On The Map

The quartet's first "official" performance was at The Gate Of Horn. "We spent days trying to come up with a name for ourselves," Makem says. "We came up with every name in the book. We had wads and wads of paper with names and we couldn't all agree on any of them. We were going to go to Chicago without a group name. But when we got there, the marquee said 'The Clancy Brothers And Tommy Makem.'"

The group quickly became a favorite of Greenwich Village's folk music crowd. "We'd be playing at Gerde's Folk City," Makem recalls, "and there would be all kinds of people there. I remember once when Liam and I were performing and this guy came up to us and asked if we would let the girl who was with him sing. They had come from Colorado. She was on crutches and had a cast on her leg. She had been skiing. It was apparently her first time in New York, so, we let her come up and sing. She turned out to be Judy Collins."

The Clancy Brothers And Tommy Makem hit their peak after their debut appearance on *The Ed Sullivan Show.* "We had been performing at The Blue Angel," Makem says, "A very prestigious nightclub. *Time* magazine and *Newsweek* and *The New York Times* covered us. The 'Ed Sullivan' people came in and got us on to the show. The night we were on, one of the big acts got sick. We were supposed to be singing two songs but the producers asked if we could improvise a few more songs. We ended up doing eighteen minutes. It was longer than anyone had ever done."

Although the folk boom dissipated, The Clancy Brothers And Tommy Makem continued to be successful. "We were lucky in that we not only had a big folk following," Makem explains, "but also a big Irish and Irish-American following. It kept us doing concerts during the lean years."

Makem left The Clancy Brothers in 1969. "I was in a comfortable groove," he reflects, "but I was beginning to stagnate mentally. It was very difficult to get away from doing the same songs over and over. We kept filling concert halls and getting well-paid for it. But this was a personal thing. I was stagnating. So, I took off. Certainly, we didn't have a knife-fight or anything like that. We're still good friends."

Makem reunited with Liam Clancy in 1975. "We got together at a music festival in Cleveland, Ohio," he recalls. "We were both booked separately and, then, we got back on stage and did a set together. We stayed together as a duo until 1988." As this book went to press we learned that Liam's brother, Tom Clancy, had passed away.

Makem released two albums in 1990. *Rolling Home* focused on songs about the environment and the tragedy of war. *The Tommy Makem Songbag* featured re-recordings of old songs plus a few new ones. "I used the same musicians as the last album. We tried to keep all the verve and excitement that The Clancys and myself would have used," Makem said.

"The environment is possibly the most important thing that we have to deal with," said Makem. "It's been taking a pounding for so long that it's time to do something about it. What we're handing over to our children is a terrible misuse of what was handed down to us. The subject of war should be the last thing on anybody's mind, but, it's not."

"We were lucky in that we not only had a big folk following but also a big Irish and Irish-American following."

Simon Nicol

FAIRPORT CONVENTION

In England in the 1960's, traditional music was blended with more contemporary influences by groups such as Pentangle, Steeleye Span and The Incredible String Band. Fairport Convention, however, remains the most enduring and influential band. Although they've never had a Top Ten single, the group has withstood numerous personnel changes.

Fairport Convention's present incarnation features the group's longest-lasting lineup. Included are founding member Simon Nicol on guitar; Dave Pegg on bass; Dave Mattacks on drums; Ric Sanders on electric fiddle; and Martin Allcock on guitar and mandolin. "We've been together for four-and-a-half years," Nicol says from his home in the Muswell Hill section of London. "It's much better balanced. The musicians are much more complementary to each other. Also, with age, comes a certain degree of advanced tolerance."

An English Response To American Folk

Formed in 1967, Fairport Convention initially reflected an English response to early 1960's American folk music. "We were interested in American singer-songwriters," Nicol recalls. "People like Phil Ochs, Richard and Mimi Farina, and Joni Mitchell. We were very influenced by what The Byrds did with Dylan's material. It was much harder to find in England than it was to find bands that played the Mersey Beat."

Fairport Convention has never enjoyed widescale commercial success. "We've never had a heyday," Nicol says, "no day of fashionable acclaim. We're just a working band that exists outside the music industry." Fairport Convention is, however, much more than just a group of musicians punching a time clock. "All the bands have had their own flavor," Nicol explains. "There's a certain spirit that links all the different lineups. We don't take ourselves too seriously. Fairport is a lucky band to be in."

According to Nicol, the most difficult period of the band's history followed the departure of Richard Thompson in 1971. "It was probably hardest for me," Nicol reflects. "I had never played guitar without him." The situation proved so difficult that Nicol temporarily left the band. "I took five years off for good behavior," he says.

Nicol returned in 1976. The band, however, seemed to have run its course by the late 70's. In 1979, Fairport Convention performed, what they believed was, their "Farewell Tour." "We had done all that we could do with that lineup," Nicol remembers. "(Dave) Swarbrick had a ringing in his ears and wanted to stop playing electric music. We had to decide whether we were going to replace him or become an acoustic band. Instead, we decided to call it quits."

It didn't take long for the band to recuperate. In 1980, the first "Fairport Convention Reunion" was held in Cropedy. "More people came than we expected," Nicol recalls. "It created a momentum that has kept us going." Fairport Convention was "officially" reunited in 1983 with Sanders replacing Swarbrick. "(Sanders) has a much broader spectrum of music at his command," Nicol says. "As a result, we're much more eclectic than in the past."

Fairport Convention's "Twentieth Anniversary Reunion" in 1987 was filmed and featured during Paul Kovit's video-documentary, *Fairport Convention: It All Comes 'Round Again.* "(Being the subject of a video) is a marvelous asset," Nicol says. "It was really done well. It's very lucid. It doesn't drop a beat. It answers all the questions about Fairport and clears up a lot of the confusion."

Fairport "Alums"

Richard Thompson, Fairport Convention's original lead guitarist, has gone on to even greater fame since leaving the band in 1970. Continuing to base his compositions on reworkings of Playford's tune collection of 1561, *The English Dance Master,* Thompson combines ultra-subtle guitar playing with contemporary-minded lyrics. His collaborations with his ex-wife, Linda Thompson, culminated in the influential album *Shoot Out The Lights* which *Rolling Stone* included in its list of top albums of the 1980's. Since then, Thompson has alternated between solo acoustic shows and performing with an electric band. Thompson's guitar playing has also been featured on albums by Loudon Wainwright III and Michael Doucet's *Cajun Brew.* French, Frith, Kaiser And Thompson, the band that he formed with avant-garde musicians John French, Fred Frith and Henry Kaiser, has resulted in two albums.

Although he's never performed in The United States, Ashley Hutchings, bassist and Fairport Convention's founding father, has been one of the leading forces of British folk-rock. Since leaving Fairport in 1969, Hutchings has gone on to form many other influential bands including Steeleye Span and The Albion County Dance Band. In recent years, Hutchings has toured with a band that featured Clive Gregson and Dave Mattacks.

Sandy Denny, who sang and wrote songs for Fairport Convention, Fotheringay and The Strawbs, died on April 21, 1975. Her influence, however, remains extremely powerful.

Founding member Iain Matthews, who recently returned to the Gaelic spelling of his first name, left Fairport in 1969. In the years immediately afterwards, he had several hits, including a version of Joni Mitchell's "Woodstock" that reached number one in the United Kingdom. Although he's been relatively inactive since emigrating to The United States in the early 1970's, he returned to the studio in 1987 to record *Walking A Changing Line,* which featured songs by Jules Shear. His most recent outing, *Pure And Crooked,* was a return to the folk-pop sound of his earlier work.

Dave Swarbrick, who played with Fairport Convention from 1969 until 1979, was a founding member of the acoustic, tradition-based group, Whippersnapper. He recently left the group and was replaced by guitar player Martin Simpson.

STEELEYE SPAN

Steeleye Span has gone through a number of personnel and musical changes since their inception by Ashley Hutchings in 1969. Lead vocalist Maddy Prior, however, has been at the heart of the band since the beginning. The group reached its commercial

"All the bands have had their own flavor. Fairport is a lucky band to be in."

Triona Ni Domhnáill

peak in the mid-1970's when they focused on a more electric, pop-minded sound and had Top-40 hits with "All Around My Hat" and "Thomas The Rhymer." Their 1974 album *Now We Are Six* was produced by Ian Anderson of Jethro Tull. *Now We Are Six* featured David Bowie on saxophone on the Phil Spector tune, "To Know Him Is To Love Him." Temporarily disbanded in 1978, the group reunited two years later. Their latest recording, *Tempted And Tried: A 20th Anniversary Celebration* is a return to the roots of traditional songs. The album's original tunes were composed by mandolin player/fiddler Peter Knight, who joined in 1970, and by guitarist Robert Johnson.

TRIONA NI DOMHNÁILL

The Bothy Band was one of the first bands to bring traditional Irish music up to contemporary standards. "The first two years, we played some great music," vocalist Triona Ni Domhnáill recalls. "We were all fired up and we weren't worn down by the road. We didn't make any money but it didn't matter." The group eventually drifted apart. "We felt jaded by the road and our lack of management," Ni Domhnáill remembers.

After emigrating to The United States, Ni Domhnáill settled in Chapel Hill, North Carolina (and eventually, in Portland, Oregon). "I met Mike Cross in a bar in Nashville," she recalls. "He was very into The Bothy Band and invited me to come to Chapel Hill to stay for a while and meet musicians. He paid my fare. I didn't have any money." Before long, Ni Domhnáill was performing with a new band. "Touchstone came together at a jam at Mike's house," she says. "We played some original tunes, some traditional tunes and some tunes from Nova Scotia."

Touchstone had a minor hit when they recorded Claudia Langille's tune, "Jealousy," the title track from their second album. "We wanted to get airplay," Ni Domhnáill explains. "It's as close as we got to playing rock. It might not have gotten on the album but we needed another track."

Ni Domhnáill and her brother, Michael O'Domhnáill, who played guitar for The Bothy Band, currently perform and record with two bands that feature Scottish accordion player and keyboardist Phil Cunningham. Nightnoise is shared with fiddler Billy Oskay and flautist Brain Dunning, while Relativity also features Cunningham's younger brother, Johnny, on fiddle.

Other members of The Bothy Band have continued to influence the music of Ireland. Flute player Matt Malloy has recorded several traditional albums, while

Manus Lunny's older brother, Donal, who also performed with Planxty and Moving Hearts, has become one of Ireland's leading producers of tradition-rooted recordings. Fiddler Kevin Burke is currently performing with Patrick Street, the band that he formed with former DeDanaan accordionist Jackie Daly and ex-Planxty members Andy Irvine (mandolin and bouzouki) and Arty McGlynn (guitar).

JOHNNY CUNNINGHAM

In Scotland, the folk revival was sparked by bands such as The Tannahill Weavers, The Boys of Lough and Silly Wizard. Silly Wizard began as house band for the Triangle Folk Club in Edinburgh. "It was an effort to start creating music that was more honest," Johnny Cunningham remembers.

Cunningham began playing at the age of five. "My grandfather brought (my brother) Phil and I mouth organs," he remembers. "We used to play in a mouth organ band. Phil got into playing the accordion, which was a natural progression. They tried me on accordion but I was totally useless. I tried piano lessons but I was useless on that as well. My grandmother got me a fiddle when I was about seven. The fiddle and accordion in Scotland always went together."

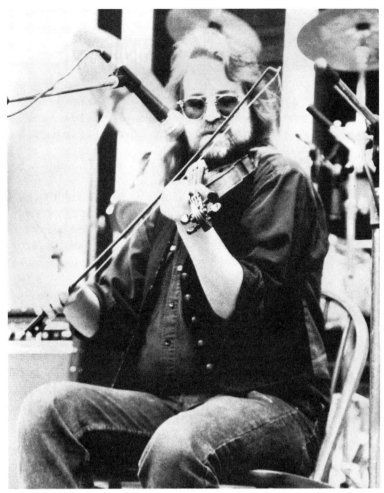

Johnny Cunningham

Silly Wizard

The Cunningham brothers and Silly Wizard first came to the United States in 1979. "The Philadelphia Folk Festival was the first concert we ever did in the states," Cunningham says. "There used to be six of us but at that gig there was only five. That was how the lineup remained until I left."

Cunningham emigrated to The United States in 1980 and tried to leave Silly Wizard. "I felt I'd gone as far as I was going to go," he recalls. "One of the best things about my leaving was that the band had to change how they put things together. They called me up a couple of years later. I hadn't even seen anybody until we did that live album in Sanders' Theater (on the campus of Harvard University). I was sitting in Philadelphia when the phone rang. It was my brother. He asked if I'd like to come and do a live album. I said "Sure, why not? When are you going to do it?" He said 'Tonight. There's a ticket waiting for you at the airport.' After that, it was like a progression. They always asked in ways that I couldn't say no. I did all the tours with them until two years ago when we disbanded."

Solo Work

Cunningham recorded two solo albums, *Thoughts From Another World* and *Fair Warning*. "The first one was done in 1980," he says. "It was before the New Age thing started. It was a concept album but the critics didn't know what to do with it. I recorded everything to sound false. The hammer dulcimer, for example, sounded like a piano. I muted all the fiddles. It was meant to be a thought process. It was the way that I was looking at Scotland now that I was away from it. It was a false view because you're always remembering only the good things and forgetting the rest."

"By the time I made the second album," he continues, "the New Age thing was happening but I wanted to do something else. I wanted to do a lot of traditional tunes. I don't want to do what's expected of me. There's no joy in that. I've been lucky in my career in that I've always been able to do exactly what I've wanted to do. It might not be good discipline-wise, but it's great for the head."

Cunningham also recorded two albums with Relativity, a band he formed with his brother and Triona Ni Domhnáill and her brother, Michael O'Domhnáill. "(Triona and Michael) come from Donegal, which is in a part of Ireland that's very close to Scotland," he says. "The Bothy Band had always done Scottish songs. Michael and Triona were well-versed in Scottish music. Phil and I have been playing Irish music for a good fifteen years."

Over the past couple of years, Cunningham has shifted his attention from the Celtic music of Silly Wizard and his other bands to rock. He currently plays with The Raindogs, the rock band that he formed with ex-members of Red Rockers. "It wasn't really a natural transition," he reflects, "But I felt that I'd gone as far as I could with folk music. Lyrically, I was looking for something else."

Silly Wizard's lead vocalist Andy M. Stewart has continued to write deeply romantic songs. His 1987 album *Dublin Lady* was a collaboration with guitarist, bouzouki, bodhran player and vocalist Manus Lunny and featured guest appearances by Phil Cunningham on accordion and fiddler Aly Bain of The Boys of The Lough.

THE BATTLEFIELD BAND

"We're not living in a time warp, we're pushing the traditions forward."

The traditional Scottish instrument, the bagpipes, has been featured in a variety of innovative musical settings. "Taking a bagpipe into a band was a big step," recalls Alistair Russell, acoustic guitarist-vocalist of The Battlefield Band. "But sound systems made it possible for other instruments to be heard."

Acoustic Rock to Contemporary Folk

The Battlefield Band has incorporated the bagpipes into everything from traditional folk tunes to 50's-style rock 'n' roll. "We started off as an acoustic band playing rock music," keyboardist Alan Reid, who joined the band a few weeks after it was formed in 1970, remembers. "We played stuff like The Byrds, The Band and whatever was on the Top Forty."

The band began playing folk music in the mid-70's. "We started playing English folk music and Irish folk music," Reid recalls. "It took us a few years before we started playing Scottish music. That coincided with the first time that we played in a folk club. Prior to that, we played in bars. People wanted to hear country and western music. But when we first went into a folk club, we discovered that people would listen and not make any noise when we played. There was hardly a sound. The novelty of this really blew us away."

The Battlefield Band continued to evolve musically after the arrival of Russell and multi-instrumentalist Dougie Pincock in 1984. "We started to pull in different kinds of music," Russell remembers, "Over the past few years, it's evolved so that we haven't placed any theoretical limits on the material that we do. If we felt like doing it, we did it. Fortunately, our instincts coincided with what the audiences wanted."

The band's 1986 album *Anthem For The Common Man* ranks among contemporary folk music's most influential recordings. "Some people in England thought it was an attempt to make a political statement," Russell remembers. "It coincided with the miner's strike. Some people thought that we were making some kind of social comment. But it was coincidental. We chose the songs that we wanted to record and looked for a common theme. We had a song called 'Anthem' and a song 'I Am The Common Man,' so, we added them together and made the album title."

The album was significant for the group because it included their earliest attempts at songwriting. "After playing traditional music for awhile, two things happen," Russell explains. "One is that you run out of material no matter how many dusty old books you go through. The folk revival in Europe is so old that every song has already been done. The other thing is that when you look at these songs, you realize that they've got social relevance to the time when they were written. You might as well write songs that have social significance now." "We're not living in a time warp," Reid continues. "We're pushing the traditions forward."

The Battlefield Band

Robin Williamson

The Battlefield Band's 1990 release *Home Ground* was recorded during a concert performance in Scotland. "When we do the spoof that we do of 'Land Of A Thousand Dances' it lasts ten minutes and has every kind of music in it," Russell explains. "There's no way that we record it in a studio and get the right atmosphere. That one song was the inspiration to record a whole live album." The album features a version of Creedence Clearwater Revival's "Bad Moon Risin.'" "We've been playing it for so long," Russell says, "that we wanted to lay it to rest."

The Battlefield Band also recently released *Music In Trust* (also featuring other musicians), a series of albums that were recorded for a BBC television series. "It was done for the National Trust for Scotland's Properties," Russell explains. "It called for music that we had to create."

The group has gone through a number of personnel changes over the past twenty years. Recently Dougie Pincock and founding member Brian McNeil left. Pincock and McNeil have been replaced by ex-Ossian piper Ian MacDonald and fiddle and keyboard player John McCusker.

ROBIN WILLIAMSON

Glasgow-born and Los-Angeles based multi-instrumetalist, singer, songwriter, and storyteller Robin Williamson has fused the ballad tradition with an eclectic variety of folk and popular influences. As co-founder of the Incredible String Band, Williamson helped to spark the late 60's revival of British Isles music. Since the band's breakup in 1974, Williamson has remained musically active. In the early 1980's, he recorded three albums with "Robin Williamson's Merry Band" that incorporated music and poetry. Subsequent solo work includes a Celtic-rock album (*Ten Of Songs*), a series of traditional Celtic harp albums, (*Legacy of the Scottish Harpists*) and the soundtrack of a 1983 production of ancient Welsh legends (*Music for the Mabinogi*).

ALAN STIVELL

The Celtic harp tradition has produced some of the British Isles' most beautiful-sounding music. "I was eight years old," Alan Stivell recalls from his home in Brittany, "when my father built his first instrument, a sixteenth century-style metal string harp. I fell in love with it."

Stivell (which means "source, spring, fountain" in Breton) was born Alan Cochevelou in 1944. Classically trained in Paris, Stivell developed a distinctly personal playing style. "I started to play in the medieval style," he remembers. "I adapted fingerpicking later. It helps me get a lot of interesting rhythms. On most of the things that I do, I use double picking."

"I like the middle strings," he continues. "They've got a special, hypnotic sound. It's very close to the sitar—very rich in high harmonies. The bass is very powerful. There's a big range of sounds or vibrations. I don't like silence between notes. I want everything to be linked together—a long, very rich sound."

Stivell's sound is rooted in the Celtic traditions of his native country. "Brittany is a storehouse for the ancient type of music that was played before the Middle Ages," he says. "There's a unity between the Celtic nations. We've got a lot of the same feelings, but we express them in different ways. Brittany has more of a French and Latin influence than Ireland."

Stivell played an important role in the Anglo-Celtic folk revival of the mid-1960's. "It became a real movement," he reflects. "Not only in terms of the younger generation but also in a real cultural aspect. It changed a lot of things. We felt very important."

Rare Air

Stivell has recorded in a wide variety of settings—everything from solo and duo recordings to epic works requiring 75 musicians and singers. "It's not the same approach at all," he says. "Playing solo, there's much more intimacy with the instrument. But I also like being on a large stage with a lot of musicians. You get a different relationship with the audience." His second album *Renaissance Of The Celtic Harp* (released in 1966) achieved cult status when it was used as background music and environmental enhancement for some of Timothy Leary's LSD experiments at Harvard University.

"There's a unity between the Celtic nations. We've got a lot of the same feelings but we express them in different ways."

RARE AIR

The Ontario-based quartet Rare Air is centered around the Highland bagpipes playing of Patrick O'Gorman and Grier Coppins and the hand drumming of Trevor Ferrier. They spent a year in Brittany studying music and the traditional playing of their instruments. The group fuses a number of influences to create a distinctive, hard-driving, contemporary sound.

Will Ackerman

New Instrumentals

New Age Music is a misnomer. Most performers refuse to be categorized as such. We refer to the music here as "New Instrumentals." "If I find the individual who is responsible for the term 'New Age Music,'" Windham Hill founder Will Ackerman says, "I'll nail his forehead to the wall. To me, it was the end. It, then, was codified. It was identified and easily imitable. It ceased to be an innocent and genuine musical movement and became a marketing ploy."

"It's a hard category to describe," Ken LaRoche of the New Hampshire-based group, Doah, explains, "It encompasses so many aspects of music. To me, New Age music merges folk music, jazz, world music and rock. There's been a change in people's consciousness and they want things that soothe the soul."

New Age music can be traced to the Third Stream music of the late 1950's. Originally coined by Gunther Schuller of The New England Conservatory of Music, the term "Third Stream" describes a blend of jazz improvisation and classical technique. Third Stream music has evolved to the point that it now refers to the interplay of any diverse musical cultures.

WILL ACKERMAN AND WINDHAM HILL

Despite Will Ackerman's refusal to term Windham Hill's music as "New Age," the Stanford, California-based record label became the leading producer of New Age-style music. "Vollenweider was doing what he was doing in Switzerland," Ackerman says, "and Kitaro was doing what he was doing in Japan. That meant that it was taking place at the same time in Switzerland as it was in Japan as it was in The United States. George Winston was sitting in a living room in Santa Monica, while Michael Hedges was in Oklahoma. It was a movement, something very phenomenal was happening. It was probably a reaction to what was happening sociologically."

A Search For The Turtle's Navel Finds A Significant Record Label

Ackerman initially began the label to distribute his first album *Search For The Turtle's Navel*. "On weekends, I would go to reverberative places at Stanford University," he recalls. "I'd get out there at 9 o'clock at night and, sometimes, play until 2 AM. I'd trance out and play the guitar. When I looked up, there would be one or two hundred people sitting there. Other guitar players started stopping by. People started saying that they'd like a recording. At first, I'd go into somebody's house and play into a cassette recorder. Finally, I told everybody that asked me that if they gave me five dollars, I'd bring them a record."

Sales for the record exceeded Ackerman's expectations. "We printed three hundred copies," he explains. "I truly did not think I would sell three hundred records. But that was the minimal order that the pressing company would print. I thought that I would have one hundred and twenty of them for the rest of my life. But, the three hundred copies sold out pretty quick. It took less than a month. I started getting these big orders."

Windham Hill Modeled After Takoma

The label was modeled after guitarist John Fahey's company, Takoma Records. "*Search For The Turtle's Navel* was part autobiographical," Ackerman remembers, "but it was also a tribute to Fahey's *Voice Of The Turtle*. Even right down to the liner notes, it was all a tribute to Fahey. I think he's sort of resentful of all the people that have come up and left him behind. I still look to him as a major influence."

Another influence was the music of Robbie Basho. "His objective was to create a classical discipline for the steel string guitar," Ackerman says. "He taught me to play

"If I find the individual who is responsible for the term 'New Age Music,' I'll nail his forehead to the wall."

the guitar on my left knee. What he did by borrowing from Indian sarod music and adapting it to a very linear style on guitar was essential. Taking a folk instrument and adapting it to a linear, melodic, single-note style was fairly revolutionary to me."

George Winston Puts Windham Hill Through The Roof

Windham Hill's earliest releases were albums by Ackerman and his cousin, Alex De-Grassi. The label didn't come into its own, however, until the release of George Winston's album *Autumn.* "(Winston) and I used to talk on the phone and send letters to each other," Ackerman recalls. "He's got a record collection a few miles long. He's incredibly knowledgeable. He's brilliant. He knows, he cares, he cross-references. It's computer-like. He wrote to me about all kinds of things. 'Did you hear this? Have you heard that?' This went on for about a year or more. I did a gig with DeGrassi at McCabe's in Santa Monica," he continues "and George came up to me afterwards and invited me to come back to his house to jam. I never jam and I never go back to somebody's house. I like to go back, by myself, to my room. This time, however, I said, 'Sure, Why not?' When we got there, he took out a guitar. I heard some of the best slide guitar that I'd ever heard in my life. I said 'Let's do a record.' When it came time to go to bed, he asked if he could play a little piano while I tried to get to sleep. Then, he played two transcriptions of my tunes and a transcription of DeGrassi's 'Turning, Turning Back' note-for-note. It's one of the densest things ever written. Listening was just mind-boggling. Then he went into the whole album of 'Autumn.' When I woke up in the morning, I asked, 'George, what was that?' He said, 'Well, that's just my piano composition.' I said, 'I liked your guitar, but, I loved your piano.'"

The album received phenomenal commercial and critical success. "It put us through the roof," Ackerman says. "It got four-star reviews in *Rolling Stone.* That was our flare to the nation and the industry. We owe that record a great deal." The success of the label, however, put a strain on Ackerman's creativity. "It became a big responsibility," he explains. "I became a father figure to more people than I could possibly handle. I went through a weird illness and had a bad period of time."

The Windham Hill label underwent troubled times in the mid-1980's. "Losing De-Grassi, Mark Isham, Liz Story and Shadowfax was difficult," Ackerman recalls. "There was a period of 'What did we do wrong?' Recently, however, Windham Hill's bad luck has reversed itself as major acts have returned, along with diverse new artists. "As it turned out," Ackerman says, "everyone felt that Windham Hill was a really good company. DeGrassi just re-signed with the label. I produced the new Liz Story album. Mark Isham is doing new projects for us. Chuck Greenberg (of Shadowfax) just sent us demo tapes of his new material."

Windham Hill Shifts Attention To Singer-Songwriters

Windham Hill recently shifted its attention towards singer-songwriters. "I was watching MTV and a Tracy Chapman video came on," Ackerman reflects. "It had a wonderfully hypnotic, repetitive, guitar line. I just went nuts. We've got to find music that's this chancy. We've got to find people that are this talented. We can't sit around and just do more piano solos. I was tired of self-imitation."

The next morning, Ackerman called a staff meeting. "I told everyone that there were people like Tracy Chapman on earth, go find them," Ackerman remembers. "I issued a memo that we weren't even listening to solo piano or guitar demos anymore." The label's first singer-songwriter release was a sampler album, *Legacy.* "Windham Hill has had a history of doing samplers," Ackerman says. "It gives us a way to evaluate different artists."

PAUL WINTER

Among the earliest experiments at creating a meditative, New Age style of music was the work of The Paul Winter Consort in the early 1970's. "There's no fixed notion of what we play," Winter explains from his home in Connecticut. "It's been constantly evolving. As we've traveled, it's expanded. It's grown into a much broader idiom. Every time I've seen an instrument—whether it was a cello, English horn, harp or a twelve-string guitar—I've been interested."

Winter began his musical career in the early 1960's as leader/saxophonist of a high school BeBop jazz band, The Paul Winter Sextet. A state department-sponsored tour of Latin America served as an introduction to world music. "We played twenty-three countries," Winter remembers. "We saw a world that we never dreamed existed. We heard lots of music. I, especially, fell in love with Brazilian music. It was a big turning point."

Following the band's return to the United States, they became the first jazz band to perform at The White House. "It was quite wonderful," Winter recalls. "The East Room is a very live-sounding room. We sounded so loud that the guards were afraid that the painting of George Washington was going to fall off the wall. It was shaking so much."

Paul Winter

Renaming the band The Paul Winter Consort, Winter continued to explore a variety of world music and rhythms. Winter and The Paul Winter Consort reached their commercial peak in 1972 with the George Martin-produced album *Icarus*. The title track, which musically interpreted the ancient myth, was composed by guitarist Ralph Towner. "(Towner) wrote it within thirty minutes after I put a twelve-string guitar into his hands for the first time," Winter recalls. "He was trained as a classical guitarist, while the twelve-string was essentially a folk instrument. But he's such an amazing musician that he immediately came up with something."

Whale Songs

In 1968, Winter heard some of the earliest recordings of Whale songs. "I heard some tapes of humpback whales," he recalls, "and became completely entranced. It led me to learn more about whales and it led to my first wilderness trips. Once you've experienced a wilderness trip, you're hooked." Winter's latest album *Wolf Eyes* was initially released in Japan as *The Best of Paul Winter.* "For a long time, people have been

"We saw a world that we never dreamed existed."

Leo Kottke

asking me to do something by myself," Winter explains, "something oriented to the sound of the soprano sax. I've been involved with The Wolf Recovery Program, a campaign to reintroduce the wolf to Yellowstone Park. We used the tune 'Wolf Eyes' as the title track to bring attention to the campaign."

Winter has also used music to further human relations. In 1985, the Consort toured with Soviet poet Yevgeny Yevtushenko, providing musical accompaniment for his recitations. The group's 1987 album *Earthbeat* features the choir-like vocals of the Dimitri Pokrovsky Singers. "(The album) was the result of our tour of the Soviet Union in 1986," Winter explains. "We met them at our last show in Moscow. We stayed up all night jamming. We talked about doing something together but it seemed like a far-fetched pipedream. Nothing like it had ever been done before."

LEO KOTTKE

John Fahey's influence can be heard through the playing of many solo guitar players. "(Fahey) is responsible for the type of fingerstyle guitar playing that I'm into," Leo Kottke says from his home in Minneapolis. "He was the first to record it." Kottke initially attracted attention in 1970 when he recorded *Six And Twelve String Guitar* for Fahey's Takoma Record label.

Kottke's most recent albums are all-instrumental and feature acoustic guitar occasionally accompanied by synthesizer and cello. "I hadn't written any lyrics in a while," Kottke confesses. "The label—Private Music—has only recorded instrumental music in the past. So, it all worked out."

Born in Athens, Georgia, Kottke was raised in twelve different states. "It was great for my music," he says. "It exposed me to all the different attitudes that people have towards music." Kottke's earliest years were spent listening to classical music and studying trombone. "Playing trombone for nine years," he points out, "made no small dent on my playing. I was seventeen or eighteen years old before I heard blues or country music. All my early musical memories go back to my classical past."

Damage to both his ears has had a strong effect on his music—his left ear was impaired by a cherry bomb as a youngster, his right ear was damaged during target practice while serving in The Navy. "It's probably amplified the intuitive side of my playing," he reflects. "If I had had more of a hearing orientation, I probably would've learned the standard vocabularies much faster. On most of my tunes, I stick to the bottom end. It's where my ears are most comfortable."

PIERRE BENSUSAN

One of the most distinctively personal styles in contemporary folk music is that of Pierre Bensusan. Combining a wide range of ethnic and popular influences—from North African music to American bluegrass and Irish pipe music—the Paris-based guitarist has created a unique instrumental sound. He described it during a recent interview as "impressionistic waves of sound, feelings and atmospheres."

Open guitar tuning—DADGAD—forms the basis for much of Bensusan's music. "A lot of it is inspiration," he explains. "I try to focus on the music and the sound rather than digital tuning. It has a lot to do with inspiration."

Bensusan brings superlative imagination, extreme sensitivity and technical proficiency to his music. As a result, his compositions have often been categorized as "New Age Music." However, he resists categorization. "I don't feel the need to be limited to any one music label," he states. "I've been developing a personal fusion of music since the day I was born. My parents were into all kinds of music."

Pierre Bensusan

Drowned in the Anglo Culture

Although he studied classical piano as a youngster, Bensusan became enchanted with American folk music of the 1960's. "As a teenager," he remembers, "I was into Cat Stevens, Simon and Garfunkel and Crosby, Stills and Nash. I was touched by the way they expressed themselves. The overall sound was very inspirational. We were completely drowned in the Anglo culture," he continues. "Movies, music, TV. America was very good at selling itself. But France had Impressionism. There was Jacques Brel and other singer-songwriters." Teaching himself to play guitar, Bensusan was deeply influenced by the banjo playing style of Bill Keith, using chords of combined fretted and open strings. After meeting Keith at a Paris folk club, Bensusan joined him and Jim Rooney as a bluegrass mandolinist. "They gave me chance to express myself," he recalls. "We played in Switzerland, Germany and France. But I stopped playing bluegrass a long time ago."

After playing with Keith and Rooney for a year, Bensusan assembled a group of France's finest acoustic musicians and recorded his debut solo album *Pres De Paris*. It received the prestigious Grand Prix du Disc for best Folk album of the year at the 1976 Montreux Jazz Festival. Bensusan recently signed a recording contract with CBS Masterworks. "It's like being in a dream," Bensusan reflects. "It'll be the first time that my music will be well-distributed in France."

"I don't feel the need to be limited to any one music label."

Tracy Moore

TRACY MOORE

A finely tuned sense of humor gives twelve-string guitarist Tracy Moore's music its unique charm. "I'm always looking on the lighter side of things," he says from his home in Boston. Moore often uses whimsical titles for his compositions. "I like very outrageous, non-new age kinds of titles," he explains.

Born in Seattle, Moore moved to Boston in 1987. "I really like New England," he says. "It's got a great sense of history. There was a strong music scene in Seattle but I felt like there was no place left for me to go. I wanted to become part of a larger scene."

Moore bought his first guitar from Sears. "It came with a music book," he remembers. "After school, I went over the book with my mother. I picked it right up. About four or five years ago, I bought my mother a classical guitar just to say 'thanks.'"

Moore attended Western Washington University in Bellingham, Washington. "I didn't quite graduate," he says. "I was originally a Music Education major. But by the time that I was ready to student teach, a lot of funding had been cut. All the guitar programs in the schools were cut."

Left School to Join The Circus

Moore's performance techniques were strengthened when he left school and joined the circus. "I was into juggling, clowning and fire eating," he recalls, "and joined a circus that had a Renaissance theme. I hardly took my guitars out of their cases. But it taught me a lot about dealing with an audience and being comfortable. It taught me a lot about stage presence."

Moore's playing reflects a variety of musical influences. "I like the music from the Renaissance era," he explains, "especially the lute music. It's got a great sense of melody. It's got a nice, solid, dance meter. I like Tower of Power. They're a real tight horn section. I like a lot of the music from the swing era. I really like what Leo Kottke has done with the twelve-string. He's my original influence."

Moore's guitar was built in 1977 by the now retired Yugoslavia-born and San Diego-based guitar builder Bozo Podunavac. "It's got a really rich, resonant bass," he says. "It sustains forever. People have compared it to a harpsichord or a church organ." Moore has used the instrument to create his own distinctive sound. "The bottom four strings are an octave apart," he says. "I've developed a technique that allows me to catch two notes at once. The melody creates a harp-like effect."

Moore recently completed an album with cello player Seth Blair. Future plans include an album of traditional music from around the world and a hoped-for collaboration with Philip Boulding of Seattle-based duo, Magical Strings. "I really love the sound of his metal harps," Moore explains. "I want to see what can be done with a twelve-string. I hope to be able to make my living doing this."

Moore has recorded two albums— *Sky Piece* and *A Peculiar Point Of Balance.* "The first album was just a tip of the hat," he says. "The second features more of my own voice."

DAVID NEIMAN

The hammer dulcimer is one of the world's oldest string instruments, tracing back over one thousand years to ancient Persia. Traditional jigs and reels are the instrument's usual repertoire. But David Neiman has taken it much further. "My first thoughts about deviating from the traditional tunes," he says from his home in Cambridge, Massachusetts, "came very early in my playing. I have a background in classical guitar, so I gave a lot of thought to adapting the songs that I did on guitar to dulcimer."

David Neiman

Neiman's repertoire spans from Bach to Balkan to contemporary folk-pop. "One of the things that I played when I won the (national hammer dulcimer) championship (in Winfield, Kansas in 1987) was Rodgers and Hammersteins' 'My Favorite Things.' I played it more in the John Coltrane style." Neiman has recorded two solo albums, *Spectrum* and *Early Works.* "The first one is a collection of many different styles," he explains. "The second is an all early classical music recording—Bach, Telemann and Vivaldi."

Neiman was first exposed to hammer dulcimer in 1978. "I saw someone playing in Boston Common," he remembers. "It had a beautiful sound." A year and a half later, he built his own instrument. "I was in love with it before I even played it," he recalls. "I had created it." Within seven months he was playing with college bands. "I always needed lessons to keep going on the guitar," he says. "But with the dulcimer, there was no one to take lessons from. I was very self-motivated. It was such an intriguing instrument that I always wanted to learn more."

Neiman has performed concerts, festivals and workshops throughout the United States, Europe and Japan. He currently plays an eighty-stringed instrument built by Sam Rizetta, former dulcimer player for the folk-fusion group Trapezoid. "I really love its tone," he reflects. "It's very responsive and it's got a great dynamic range."

Jay Ansill

JAY ANSILL

In recent years, the harp tradition has been expanded by players such as Philadelphia's Jay Ansill and Cambridge, Massachusetts' Deborah Henson-Conant. "I'm not trying to recreate the traditional sounds," Ansill explains backstage at The Philadelphia Folk Festival. "It's important to realize that the traditions have never stopped. I've got a great sense of tradition but I'm not afraid to play with it."

The harp playing of Robin Williamson is a major influence on Ansill's music. "I saw Robin with his Merry Band in 1979," Ansill remembers. "It knocked me out. It made me want to be a musician. It was a very powerful performance. In the 1960's, Robin was one of the first to incorporate real ideas of literature, dreams and childhood memories into his music," Ansill continues. "(Williamson's band) The Incredible String Band hit so big in Britain that it had a real influence on treating songs as poetry."

Origami and James Joyce

Ansill's playing is influenced by his interests in origami, the traditional Japanese art of paper-folding. "I've been into origami since I was in the second grade," he explains. "The harp is in a diatonic scale. It's a simple scale and you can't get the range of tonalities that you can get with a piano or guitar. But I wanted my music to be as complex as possible. Origami is very similar. You start with a very simple base and push it to its limits."

Literature has also had a great effect of Ansill's compositions. "I get a lot of ideas from literature," he says, "especially from James Joyce. He played with language, mixing everything and putting it together. He suffered a lot. He was uncompromising. But it was the only way to put across what he wanted to put across. It was something that was in his heart and inside his brain."

DEBORAH HENSON-CONANT

Deborah Henson-Conant's harp sounds a great variety of tone colors. "It tends to absorb and reflect everything that it comes close to," Henson-Conant explains from her home in Cambridge. "People think of the harp as being limited. But that's just another myth. The harp is one of the richest instruments in terms of tone color. Harps can give a range of tone qualities from utmost delicacy to real raunchiness. It has the ability to play very low notes loudly and, when you effect them with the foot pedals, you get some very raunchy sounds."

Henson-Conant's Background

Born in Stockton, California, Henson-Conant spent the early years of her life traveling. "We moved a lot when I was a kid," she recalls. "Every one of my relatives had a piano in their living room. I used to make up stories and create a soundtrack as I went along." Henson-Conant's love of storytelling is reflected in each tune. "My music is becoming more and more an abstract form of telling a story," she explains.

"Music was an expression of love," Henson-Conant reflects. "Music was a functional part of my life and of my learning." Folk music was also an early influence. "I loved to listen to Burl Ives when I was a young girl," she explains. "The forms of folk music are similar to children's songs."

Although she took a few harp lessons as a youngster, she didn't take the instrument seriously until she was in college. "They needed a harper," she recalls, "so, they offered to pay for my lessons. I was ready emotionally and mentally enough to commit myself to learning on that level. It's hard for children to have the concentration that I needed. But, at the age of twenty-two, I could be fascinated by how my fingers moved. I could be amazed by the Zen of it."

Deborah Henson-Conant

Jazz

Henson-Conant helped introduce the harp to contemporary jazz. "I was very excited about working with a musical form that would spawn rich improvisation," she says. "Jazz is one of the few forms of music based on improvisation."

Henson-Conant has performed in a variety of settings—from solo performances to large ensembles. "One of the exciting things about jazz," she says, "is that it's such an open script. If you know the form, you can play with other musicians. It's like being a child. If you know the basic games, you can play with other people. Once you've got the structure," she continues, "then, it's what you do with it that's important. It becomes a structure for imagination. Each player brings out something different in every other musician. It causes me to discover all the different music inside myself."

Henson-Conant uses two different harps. "I have two Chromatic or Pedal Harps, the standard orchestra model," she says. "One was built in the 1920's and is quite small for a Concert Harp. It's got a narrow soundboard and less of an acoustic sound. It responds more cleanly to amplification. My other harp is so old that the soundboard has bowed up. As a result, it has a very rich series of overtones. I use it for recording. The acoustic sound is beautiful."

Babatunde Olatunji

World Music

Although New Age Music has become what Windham Hill's

Will Ackerman calls "a waning renaissance," the popularity of ethnic and world music has steadily increased. The field of world music is vast and we introduce here only a very few performers who are well-known to folk music stages.

African and African-derived music has played an important role throughout the musical history of The United States. Jazz, blues, rock 'n' roll and reggae provide examples of its influence. Great African drummers such as Babatunde Olatunji have spread the gospel of African rhythms in the U.S., while American music has equally influenced African pop-rock musicians such as King Sunny Ade from Nigeria, The Bhundu Boys from Zimbabwe, and the White South African Johnny Clegg.

Latin music, from South America to the Salsa sounds of New York, is increasingly popular. Many other traditions are also emerging. North American performers such as Doah and Mickey Hart draw upon these influences to create new sounds.

LADYSMITH BLACK MAMBAZO

In recent years the vocal styles of Ladysmith Black Mambazo have attracted attention to the music of South Africa. Although the group has been together through 19 years and 25 South African-produced albums, it was their startling performance on Paul Simon's Grammy award-winning *Graceland* album and world tour that introduced them to American listeners. Ladysmith Black Mambazo has also been featured on *The Tonight Show, Saturday Night Live* and on the cover of *Rolling Stone.* "(Performing with Simon) was our opportunity to show the world what we could do," Joseph Shabalala, the group's forty-nine year old founder and lead singer, says from his hotel room in Washington, D.C. "Since then, we've been to so many different places."

Although Simon paid the group triple union scale—the same as New York studio musicians—*Graceland* was publicly censured by the African National Congress and other anti-apartheid organizations in the United States for violating the United Nations' cultural boycott of South Africa. "I don't want to argue with people," Shabalala says. "I don't know anything about politics. I grew up on a farm. But, I believe musicians have to work together."

Simon subsequently produced Ladysmith's 1987 album *Shaka Zulu.* "When we met," Shabalala explains, "(Simon) said that he had been looking for me. He said that he had seen us on the BBC singing in German. He's a very wise man. He's got great ears. When you record with him, he's able to listen and make suggestions."

Ladysmith Black Mambazo, whose name means "The Black Axe of Ladysmith," was formed in Ladysmith, Emnambithi district, a rural grassland two hundred miles from Durban. At first, the group sang like all the others that were singing in the Cothoza Mfans or Isicathamiya style. Their harmonies were initially based on the songs heard in the men's hostels, the single-sex dormitories where South Africa's immigrant workers are housed. "Our brothers and fathers sang like this when they came back from working in Johannesburg," Shabalala explains. "At home, we sing with girls. We're always singing. We sing at parties. We sing at home. When the men were away, they would sing when they felt homesick. Most sang in a rough bass voice but a few sang in a higher pitch. We copied this."

Inspired By A Dream

In 1963 Shabalala was inspired by a dream to develop a new kind of harmony. "When I went to sleep," he remembers, "I heard a very nice sound. Then, I saw children that were floating up to the sky and singing." When Shabalala tried to introduce the new harmony style to the group, he found them resistant. "They said 'No, this harmony is

Casselberry-Dupree

too difficult. You want us to sing like a man who is talking.' But, we must tell a story," Shabalala continues. "They were used to singing the same words over and over again. So I left and started a new group." Although they've recorded in German and English, most of Ladysmith Black Mambazo's songs are sung in Zulu.

CASSELBERRY-DUPREE

The sounds of Jamaica and the reggae of the late Bob Marley are important influences on the music of Casselberry-DuPree. "(Marley) was such a prolific songwriter," Judith Casselberry explains from her home in Boston. "His last recordings showed the influence of a lot of different styles."

Judith Casselberry and Jaque DuPree met while attending Erasmus High School in Brooklyn. Their music combines a variety of influences. "What we have in common is that most of our music is based on folk music from around the world. We started out with acoustic guitars and vocals, so, it's not a heavily electrified sound. Stylistically, we use Caribbean, African and American influences, especially from the American South—slave chants and blues."

Toshi Reagon, the daughter of Sweet Honey In The Rock's Bernice Reagon Johnson, has been playing bass with Casselberry-Dupree since 1985. "She hears it as a more melodic instrument," Casselberry says. "It fits our sound really well."

Percussionist Annette A. Aguilar adds a rhythmic edge to the group's sound. "We've been working with Annette for nine years," Casselberry explains. "She's Nicaraguan by descent and played congas in the streets with her brothers. As she got older, she started getting serious about music so she went to San Francisco State College and majored in music. After she got her degree, she went to New York to the Manhattan School Of Music and got her master's degree in classical performance. She plays every percussion instrument from marimba, tympani and trap drums to the things that she plays with us."

Messages—Personal, Spiritual, Political

Getting their message across is the prime motivation behind Casselberry-DuPree's music. "That's what we're all about," Casselberry claims. "It can be perceived as political but it can be personal or spiritual in nature. Some things that start off as personal issues can be perceived as political issues by the world at large. If somebody's telling that I can't do something because I'm a Black woman, then it's personal, but it evolves into a political issue."

FORTALEZA

The pan pipe and drum traditions of South America's Andes Mountains are preserved by Fortaleza. "People used to think that this was just the music that the natives played," John De La Zerda, the group's Bolivian-born leader says from his home in Medford, Massacusetts. "If, for example, a guy from a good family liked these instruments, his mother would say, 'What are you doing? This music is just for the peasants.' But during the last twenty-five years and mostly, the last ten years, this music has become the first music of the Bolivian people. We've started to appreciate our music and our culture more than before. We have a rich traditional culture."

Instruments

"The woodwinds are mostly what we call sigus in the Quechua language, or zampañas in Spanish," De La Zerda explains. "They have two sets of reeds and come in a family of sizes from the small ones, which have a very high pitch, to the big ones, which we call the toyos, which are fifty-five inches in length and have a deep, bass sound. "The drum, or wangara, is made of hollowed wood or a tree trunk covered with goat or lamb hide. You've got to hang it from your shoulder and play it with a stick."

Fortaleza

Fortaleza also uses the charango, the string instrument that was introduced by the Spanish in the seventeenth century. "The charango has ten nylon strings," De La Zerda says. "It was originally made from the shell of an armadillo. You can also find it made of wood, which we call the vegetarian model."

"It's mostly played in a fast, flamenco style," he continues. "You have to strum very fast. Sometimes, you can't even see my fingers when I play. They're moving so fast. It's used mostly for rhythm to accompany the songs but you can also strum very slow. You can use it as a melodic instrument."

Fortaleza moved to The United States in the early 1980's. "We were invited by the Organization of American States for a tour," De La Zerda recalls. "We weren't thinking of staying but we were encouraged by the fantastic reception. We decided to stay and contribute our music to the universal culture of The United States."

The group's latest album *Soy De Sangre Kolla, Quechua Y Aymara* (We Are Of Kolla, Quechua And Aymara Blood) was their debut for the Chicago-based Flying Fish record label. Their next album *Fortaleza—Bolivian Folk Music* is all instrumental.

"We've started to appreciate our music and our culture more than before."

Flor de Caña

FLOR DE CAÑA

Flor de Caña was formed in spring 1984 to perform a three week series of concerts in Nicaragua. "It was organized by Arts For A New Nicaragua," songwriter and instrumentalist Willie Sordillo remembers. "They were a solidarity organization that sent guitars and sound systems to Nicaragua. Eventually, they decided to send a group of North American musicians and painters."

Sordillo was initially unsure of the project. "It was a completely bizarre idea," he says. "Everyone came from a different background. Most were used to playing solo. Laura Burns usually performed as a duo with Roger Rosen. We got together in May or June and we had to be ready by August. I didn't think we could do it."

The group managed to pull things together and the tour was a success. "It was sloppy at times," Sordillo recalls, "but it worked out." The tour was sponsored by the since-defunct Center for Popular Culture. We played all over the country. We performed on street corners, rec halls, schools—rarely in auditoriums." After they returned to the United States, the musicians were eager to share their experiences.

Latin American Music—Beautiful and Fun to Play

"Four of us—Rosemarie Straijer-Amador, Brian Folkins-Amador, Laura Burns and myself—decided to form a band," Sordillo continues, "along with Sue Kalt, who wasn't on the trip. We took our name, Flor de Caña, from a Nicaraguan rum—the national drink." "(Latin American music) is beautiful and fun to play," says Sordillo. "But there's also a political motivation. We're interested in providing a connection between Latin America and here. We have a responsibility to promote peace and awareness."

Although not all of the musicians had a natural connection to Latin American music, they've been able to use traditional music to create their own sound. "We were originally very folkloric," Sordillo says, "but it made more sense to find our own individual voice. We've tried to learn from the traditions instead of mimicking them. Most Nueva Canción performers sing in the style of a particular country but we're taking more of a pan-American approach. We incorporate traditional instruments but we add saxophone and keyboards. Brian is trained as a flamenco guitarist. It's not an authentic folk style. It's much more eclectic."

TEX-MEX

Doug Sahm

Doug Sahm combines Conjunto and country music with blues and rock 'n' roll to create a distinctive Tex-Mex-goes-Cosmic-Cowboy sound. His most recent project is The Texas Tornados, a band that he formed with Augie Meyer, Flaco Jimenez and Freddy Fender.

The Texas Tornados

The Texas Tornados signed a four album contract with Warner Brothers. "We just did an album in Texas," Sahm says during a recent interview. "It's a big deal—big dollars and the whole smear. It's a monster. It's kind of a Tex-Mex radio-oriented record. It's different from anything that I've ever done before. This is aiming at radio's jugular. It's probably going to break into the rock 'n' roll market. It's the most excitement that we've generated in twenty years. We've been dubbed 'The Tex-Mex Wilburys.' It hit the bullseye with the record companies."

Flaco Jimenez and Freddy Fender

The traditional Conjunto music of the Texas and Mexican border can be

Flaco Jiminez

heard through the accordion playing of Flaco Jimenez. Jimenez' music was little known outside of San Antonio until 1973 when he performed on Sahm's album *Doug and Friends*. He subsequently recorded with Ry Cooder and Peter Rowan and performed on the 1988 Dwight Yoakam/Buck Owens hit "The Streets of Bakersfield."

The Texas Tornados also fulfills Sahm's lifelong dream of working with Freddy Fender. "(Fender) was my hero," Sahm explains. "There's another Freddy Fender inside Freddy Fender. Twenty years before there was 'Till The Teardrops Fall' he had a lot of local hits in Texas."

The Sir Douglas Quintet

Sahm put the original Sir Douglas Quintet together in 1964. "(Legendary New Orleans-based record producer) Huey Meaux brought us together," he recalls. "We played a gig with The Dave Clark Five. We were the first American band to challenge the British hold on rock 'n' roll."

The ambient tone-color of The Sir Douglas Quintet's sound was provided by organist Augie Meyer. "When we met he was working in his mother's grocery stores," Sahm remembers. "He was playing with a band called 'The Goldens.' He had the only Vox organ in Texas."

Hankus Netsky and Judy Bressler

Although they had several minor hits in the mid-1960's, the days of the original Sir Douglas Quintet were short-lived. By the early 1970's, Sahm was recording solo albums. Sahm reached his commercial peak with the album *Doug Sahm And Band*, which featured guest appearances by Bob Dylan, David Bromberg, Dr. John, and Flaco Jimenez. "It was (Atlantic Records president) Jerry Wexler's pet project," Sahm recalls. "It was a lot of fun. It was one of the best jam sessions I've ever played."

THE KLEZMER CONSERVATORY BAND

Klezmer, the centuries-old dance music of European Jews, has been brought up to date by such groups as Klezmorim, Kapelye and the Klezmer Conservatory Band. "It's a very emotional and expressive music," Hankus Netsky, saxophonist/pianist/director of the Klezmer Conservatory Band, says from his office at the New England Conservatory of Music. "It's an Old World sound but it expresses raw sentiments and emotions."

From the beginning, Jewish music has blended with other musical traditions. The elements that make it Jewish come from a combination of

"The core of the music only comes out when people dance."

the cries of the cantorial tradition, the rhythmic energy of Hassidic music and the accents and irony of the Yiddish language." Dance is essential to Klezmer music. "The core of the music," Netzky claims, "only comes out when people dance."

Although Klezmer was once performed almost exclusively for a Jewish audience, its following has crossed cultural and religious barriers. "Since the revival of the music," Netsky says, "we've picked up a large non-Jewish following. We've been playing folk festivals as much as Yiddish festivals."

The Klezmer Conservatory Band was formed in 1979 as an outgrowth of informal jam sessions. "I was inspired by (Irish musician) Mick Moloney," Netsky recalls. "He organizes great jam sessions of Irish music. I thought about doing the same thing for Jewish music."

Netsky attracted musicians from a variety of backgrounds. "What they were all versed in," he says, "was their ability to learn different kinds of music. Most of the musicians were in the Conservatory's Third Stream department and were pretty much fair game for any kind of music. (Vocalist) Judy Bressler came to the Conservatory to learn Klezmer music. But only one third of the group had had some background in Jewish music. Most had a background in jazz or folk music."

DOAH

A multitude of influences are blended into the music of Doah. The group performs on seventy different instruments, ranging from African balafon and kalimba to synthesizer and acoustic guitar. The group projects what founding member Ken LaRoche called before a recent performance at Nightstage in Cambridge, "the positive, uplifting side of life."

Doah was formed as a duo by classically-trained flautist LaRoche and jazz-oriented guitarist Randy Armstrong in 1974. Ohio-born Armstrong had played with rock and pop bands from the age of fifteen. During a tour of northern New England, he fell in love with the area. After his band broke up, he and his wife moved to the White Mountains of New Hampshire.

Determined to continue playing music, Armstrong was, nonetheless, frustrated by the lack of musicians in the Granite State. Compiling a list of over one hundred New England musicians, he loaded up his VW bug, and went off in search of a musical partner. "I was completely open," he reflects. "I had been playing rock 'n' roll but I was getting into acoustic-oriented music. I wanted to expand my personal horizons."

Doah

Armstrong Meets LaRoche

Armstrong's search led him to Peterborough, New Hampshire-born Ken LaRoche. LaRoche had performed with the New Hampshire Philharmonic Orchestra while still in high school. "My teacher was the first chair flautist in the orchestra," he explains, "and she was very supportive." His musical interests, however, were extremely wide. When Armstrong showed up on his doorstep, LaRoche was playing in an avant-garde jazz group. "I wanted to keep the same energy level as jazz," he says, "but I wanted to channel it into something more accessible."

Prayer, Meditation, Chanting and Worship

Agreeing to pool their resources, Armstrong and LaRoche took their name, Do'A, from the Arabic/Persian word signifying a call to prayer, meditation, chanting and worship. The group recently added an "h" to the original spelling of their name. "It meant very little musically or philosophically," claims LaRoche. "For the past fourteen years, a number of people misconceived our name to be D-O-A. But, now, there's a punk group and a movie by that name. Of course, there's also the medical term."

Simple instrumentation was used, at first, Armstrong on acoustic guitar and La-Roche on bamboo flutes and kalimba. They soon became obsessed, however, with collecting, studying and playing instruments from around the world. "I had a dream," Armstrong remembers. "I was walking down a cobblestone street that looked very much like Old Jerusalem. A man in a striped turban motioned for me to follow him into a store. In the store, there were all these instruments hanging in the window. I kept studying them, very perplexed. I wasn't really sure what was going on. After that, I was led into a room where Abdu'l-Baha, the son of Baha'u'llah, the Prophet-founder of the Ba'hai faith, was sitting before me. It was a very powerful feeling. I wanted to turn away, because I didn't think that I was worthy to be there. But I couldn't take my eyes off of him. He was sitting there smiling and he began showing me instruments, from around the world, one at a time."

The Ba'hai Faith

The dream had particular significance because of Armstrong and LaRoche's involvement with the Ba'hai faith. "Ba'hai emphasizes the oneness of all humanity," Armstrong explains, "and the need to explore bringing cultures together. I heard about Ba'hai from Jim Seals of Seals and Crofts while I was in Ohio. I later found out that there was a course in Ba'hai given at Ohio State University. My wife and I took the class and found that the principles of Ba'hai worked well with our principles of life."

LaRoche had also, independently, "discovered" Ba'hai. "As a youngster, I did a lot of soul searching," he says, "I investigated a lot of different viewpoints and philosophies and I found that I agreed with a lot of the principles of Ba'hai. It's truly a worldwide faith. The whole earth is linked together in a communication and travel sense. We're trying to develop a worldwide sense of community. But we're also making sure that we keep and appreciate the diversities between us."

Since 1983, Doah has performed as a quintet with the addition of drummer/percussionist Marty Quinn, saxophonist Charlie Jennison and present bassist Volker Nahrmann. "It's a fulfillment of our vision of orchestration," LaRoche explains. "We've always heard our music as being very orchestrated. The excitement factor is driven by the rhythm. I tend to miss the sensitivity of the duo setting, though we've been striving for a more subtle interplay within the ensemble."

MICKEY HART

In addition to playing drums with The Grateful Dead since 1967, Mickey Hart has combined the curiosity of an ethnomusicologist with state-of-the-art technology to collect, record and document the traditional music of the world's cultures. "Music is a worldwide phenomenon," Hart says from his home in San Francisco. "Humans must have music. They crave it like food." Hart initially began producing tapes for friends as a hobby, working with Dan Healy, a recording and sound man for The Dead. As The Dead's tours began to take them around the world Hart increasingly sought out indigenous musicians.

The Salem-based CD company Rykodisc has released a series of Hart's recordings. Performers include West African drummer Babatunde Olatunji; Sudanese folksinger Hamza El Din; The Gyuto Monks Tibetan Tantric Choir; Dafös (featuring Hart with Brazilian percussionist Airto Moreira and vocalist Flora Purim); and The Rhythm Devils (featuring Hart with fellow Grateful Dead members Phil Lesh and Bill Kreutzmann). "Rykodisc made me an offer that I couldn't refuse," Hart recalls. "They wanted to release all the recordings that I've made over the years. I've been farming them out to record companies around the world."

Hart is seriously concerned with the preservation of the world's music. "A lot of music is endangered," he claims. "A treasure is contained in the music of the world, given to us by the people who came before us. But it's not just the past. It's also the future. We've got to perpetuate it for the kids. It's like the herbs in the rain forest or a giraffe. We've got to make sure that these things aren't lost forever."

Social awareness is also essential to Hart's recordings. The Gyuto Monk's album, *Freedom Chants From The Roof Of The World*, for example, was recorded to attract attention to the plight of the Tibetans.

Music To Be Born By

Hart's most unusual recording is *Music To Be Born By*, which was originally created for the birth of Hart's six year old son Taro. Based around a recording of Taro's heartbeat in the womb, *Music To Be Born By* makes a natural soundscape that benefits mother and child before, during, and after childbirth. "Our culture has no music for being born," Hart says. "The healing has been washed out."

Hart experimented for months before deciding to record his son's prenatal heartbeat. "A week before he was born," Hart remembers, "I realized it had to come from the heartbeat. It's trustworthy. A woman can count on it. It gets into a groove. Many babies have been born to it." Babies born listening to the album experience, according to Hart, a "calmness" whenever it's played. "It's hard to tell the reasons why," Hart explains, "but it calms them down."

Hart's reputation as a record producer and folk archivist led to his being appointed to the board of directors of Folkways Records. He's currently supervising the transfer of the Folkways catalogue to digital masters for release as CDs. "Folkways is the grand old collection of (the late) Moses Asch," Hart says. "There's something like two thousand titles. I'm going to be bringing them into public domain. (Cambridge-based) Rounder Records is going to distribute them."

Hart's recently released book *Drumming At The Edge Of Magic* (Harper San Francisco) provides a good introduction to world percussion music. Despite his tight schedule, Hart continues to play over eighty concerts a year with The Grateful Dead. "Everything has transformational value," Hart says. "Jerry (Garcia's) return (after recuperating from a coma in 1986) was a real shot in the arm. Since then, we've been progressing amazingly."

"Humans must have music. They crave it like food."

Conclusion

We hope we have identified many of the important trends in contemporary folk music by highlighting many of the most influential performers on the current scene. If we have made any errors of omission or commission, we apologize.

For every performer included in this book there are many more who could have been included—Pierce Pettis, The Pogues, Pentangle, Billy Bragg, Mike Seeger, a myriad of bluegrass, blues, Cajun, and world music performers. The list is endless. We will include many of them in future books in this series.

We will also investigate other topics such as the out-migration of folk artists to the Pop and Country realms. Many contemporary folk musicians, some of whom appear in this book, hesitate to refer to themselves as such. There is more green to be made in established, money-making categories of the music business. Suzanne Vega and Tracy Chapman, for example, helped to start folk music's current reinvigoration with their respective folk-oriented hits "Luka" and "Fast Car." Yet each of these artists do not retain any association with "folk music." Some members of the folk music community which helped to encourage their work feel that Vega and Chapman have turned their backs on them. In the Country area, performers such as Mary Chapin-Carpenter, Lyle Lovett and Cliff Eberhardt are successfully crossing over from folk music.

There is nothing wrong with artists crossing over from one category to another, with diverse traditions influencing each other. Indeed, that is one of the defining aspects of the contemporary folk process. Given the explosion of talent we have seen in these pages, we suspect that in the coming years "folk music" will once again become a proud—and even lucrative—moniker.

BIBLIOGRAPHY OF SUGGESTED READING

I. THE OLD SCHOOL

Baez, Joan. *And A Voice To Sing With.* New York: Simon & Schuster, 1989.

Brand, Oscar. *The Ballad Mongers: Rise Of The Modern Folk Song.* Westport, Conn.: Greenwood Press, 1961.

Carawan, Guy and Candie, ed. *Ain't You Got The Right To The Tree Of Life?* Athens, Georgia.: University of Georgia Press, reprint, 1989.

_____. *Sing For Freedom.* Bethlehem, Penn.: *Sing Out!,* reprint of *We Shall Overcome* and *Freedom In a Constant Struggle,* 1990.

Denisoff, R. Serge. *Great Day Coming: Folk Music And The American Left.* New York: Penguin Books c/o Viking Press, 1973.

_____. *Sing A Song Of Social Significance.* Bowling Green, Ohio: Bowling Green University c/o Popular Press, 1972.

Dunaway, David King. *How Can I Keep From Singing: Pete Seeger.* New York: Da Capo Press, reissue, 1990.

Green, Archie. *Only A Miner.* Champaign, Ill.:University of Illinois Press, 1972.

Guthrie, Woody. *Born To Win.* New York: MacMillan, 1968.

_____. *Bound For Glory.* New York: New American Library c/o Pearson, reissue, 1970.

_____. *Woody Sez.* New York: Grosset & Dunlap, reissue, 1975.

Klein, Joe. *Woody Guthrie: A Life.* New York: Ballantine, c/o Random House, 1980.

McGregor, Craig. *Bob Dylan: A Retrospective.* New York: Da Capo Press, reissue, 1990.

Miller, Terry E. *Folk Music In America.* New York: Garland Publishing, 1986.

Palmer, Roy. *The Sound Of History: Songs & Social Comment.* New York: Oxford University Press, 1988.

Rodnitzky, Jerome L. *Minstrels Of The Dawn: The Protest Singer As Cultural Hero.* Chicago, Ill.: Nelson-Hall, 1976.

Scaduto, Anthony. *Dylan.* New York: Grosset & Dunlap, 1971.

Seeger, Pete. *The Incompleat Folksinger.* New York: Simon & Schuster, 1972.

Shelton, Robert. *No Direction Home: The Life And Music Of Bob Dylan.* New York: William Morrow, 1986.

Von Schmidt, Eric and Jim Rooney. *Baby Let me Follow You Down: The Illustrated History Of The Cambridge Folk Years.* Garden City: Anchor c/o Doubleday & Co., 1979.

Willens, Doris. *Lonesome Traveler: The Life of Lee Hays.* New York: W.W. Norton & Co., 1988.

Wolliver, Robbie. *Bringing It All Back Home: 25 Years At Folk City.* New York: Pantheon Books, 1986.

II. SINGER-SONGWRITERS

Bohlman, Philip V. *The Study Of Folk Music In The Modern World.* Bloomington, Ind.: Indiana University Press, 1988.

Hood, Phil, ed. *Artists Of American Folk Music.* New York: William Morrow & Co., 1986.

Near, Holly. *Fire In The Rain, Singer In The Storm.* New York: William Morrow & Co., 1990.

III. BLUEGRASS & STRING BAND MUSIC

Cantwell, Robert. *Bluegrass Breakdown: The Making Of The Old Southern Sound.* Champaign, Ill.: University of Illinois Press, 1984.

Country Music Foundation. *Country, The Music And Musicians.* New York: Abbeville Press, 1988.

Kochman, Marilyn, ed. *The Big Book Of Bluegrass: The Artists, The History, The Music.* Milwaukee, Wis.: Hal Leonard Publishing,1988.

Razaf, Henry. *The Folk, Country & Bluegrass Musicians' Catalogue.* New York: St. Martin's Press, 1982.

Stambler, Irwin and Grellin Landon. *The Encyclopedia Of Folk, Country & Western Music.* New York: St. Martin's Press, 1983.

Willoughby, Larry. *Texas Rhythm, Texas Rhyme.* Austin, Tex.: Texas Monthly Press, 1984.

IV. BRITISH ISLES

Carlin, Richard. *English & American Folk Music.* New York: Facts on File, 1987.
O'Neill, Francis. *Irish Minstrels And Musicians: The Story Of Irish Music.* New York: Mercier Press, 1987.

V. BLUES

Barlow, William Brook. *Voices From The Heartland: A Cultural History of The Blues.* Ann Arbor, Mich.: UMI Research Press, 1986.
Blackwell, Lois S. *The Wings Of A Dove: The Story Of Gospel Music In America.* Norfolk, Vir.: Donning Co., 1978.
Charters, Samuel. *The Legacy Of The Blues: Art And Lives Of Twelve Great Bluesmen.* New York: Da Capo Press, 1977.
_____. *Sweet As The Showers Of Rain.* New York: Oak Publications, 1977.
Ellison, Mary. *Extensions Of The Blues.* New York: Riverrun Press, 1989.
Evans, David. *Big Road Blues: Tradition And Creativity In The Folk Blues.* New York: Da Capo Press, 1988.
Ferris, William. *Blues From The Delta.* New York: Da Capo Press, 1988.
Govenar, Alan. *Meeting The Blues: The Rise Of The Texas Sound.* Colorado Springs, Col.: Taylor Museum, 1989.
Guralnick, Peter. *Feel Like Going Home.* New York: Harper & Row, 1988.
Harris, Sheldon. *Blues Who's Who.* New York: Da Capo Press, 1981.
Haskins, James. *Black Music In America, A History Through Its People.* New York: Thomas A. Crowell Publishing c/o Harper & Row, 1987.
Oliver, Paul, Max Harrison and William Bolcom. *The New Grove Gospel, Blues And Jazz With Spirituals And Ragtime.* New York: W.W. Norton & Co., 1983.
Roach, Hildred. *Black American Music: Past And Present.* Melbourne, Fl.: Robert E. Krieger, Co., 1985.
Southern, Eileen, ed. *The Black Perspective In Music.* New York: Foundation For The Research In The Afro-American Creative Arts, Inc., 1989, recently discontinued.
Jackson, George P. *White & Negro Spirituals.* New York: Da Capo Press, 1975.
Lee, Peter and David Nelson, ed. *Living Blues Directory.* University, Miss.: Center For The Study of Southern Culture, 1989.
Tilford, Brooks. *America's Black Musical Heritage.* New York: Prentice-Hall, 1984.
Walker, Wyatt Tee. *Somebody's Calling My Name: Black Sacred Music And Social Change.* Valley Forge, Penn.: Judson Press, 1979.

VI. LOUISIANA

Ancelot, Barry. *The Makers Of Cajun Music.* Austin, Texas: University Of Texas Press, 1984.
Broven, John. *South To Louisiana: The Music Of The Cajun Bayous.* Gretna, Louisiana: Pelican Publishing, 1983.
Hannusch, Jeff a.k.a. Almost Slim. *I Hear You Knockin': The Sound Of New Orleans Rhythm & Blues.* Ville Platte, Louisiana: Swallow, 1985.
Savoy, Ann Allen. *Cajun Music: A Reflection Of A People.* Eunice, Louisiana: Bluebird, 1984.

VII. NEW INSTRUMENTALS

Birosik, Patti Jean. *The New Age Music Guide.* New York: Collier/MacMillan Publishing, 1989.
Campbell, Don. *The Roar Of Silence: Healing Powers Of Breath, Tone & Music.* Wheaton, Ill.: Theosophical Publishing House, 1989.
Schaefer, John. *New Sounds: A Listener's Guide To New Music.* New York: Harper & Row, 1987.

VIII. WORLD MUSIC

Adzinya, Abraham Kobena, Dumisani Moraire and Judith Cook Tucker. *Let Your Voice Be Heard: Songs from Ghana and Zimbabwe.* Danbury, Conn.: World Music Press, 1989.

Allen, R. *Voices Of The Americas: Traditional Music & Dance From North, South & Central America & The Caribbean.* New York: World Music Institute, 1988.

Gerard, Charley with Marty Sheller. *Salsa!: The Rhythm of Latin Music.* Crown Point, Ind.: White Cliffs Media, 1989.

Hart, Mickey. *Drumming At The Edge Of Magic.* San Francisco: Harper San Francisco, 1990.

Locke, David. *Drum Damba: Talking Drum Lessons.* Crown Point, Ind.: White Cliffs Media, 1989.

_____. *Drum Gahu: The Rhythms of West African Drumming.* Crown Point, Ind.: White Cliffs Media, 1987.

Rubin, Ruth. *Voices Of A People: The Story Of Yiddish Folk Song.* Hatboro, Penn.: Legacy Books, 1988.

Sapoznick, Henry. *The Compleat Klezmer.* Hillside, New Jersey: Tara Publishing, 1987.

IX. MISCELLANEOUS

Baggalear, Kirstin. *Folk Music: More Than A Song.* New York: Thomas A. Crowell Publishing c/o Harper & Row, 1976.

Christgau, Robert. *Christgau's Record Guide.* New York: Ticknor & Fields Publishing, 1981.

Gusikoff, Lynne. *Guide To Musical America.* New York: Facts on File, 1984.

Jablonski, Edward. *The Encyclopedia Of American Music.* New York: Doubleday & Co., 1981.

Marsh, Dave and John Swenson, ed. *The Rolling Stone Record Guide.* New York: Rolling Stone Press, 1979.

Sandberg, Larry and Dick Weissman. *The Folk Music Sourcebook.* New York: Da Capo Press, 1989.

Stambler, Irwin. *The Encyclopedia Of Pop, Rock And Soul.* New York: St. Martin Press, 1989.

X. PERIODICALS

Bluegrass Unlimited, Box 111, Broad Run, VA 22014.

Dirty Linen: The Journal of Folk, Electric Folk, Traditional and World Music, Box 66600, Baltimore, MD 21239.

Fast Folk Musical Magazine, Box 938, Village Square Station, New York, NY 10014.

Folk Roots, Box 73, Farnham, Surrey GU9 7UN, England.

Guitar Extra!, P.O. Box 1490, Port Chester, NY 10573.

Guitar Player, 20085 Stevens Creek, Cupertino, Ca. 95014.

Living Blues, Center For The Study Of Southern Culture, University, MS 38677.

Old-Time Herald, P.O. Box 51812-WC, Durham, NC 27717.

Shiron L'Shalom, 155 Winslow Ave., Norwood, MA 02062.

Sing Out!, Box. 5253, Bethlehem, PA 18015.

World Music Connections, P.O. Box 561, Crown Point, IN 46307.

SELECTED DISCOGRAPHY OF FEATURED PERFORMERS

I. THE OLD SCHOOL

Joan Baez. *Joan Baez,* Vanguard (1960).
_____. *Volume Two,* Vanguard (1960).
_____. *Diamonds & Rust,* A&M (1975).
_____. *Recently,* Gold Castle, (1987).
_____. *Diamonds And Rust In The Bullring,* Gold Castle (1989).
_____. *Speaking Of Dreams,* Gold Castle (1989).
David Bromberg. *David Bromberg,* Columbia (1972).
_____. *How Late'll Ya Play 'Til?,* Fantasy (1976).
_____. *Sideman Serenade,* Rounder (1989).
Guy Carawan With Candie Carawan & Friends. *Tree Of Life/Arbol De La Vida,* Flying Fish (1990).
Ronnie Gilbert. *Love Will Find A Way,* Abbe Alice (1989).
Ronnie Gilbert and Holly Near. *Lifeline,* Redwood (1983).
_____. *Singing With You,* Redwood (1986).
Arlo Guthrie. *Alice's Restaurant,* Reprise (1967).
_____. *Running Down The Road,* Warner Brothers (1969).
_____. *Hobo's Lullaby,* Warner Brothers (1972).
_____. *Someday,* Rising Son (1986).
Arlo Guthrie and Pete Seeger. *Together,* Warner Brothers (1975).
_____. *Precious Friend,* Warner Brothers (1982).
H.A.R.P. (Holly Near, Arlo Guthrie, Ronnie Gilbert, Pete Seeger). *HARP,* Redwood (1985).
Odetta. *Sings Dylan,* RCA (1965).
_____. *Ballads And Blues,* Vanguard (1966).
_____. *Movin' It On,* Rose Quartz (1987).
_____. *Christmas Spirituals,* Alcazar (1988).
Tom Paxton. *Rambling' Boy,* Elektra (1964).
_____. *The Marvelous Toy & Other Galimaufry,* Flying Fish (1984).
_____. *Folk Song Festival,* Pax (1986).
_____. *A Paxton Primer,* Pax (1986).
_____. *Baloon-aloon-aloon,* Pax (1987).
_____. *A Child's Christmas,* Pax (1988).
_____. *Politics Live,* Flying Fish (1988).
_____. *The Very Best,* Flying Fish (1988).
Peter, Paul and Mary. *In Concert,* Warner Brothers (1965).
_____. *Ten Years Together,* Warner Brothers (1970).
_____. *Flowers And Stones,* Gold Castle (1990).
Tom Rush. *Classic,* Elektra (1970).
_____. *Late Nite Radio,* Nite Light (1984).
Buffy Sainte-Marie. *Best Of,* Vanguard (1973).
_____. *Best Of, Volume 2,* (1974, Vanguard (1974).
Bill Staines. *The First Million Miles,* Rounder (1989).
John Stewart. *Dream Away Dream Babies,* RSO (1979).
_____. *Dream Babies Go Hollywood* (1980, RSO)
Noel Paul Stookey and Bodyworks. *In Love Beyond Our Lives,* Gold Castle (1990).
Dave Van Ronk. *An American Songbook,* Gazelle (1990).
_____. *Peter And The Wolf,* Alcazar (1989).
_____. *Goin' Back To Brooklyn,* Reckless (1984).
The Weavers. *Together Again,* Loom (1981).
_____. *The Best Of,* MCA (1983).
_____. *At Carnegie Hall,* Vanguard (1985).

II. SINGER-SONGWRITERS

Greg Brown. *The Iowa Waltz,* Red House (1981).
_____. *44 & 66,* Red House (1984).
_____. *In The Dark With You,* Red House (1985).

_____. *Songs Of Innocence And Experience,* Red House (1986).
_____. *One More Goodnight Kiss,* Red House (1988).
_____. *One Big Town,* Red House (1989).
Buskin And Batteau. *B&B,* Silver Wing (1987).
Shawn Colvin. *Steady On!,* Columbia (1988).
John Gorka. *I Know,* Red House (1987).
_____. *Land Of The Bottom Line,* Windham Hill (1989).
Nanci Griffith. *Once In A Very Blue Moon,* Philo (1984).
_____. *There's A Light Beyond These Woods,* Philo (1986).
_____. *Lone Star State Of Mind,* MCA (1987).
_____. *One Fair Summer Evening,* MCA (1988).
_____. *Storms,* MCA (1989).
The Indigo Girls. *The Indigo Girls,* Epic (1989).
_____. *Nomads, Indians & Saints,* Epic (1990).
Patty Larkin. *Step Into The Light,* Philo (1986).
_____. *I'm Fine,* Philo (1987).
_____. *Live In The Square,* Philo (1990).
Christine Lavin. *Future Fossils,* Philo (1984).
_____. *Beau Woes And Other Problems Of Modern Life,* Philo (1986).
_____. *Good Thing He Can't Read My Mind,* Philo (1988).
_____. *Attainable Love,* Philo (1989).
Kate and Anna McGarrigle. *Kate And Anna McGarrigle,* Warner Brothers (1976).
_____. *Dancer With Bruised Knees,* Warner Brothers (1977).
_____. *French Record,* Hannibal (1981).
_____. *Love Over And Over,* Polydor (1983).
Rod MacDonald. *No Commercial Traffic,* McDisc (1983, reissue).
_____. *White Buffalo,* McDisc (1987).
_____. *Bring On The Lions,* Brambus Records, (1989).
Bill Morrissey. Bill Morrissey, Philo (1984 reissue).
_____. *North,* Philo (1986).
_____. *Standing Eight,* Philo (1989).
Holly Near. *A Live Album,* Redwood (1974).
_____. *Imagine My Surprise,* Redwood (1978).
_____. *Don't Hold Back,* Redwood (1987).
_____. *Sky Dances,* Redwood (1989).
Fred Small. *Love's Gonna Carry Us,* Aquifer (1981).
_____. *The Heart Of The Appaloosa,* Rounder (1983).
_____. *No Limit,* Rounder (1985).
_____. *I Will Stand Fast,* Flying Fish (1988).
Loudon Wainwright III. *Album III,* Columbia (1972).
_____. *Attempted Mustache,* Columbia (1973).
_____. *A Live One,* Rounder (1980).
_____. *Fame And Wealth,* Rounder (1983).
_____. *I'm Alright,* Rounder (1985).
_____. *More Love Songs,* Rounder (1986).
_____. *Therapy,* Silvertone (1989).
Windham Hill. *Legacy,* Windham Hill (1989).

III. BLUEGRASS

Auldridge, Reid & Coleman. *High Time,* Sugar Hill (1989).
Bryan Bowers. *By Heart,* Flying Fish (1984).
The Dry Branch Fire Squad. *Good Neighbors & Friends,* Rounder (1985).
_____. *Fertile Ground,* Rounder (1989).
Cathy Fink. *Doggone My Time,* Sugar Hill (1990, reissue).
_____. *When The Rain Comes Down,* Rounder (1987).
Cathy Fink And Marcy Marxer. *Fink & Marxer,* Sugar Hill (1989).
_____. *Help Yourself,* Rounder (1990).
Alison Krauss. *I've Got That Old Feeling,* Rounder (1990).
Marcy Marxer. *Jump Children,* Rounder (1987).
The Nashville Bluegrass Band. *The Boys Are Back In Town,* Sugar Hill (1990).
Northern Lights. *Take You To The Sky,* Flying Fish (1990).

The Seldom Scene. *A Change Of Scenery*, Sugar Hill (1988).
_____. *15th Anniversary Celebration*, Sugar Hill (1988).
_____. *Scenic Roots*, Sugar Hill (1990).
_____. *Act One*, Rebel (1990 reissue).
Doc Watson. *The Essential*, Vanguard (1973).
_____. *Riding The Midnight Train*, Sugar Hill (1986).
_____. *Portrait*, Sugar Hill (1987).
_____. *On Praying Ground*, Sugar Hill (1990).
_____. *Sings Songs For Little Pickers*, Sugar Hill (1990).
Doc & Merle Watson. *Guitar Album*, Flying Fish (1983).
_____. *Down South*, Sugar Hill (1984).
_____. *Pickin' The Blues*, Flying Fish (1985).

IV. BLUES

Rory Block. *Blue Horizon*, Rounder (1983).
_____. *Rhinestones & Steel Strings*, Rounder (1983).
_____. *I've Got A Rock In My Sock*, Rounder (1986).
_____. *House Of Hearts*, Rounder (1987).
_____. *Color Me Wild*, Alcazar (1990).
Clarence Gatemouth Brown. *The Original Peacock Recordings*, Rounder (1982 resissue).
_____. *One More Mile*, Rounder (1983).
_____. *Pressure Cooker*, Alligator (1985).
_____. *Real Life*, Rounder (1986).
_____. *Standing My Ground*, Alligator (1989).
James Cotton. *Mr. Superharp Himself—Live From Chicago*, Alligator (1986).
_____. *Take Me Back*, Blind Pig (undated).
James Cotton (with Junior Parker, Pat Hare). *Mystery Train*, Rounder (1990 reissue).
James Cotton (with Matt Guitar Murphy And Luther Tucker). *Recorded Live At Antone's Night Club*, Antone's (1988).
The Dixie Hummingbirds. *Love Me Like A Rock*, Columbia (1973).
John Hammond (with Dr. John & Mike Bloomfield). *Triumvirate*, Columbia (1973).
John Hammond. *Solo*, Vanguard (1976).
_____. *Frogs For Snakes*, Rounder (1982).
_____. *Live*, Rounder (1983).
_____. *Nobody But You*, Flying Fish (1987).
John Lee Hooker (with Canned Heat). *Hooker 'n Heat*, Liberty (1970).
John Lee Hooker. *Live At Soledad Prison*, ABC/Bluesway (1972).
_____. *The Healer*, Chameleon (1989).
_____. *40th Anniversary Album: Original 1948-1961 Recordings* (1989).

V. LOUISIANA

Michael Doucet With Beausoleil. *Zydeco Gris Gris*, Swallow (1985).
Beausoleil (dit Canray Fontenot). *Allons A Lafayette*, Arhoolie (1986).
_____. *Bayou Boogie*, Rounder (1986).
_____. *Hot Chili Mama*, Arhoolie (1987).
_____. *Bayou Cadillac*, Rounder (1989).

VI. BRITISH ISLES

Battlefield Band. *Home Ground/Live From Scotland*, Temple (1990).
_____. *Anthem For The Common Man*,
Bothy Band. *Afterhours—Recorded Live In Paris*, Green Linnet (1984 reissue.)
_____. *?1975*, Green Linnet (1983 reissue).
_____. *Out Of The Wind Into The Sun*, Green Linnet (1985 reissue).
John Cunningham. *Thoughts From Another World*, Shanachie (1982).
_____. *Fair Warning*, Green Linnet (1983).
Phil Cunningham. *Airs & Graces*, Green Linnet (1984).
_____. *Palamino Waltz*, Green Linnet (1989).
Sandy Denny. *Who Knows Where The Time Goes*, Hannibal (1985).
Fairport Convention. *The History*, Island (1972).
_____. *Expletive Delighted!*, Rounder (1986).
_____. *Red & Gold*, Rough Trade (1989).

_____. *The Boot*, Reunion, distributed by Dirty Linen (1983).
_____. *The Other Boot*, Reunion, distributed by Dirty Linen (1986).
_____. *The Third Leg*, Reunion, distributed by Dirty Linen (1987).
_____. *The Five Seasons*, Rough Trade (1991).
French, Frith, Kaiser And Thompson. *Invisible Means*, Windham Hill (1990).
Triona Ni Domhnáill. *Triona*, Green Linnet, (1984 reissue).
Rare Air. *Na Caberfeidh*, Flying Fish (1982).
_____. *Mad Plaid*, Flying Fish (1984).
_____. *Hard To Beat*, Green Linnet (1987).
_____. *Primeval*, Green Linnet (1989).
Silly Wizard. *Golden, Golden*, Green Linnet (1985).
_____. *Live In America*, Green Linnet (1985).
_____. *A Glint Of*, Green Linnet (1986).
Steeleye Span. *Portfolio*, Shanachie (1988).
_____. *Tempted And Tried—A Twentieth Anniversary Celebration*, Shanachie (1989).
Alan Stivell. *Journee A La Maison*, Rounder (1981).
_____. *Renaissance Of The Celtic Harp*, Rounder, (1983 reissue).
_____. *Celtic Symphony*, Rounder (1984).
_____. *Harpes Du Nouvel Age*, Rounder (1986).
Richard Thompson. *Across A Crowded Room*, Polygram (1985).
_____. *Amnesia*, Polygram (1989).
Richard and Linda Thompson. *First Light*, Chrysalis (1978).
_____. *I Want To See The Bright Lights Tonight*, Carthage (1983).
_____. *Shoot Out The Lights*, Hannibal (1982).

VII. NEW INSTRUMENTALS

Will Ackerman. *In Search Of The Turtle's Navel*, Windham Hill (1977).
_____. *Conferring With The Moon*, Windham Hill (1986).
_____. *Imaginary Roads*, Windham Hill (1988).
Jay Ansill. *Origami*, Flying Fish (1989).
Pierre Bensusan. *Solilai*, Rounder (1982).
_____. *Early*, Windham Hill, (1986 reissue).
_____. *Spices*, CBS (1988).
Deborah Henson-Conant. *On The Rise*, GRP (1989).
_____. *Caught In The Act*, GRP (1990).
Leo Kottke. *Twelve String Blues*, Oblivion (1969).
_____. *Six And Twelve-String Guitar*, Takoma (1972).
_____. *The Best*, Capitol (1978).
_____. *Time Step*, Chrysalis (1983).
_____. *A Shout Toward Noon*, Private Music (1986).
_____. *That's What*, Private Music (1990).
Paul Winter. *Common Ground*, A&M (1978).
_____. *Icarus*, CBS (1972).
_____. *Missa Gaia*, Living Music (1982).
_____. *Sunsinger*, Living Music (1983).
_____. *Concert For The Earth*, Living Music (1985).
_____. *Canyon*, Living Music (1985).
_____. *Earthbeat*, Living Music (1987).
_____. *Whales Alive*, Living Music (1987).
_____. *Wolf Eyes*, Living Music (1988).

VIII. WORLD MUSIC

Do'a. *Ornament Of Hope*, Philo (1979).
_____. *Ancient Beauty*, Philo (1981).
Do'a World Music Ensemble. *Companions Of The Crimson Coloured Ark*, Philo (1984).
Doah. World Dance, Global Pacific/CBS (1988).
Flor De Caña. *Muevéte/Move It*, Flying Fish (1988).
Fortaleza. *Soy De Sangre Kolla, Quechua Y Aymara*, Flying Fish (1989).
Ladysmith Black Mambazo. *Inala*, Shanachie (1986).
_____. *Shaka Zulu*, Warner Brothers (1987).
_____. *Umthombo Wamanzi*, Shanachie (1988).

Mickey Hart/Airto/Flora Purim. *Dafös*, Rykodisc (1989).
Mickey Hart/Taro Hart. *Music To Be Born By*, Rykodisc (1989).
Klezmorim. *First Recordings:1976-78*, Arhoolie, (1989 reissue).
_____. *Metropolis*, Flying Fish. (1981).
_____. *Notes From Underground*, Flying Fish (1984).
_____. *Jazz-Babies Of The Ukraine*, Flying Fish (1987).
Rhythm Devils. *The Apocalypse Now Sessions*, Rykodisc (1989 reissue).

OTHER FOLK RESOURCES

Record Labels

Abbe Alice, P.O. Box 8388, Berkeley, CA 94707.
Alcazar, Box 429, Waterbury, VT 05676.
Alligator, P.O. Box 60234, Chicago, IL 60660.
Arhoolie, 10341 San Pablo Avenue, El Cerrito, CA 94530.
Blind Pig, P.O. Box 56691, New Orleans, LA 70156.
Brambus Records, Vertrieb BRD 1MC Hamburg, Germany.
Folk Legacy, Box 1148, Sharon, CT 06069.
Flying Fish, 1304 W. Schubert, Chicago, IL 60614.
Gazelle Records, P.O. Box 527, Mansfield Center, CT 06250.
Gold Castle, 3575 Cahvenga Blvd. W. #435, Los Angeles, CA 90068.
Green Linnet, 43 Beaver Brook Rd., Danbury, CT 06810.
Living Music, P.O. Box 72, Litchfield, CT 06759.
Nite Light, P.O. Box 16, Hillsborough, NH 03244.
Pax Records, 78 Park Place, East Hampton, NY 11937.
Philo (distributed by Rounder).
Rebel, P.O. Box 3057, Roanoke, VA 24015.
Red House, P.O. Box 4044, St. Paul, MN 55406.
Redwood, 6400 Hollis Street, Emeryville, CA 94608.
Rounder, 1 Camp Street, Cambridge, MA 02140.
Rykodisc, Pickering Wharf, Building C, Salem, MA 01970.
Shanachie, P.O. Box 284, Newton, NJ 07860.
Silver Wing, P.O. Box 793, Village Station, New York, NY 10014.
Sugar Hill, P.O. Box 4040, Duke Station, Durham, NC 27706.
Swallow, P.O. Drawer 10, Ville Platte, LA 70586.
Temple, c/o Flying Fish.
Vanguard, 1299 Ocean Avenue, Santa Monica, CA 90401.
Warner Brothers, Box 48888, Los Angeles, CA 90048.
Windham Hill, P.O. Box 9388, Stanford, CA 94309.

Books, Audio and Video Cassettes on World, Folk and Popular Music from White Cliffs Media are distributed to bookstores by The Talman Company, or may be ordered direct.Write us for a catalog. If reordering, add $3.00 shipping/handling ($5.00 international). Indiana residents add 5% sales tax. Prices subject to change.

White Cliffs Media
P.O. Box 561
Crown Point, IN 46307-0561
(219) 322-5537 (Visa/Mastercard orders from individuals accepted).

Distributed to the book trade by
The Talman Company, Inc.
150 Fifth Avenue
New York, NY 10011
(212) 620-3182
(800) 537-8894
Fax: (212) 627-4682